To Ju

Best

Carol M Creasey

ONE MOMENT OF MADNESS

Also by Carol M. Creasey:

Biography:
My Life is Worth Living!

Fiction:
Fatal Obsession
Not Just an Affair
Evil Woman
Evil Woman...Takes Revenge
The Power of Love

ONE MOMENT OF MADNESS

CAROL M. CREASEY

UNITED WRITERS
Cornwall

UNITED WRITERS PUBLICATIONS LTD
Ailsa, Castle Gate, Penzance, Cornwall.
www.unitedwriters.co.uk

*All Rights Reserved. No part of this publication
may be reproduced, stored in a retrieval system,
or transmitted, in any form or by any means,
electronic, mechanical, photocopying, recording
or otherwise, without the prior permission of the
Copyright owner.*

British Library Cataloguing in Publication Data:
A catalogue record for this book is
available from the British Library.

ISBN 9781852001865

Copyright © 2018 Carol M. Creasey.

Printed and bound in Great Britain by
United Writers Publications Ltd.,
Cornwall.

I dedicate this book
to Imogen,
my lovely granddaughter.

PART ONE

Chapter One

1988

"Diana, you need to eat all your dinner up," said Susan Scott, trying not to sound too annoyed, as her niece Diana sat toying with her fish fingers, mashed potato and peas. After what these girls had been through, and only eight years old, it was hard to be strict with them, but Susan knew it would have been what their mother Ella would have wanted. It was these thoughts that allowed her to brush away any feelings of irritation she felt when Diana pushed her fork aside and burst into tears.

"Mummy didn't make me, I miss Mummy."

Diana's sister Rachel rose from her chair, and Susan watched as she comforted her twin. Although a mere ten minutes older, Rachel was the more practical and stable one, much easier to deal with than her volatile sister. The closeness of these two girls was touching. All they truly had now was each other, and Susan, who had never had her own children, nor wanted any, with her life full of cats and a husband who had provided her with a very comfortable lifestyle, spending much of her time hosting coffee mornings, had suddenly found herself unable to turn her back on them when their parents had so tragically died in a car crash. There was no way she could allow them to be taken into care, and even Clive had agreed.

"Just eat some, you know you can," said Rachel gently.

They both knew that their mother would have been very strict, and Diana would have eaten everything, but suddenly their lives had been turned upside down, and inside them both was fear and

7

apprehension. Without the loving arms of their mother, and the strength of their father too, they did not know what to expect.

For no other reason than because Rachel had asked her, Diana obediently took a few mouthfuls, but then she felt the nausea engulfing her when she thought about yesterday. They had stood in the church and watched two coffins being taken in, and inside, they had been told, were their parents, Mummy, who had always felt so warm and safe, and their adorable Daddy, always romping and having fun with them, making them laugh.

Rachel saw her heave, and then Diana fled for the cloakroom, from which the sound of her vomiting could clearly be heard.

"Sorry, Aunt Susan. Diana is still upset from yesterday, she can't help it."

Once again Susan secretly admired Rachel, she was so stoic and grown up for an eight year old. She was way out of her depth with children. Her sister Ella had been mother earth and she was not, but at that moment she made up her mind that she would try very hard to meet their needs; for their sakes, and also for the sake of their parents. Together with Clive, she must help them to cope with the tragic death of their parents.

Clive Scott was on his way home. He had been paying a visit to his restaurants, all situated in and around London. He had made his way in life, and now all he needed to do was make sure the restaurants were being run in the way that he wanted. He prided himself in hiring the best chefs, keeping his restaurants full and the money rolling in. No matter how hard the economy might be, there was definitely money in food. And when it came to celebrating a birthday or special occasion, even the poorest of people would pull out all the stops to give their loved one the very best, and he felt proud, because his food was the very best.

It was funny how life turned out. When he had married Susan, neither of them had really thought about having children, and then she had filled the house with cats; not that he minded, cats were sleek interesting creatures, very independent, and very low maintenance. Susan had been content for him to go and make the money, whilst she spent her time entertaining friends and enjoying the good life. But now, at the age of forty, they had inherited a family.

Clive loved his beautiful elegant wife. She had always looked after herself. She was still slim, wore good clothes, and kept her shining blonde hair immaculately groomed, wearing it in a neat bob which was chin length, with a full fringe which made her look easily in her early thirties.

He had thick hair which had touches of grey now, making him look distinguished, and his slim frame was due to regular visits to the gym. He also played golf and tennis, as did Susan.

They were a happy, contented couple, and then tragedy struck: Susan's younger sister Ella, and her husband Paul, had been killed in a head-on car crash whilst travelling home from a night at the theatre.

When they were over the initial shock of it, they had arrived at the house to find the police with a bewildered babysitter, and the twins were in bed asleep. He swallowed uncomfortably when he remembered, after electing to stay the night, how hard it had been for himself and Susan to explain to the twins that their parents had been killed in a car crash and were never coming back.

Diana, always the more emotional of the two girls, had been inconsolable, whilst Rachel, always the more placid one, had done her best to comfort her sister whilst trying to control her own tears. Then the girls had become withdrawn and silent, no doubt trying to understand how their world could have been so cruelly shattered into pieces.

They were like two little lost souls. Social workers and do-gooders were buzzing around everywhere before long, trying to organise their lives, and then Susan had said the one thing that was apparent to him. The girls should never have to go into care, it was up to them, as the nearest relatives, to give them a home, and try and help them through this trauma. Neither of them knew much about children, but at least they were family, and they could learn.

He was glad the funeral was now behind them. It had rained, the sky was grey, the wind was blowing, and this only added to the feeling of melancholy which hung over them all. In hindsight maybe the girls had been too young to attend their parents' funeral; the sight of their coffins had clearly distressed them greatly, but they had both said they wanted to say goodbye.

Taking them to the funeral parlour had not been an option, as the undertaker had gently explained to Clive that it was best to remember them as they were, because the crash had been such that their features would be unrecognisable. Of course, they hadn't told the girls that. The huge turn-out of mourners had been equally stunned that such a popular couple, with so much to live for, had been snuffed out in an instant. The two little girls, who stood hand in hand, looking so vulnerable and confused, were clearly traumatised, and the words of sympathy from everyone may have washed over them, but were gratefully received by their aunt and uncle.

Clive turned into the long driveway leading to the house which had been specially built for them. Trees lined each side, and as he reached the top, he parked the car next to Susan's little runabout. He couldn't wait to get inside and relax with his usual Scotch whisky before he ate dinner.

As he opened the front door, he saw the twins standing outside the study. To him they looked identical, with their strawberry blonde hair which was normally worn straight, or occasionally in plaits. They were both quite thin, and there was an expression of uncertainty in their huge green eyes as they caught his gaze. The only way he could tell them apart was by their behaviour. Diana was more emotional and dramatic, whereas Rachel was calmer and more practical, and willing to listen to what was said to them. She had adopted a protective role towards her sister.

Apparently Diana had been very close to Paul, her dad, who charmed her with magic tricks and was full of fun. Clive knew he could never replace Paul, and didn't want to try; he was a serious businessman. Rachel had been close to her mother Ella, and had inherited her common sense and level-headedness. Rachel had a protective arm around her sister, who was sobbing quietly. Behind them stood Susan.

"So glad to see you are home darling," she said; if only he knew how much! She was struggling to help these children with their grief. The whole situation was heartbreaking, but now Clive was home she would not feel so totally alone and useless.

"Hello Uncle Clive," Rachel said, with her arm still firmly around the shoulders of her sister, who was attempting to wipe away her tears with a large man-sized tissue. "Diana feels sick. She did try to eat her dinner."

"It's OK, don't worry about it," said Susan, trying to inject some brightness into her voice. "What would you like to do now girls?"

10

"We are going to our room now. Mummy would have said, Diana needs a good night's sleep."

"Of course, I am sure you will feel better tomorrow," said Susan, gently touching Diana's arm. You can watch the TV, or play some music quietly, we don't mind."

"Goodnight girls," said Clive, as he watched them disappear up the hall. They had come from a home which was not as wealthy as this, and had not even had a television in their room, but both Clive and Susan were aware that no amount of money and luxuries could ever replace their parents. To lose them at such a young age was heartbreaking.

Susan felt guilty about the feeling of relief that flooded through her as they went off to bed. She made up her mind she was not going to push either of them to eat until they had a chance to come to terms with this trauma. She blamed herself for making Diana sick, she should have been more sensitive to her distress.

"Our dinner is ready Clive, Sandra has only just gone home after cooking it."

"Great!" said Clive with feeling. Susan had never really learned to cook; thank goodness for their very competent housekeeper.

Whilst they sat eating their steak meal, washed down with a bottle of Beaujolais, Susan poured out her worries about how the girls were not coping, and neither was she. She didn't know how to help them, but she so wanted to.

Clive took an appreciative sip of the wine, and allowed it to slip slowly down his throat before he replied.

"Honey, it's been a trauma for all of us, but you and I have each other. They are two frightened little girls who have suddenly become orphans. They need expert help, and counselling, and we will make sure they get it."

"Oh yes, professional people can help, I never thought of that!" Susan smiled at him with gratitude. Life might be tough for all of them right now, but in time, with the right help, maybe they could all move on. Her sister and Paul would never be forgotten, but they would all learn to deal with such a tragic loss.

Chapter Two

1991

"Are you going somewhere nice, Diana?"

Rachel hid her feeling of disappointment that her sister was going off somewhere secret without her. She realised that just because they were twins, it didn't mean they had to be joined at the hip, but she had always made it her role to protect her slightly unstable sister; she felt deep inside herself, that it was what her mother would have expected her to do. At the age of eleven, and shortly due to go into senior school, Diana was feeling her feet, and she didn't always choose the right people to be her friends in Rachel's opinion. She didn't seem to be a very good judge of character.

"Just off into town to look round the shops," said Diana airily, but without her eyes meeting Rachel's. She had hoped to vanish before Rachel noticed, as she was going out with Pam for a laugh and Rachel would certainly not approve. Her sister was a bit of a goody two-shoes.

"On your own?"

There was a pregnant pause between them, Diana was wondering if Rachel would know if she lied, and then decided she would. She had already told Aunt Susan she was getting the bus into town with her new friend Pam, so she had better come clean.

"I am off to the shops with Pam."

"But you haven't got any money, you spent it all."

"Pam has!"

Rachel saw the defiance in Diana's eyes, and she knew if she didn't tread carefully, Diana would create another one of her dramas. When that happened, nobody could escape it; her tears and tantrums, and then the long silence afterwards when she sulked for days and refused to speak to anyone. Aunt Susan couldn't handle her, and Uncle Clive lacked the charm their dad had used to get through to her. Rachel loved her sister dearly, but sometimes she did find her hard work. Not only that, none of her friendships lasted long, and Pam was definitely not a good influence on her. Although only eleven, Pam swore like a trouper, something obviously learned from her parents, and spent all her time at school messing about and distracting everyone else.

"You can come too if you want," Diana was hoping Rachel would decline. At times her perfect sister, who always seemed to do the right things, and was their aunt Susan's clear favourite, really did her head in, but those bonds that they had made her weaken, and she was rewarded by the look of happiness on Rachel's face as she hurried away to get ready.

After a hasty goodbye to their aunt, who was busy feeding her cats, they ran down to the bus stop at the end of the road. Rachel swallowed her misgivings when she saw Pam waiting for them. Pam loved to shock everyone with her colourful language, and no doubt she would find a reason to air it on the bus.

Pam had dark hair, but it always looked as if it needed washing, and her skin had spots, her clothes looked as though they needed a good iron, and Rachel wondered why, out of everyone in their class, Diana had decided to be a friend of hers. She fixed a smile on her face and greeted her, only to flinch at Pam's response.

"Bloody hell Di, you didn't tell me righteous Rachel was coming!"

After that the atmosphere was so awkward that Rachel wished she had not come at all, she was clearly not wanted, and sat alone on the bus whilst the other two sat in front whispering secretly for most of the journey.

Diana was annoyed that Rachel had come, she felt like she was a minder, and at eleven, she certainly didn't need one. She didn't know why she felt the need to befriend anyone her sister would not approve of, but good quiet people bored her, she wanted excitement and adventure in her life. She still missed the fun that her father had provided, even after three years, and always felt that her aunt and uncle didn't really love her or Rachel, they had just done the right thing; although certainly the comfortable way of life they had provided was much more preferable than being in care. They seemed more interested in cats than children, and although she often had the desire to unleash some of the anger, frustration, and feelings of insecurity inside her, she did not, and most of her negativity was vented on her long suffering twin.

They spent a couple of hours going round department stores, giggling whilst they tried on shoes and hats they were not going to buy. The more the assistants eyed them with suspicion, the more fun it seemed to be for Pam and Diana, but as for Rachel, her embarrassment grew, she could feel herself colouring up, so she decided to visit the ladies' room.

"We are just popping into Woolworths before we go home," said Pam, winking at Diana.

"OK, I will come and find you."

Diana and Pam could not stop laughing as they ran across the road and into Woolworths, which was very crowded. Every time Pam thought about Rachel's 'pooky' face, it made her want to laugh even more.

"If your sanctimonious sister had not been with us, we could have nicked a couple of those hats," laughed Pam, and even though she knew it was wrong, Diana was thrilled by her daring.

"Well, she's in the loo, so let's find something in Woolies," Pam added.

They skirted round the shop until they reached the stationery counter, and wanting to prove to Pam that she could do it, Diana slid a pen and a ruler into her pocket. Pam laughed loudly, and as they made their way towards the door, they saw Rachel coming towards them, with a look of relief on her face that they were leaving the shop.

"Quick, someone else is coming," Pam suddenly hissed, and at that moment Diana panicked. She pretended to bump into her sister, using that moment, unbeknown to Rachel, to put the stolen pen and ruler into her sister's deep coat pocket.

They all headed for the door, but there was a security guard in uniform blocking their way. As they stood, wondering what to do, another man with a beard appeared from behind them. He looked grimly at them, and Rachel wondered what was wrong. Had the

14

other two been making a nuisance of themselves? She had only left them for a few minutes.

"Right young ladies, come to my office, I have reason to believe you have goods that you haven't paid for."

Rachel gasped, surely that wasn't true, but they all had no choice but to follow him into his office, and she felt as if the eyes of every assistant and customer were on them; so humiliating, whilst the other two just stared into space.

The security man also came with them, and they were ordered to empty their pockets. Rachel felt relief when Diana and Pam both had nothing in their pockets and profusely argued their innocence.

"Now you, please," said the manager, eyeing her suspiciously. When Rachel turned out her deep pocket, and the pen and ruler were there, fear and anger coursed through her as she realised what had happened. Her own sister had landed her in it.

"You are lucky that I stopped you before you went out of the doors, I will give you the chance to pay for these goods."

"I haven't got any money except my bus fare home," she said falteringly, "and it's not going to be enough."

"Then it's stealing, taking goods you cannot pay for. People who steal go to prison," he said ominously. "If I call the police you will be arrested, and do you think it's worth it, for a pen and a ruler?"

Rachel could feel the tears pricking at her eyelids, and she fought to remain in control, it wasn't only about the shame she felt, but also what her sister had done to her. The pain of that knowledge was hard to bear.

Diana knew it had been wrong to land Rachel in it, and she also knew her sister was struggling to hold back her tears. It was a prank that had back-fired on them all, and now she was sorry. Even though she was only eleven years old, she knew how to charm a man, or appeal to his better nature, and right now she had to do something to save her sister. She fixed her big green eyes sorrowfully on the bearded wonder, made her lip tremble, and gave the performance of her life.

"Please don't call the police. My sister is so sorry, she can't even speak, I know she will never do it again. It's my fault, she stole them for me because I spent all my pocket money."

John Mason, manager of Woolworths, surveyed the little green

15

eyed beauty, who had by now put her arms around her twin sister, who was shaking in an effort to contain her tears. It was a pitiful little scene. He had not really intended to call the police, kids were always nicking stuff, but they had to realise it was wrong. Maybe one day someone would invent some sort of security tab so it couldn't happen.

"You need to ask your mother or father to telephone me when you get home," he said, handing Diana a piece of paper. The other girl, who was smirking, looked a bit scruffy, and he doubted even if she told her parents, that they would ring. The twins looked as if they came from a decent home.

"Our parents are dead, we live with our aunt." Diana was glad she could use that; and it worked, his face showed awkwardness at this revelation.

Rachel had recovered her composure now, so she took control of the situation, taking the paper gently from Diana, who did not resist.

"My aunt will ring you later, and I am sorry for a moment of madness, that is all it was. It will never happen again."

Once they were allowed to go home, Rachel refrained from discussing any of it with Diana in front of Pam. She was determined to put it right, and she was prepared to take the blame for Diana with their aunt, but she was also determined that Diana would be made to realise just how betrayed she felt by her. As soon as they had left Pam behind, she spoke furiously to her.

"Diana, just because you think it's big to be friends with someone who gets a thrill out of shoplifting, just remember I don't! I will take the blame because you are my sister, but don't ever do it again!"

Diana knew she had gone too far on this occasion. She did love her sister, and had really tried her patience too much. Also she didn't want her aunt and uncle to know she had been stealing from Woolworths; so she cooled her friendship with Pam, and Rachel forgave her, because she truly believed that Pam had been the bad influence that had caused Diana to steal, and it was never mentioned again.

After a long discussion with John Mason, Susan and Clive made a life-changing decision for them and the twins. They had no idea how to cope with the situation, and Susan found it hard to believe that Rachel would have stolen anything. It was more likely to be something to do with Pam, as it was common knowledge that her brother was in a young offenders' prison, and there was no father at home. Both her and Clive believed the best way to keep the girls on the straight and narrow was to keep them away from Pam, so instead of going to the local senior school, by the time September came, the girls had been admitted to a boarding school in Scotland, and because the head felt, as twins, they needed to develop in their own way, they were put in separate classes. Susan and Clive didn't want this to feel like a punishment, it was meant for their own good.

They did have affection for the twins, but were not demonstrative, and although they didn't like to admit it, sending them to boarding school made life much easier for them, as they only saw them at holiday times when they arranged plenty of outings to keep them occupied.

Chapter Three

McArdle House was an austere building dating back to Victorian times, built out of grey stones; it was impressive, but also forbidding. A large building set in acres of grounds, which contained tennis courts and hockey pitches. It was a boarding school for girls from eleven until sixteen years, and sixth form courses were also available for aspiring students who wished to go on to university, with a separate building for that purpose.

The School was run very efficiently by Fiona McCoy, a grey haired lady in her fifties, who dressed in the same way every day; a grey tweed skirt with a white blouse, and her hair was always drawn back into a bun. Her features were severe, she rarely laughed, but underneath her tough exterior was a woman who had the best interests of her students at heart. She believed that every one of them was gifted in different ways, and any sign of talent was to be nurtured and encouraged.

She had never married, she was a tough lady, who had originally come from Glasgow, and life as headmistress of McArdle house in Edinburgh suited her very nicely. She had a group of good teachers around her to help her girls to reach their potential, and the school was so popular there was a waiting list to get in. The only reason that Clive and Susan's application had jumped up the queue was because Clive was her cousin, and also she knew about the twins losing their parents and the subsequent difficulties Clive and Susan had experienced since giving them a home.

For Fiona it was a challenge, and one that she would relish, she had heard that Rachel was bright and studious, but Diana not so much. She had met them; they were very striking looking girls with their very green eyes and strawberry blonde hair that carelessly tumbled around their shoulders, although they would have to wear plaits at school. Even at eleven, it was clear to see they would be beauties. Rachel had a calmness about her character, whereas Diana had a glint of defiance in her eyes, a girl of character, and Fiona had to make sure that character was steered the right way.

She realised that at first their new situation would be overwhelming for them. They were used to having each other, so she decided to let them share a dormitory, at least for the first term, but so their different characters could emerge, they must not be in the same class; they must learn to cope without leaning on each other, and have new friends.

When the twins arrived at McArdle House, it looked cold and forbidding. They felt like it was a punishment for the incident in Woolworths. Rachel had never dodged from taking the blame for Diana's reckless act, and although she forgave her, she made it clear it must never happen again, because the next time she would not cover up for her. Diana knew she meant business, and there was no longer Pam to impress, so she accepted her new school. Initially she didn't like being in a different class to Rachel, but her slightly excitable and daring nature made her popular and won her friends. She was always up for a laugh, although school work bored her.

Rachel kept her head down and worked hard, excelling in maths and the sciences. As they grew up, their similarity stayed the same, but their characters were completely different. Rachel was a little stockier than her sister, not as popular, and prone to be bullied a little by her classmates; but she coped with it, in her usual stoical way. Even Diana ridiculed her at times because she always toed the line, she called her boring and predictable, which she knew she was, but she couldn't change, any more than Diana could suddenly become studious.

Fiona had noticed that although not interested in being academic, Diana was good at drama. She usually took the lead part in school plays; her sense of drama, and need to be noticed were fulfilled when she was on stage. She had a stage presence, and even her singing voice was good, although she baulked at being in the school choir. At the age of sixteen, it was unlikely she would pass many of her exams, nor want to stay and go into sixth form like Rachel, so maybe her future lay elsewhere. But Fiona needed to find out, so she decided to contact her aunt and uncle first.

When Clive received the letter, he opened it quickly, hoping nothing was wrong; you just never knew with teenagers.

"Susie, here's a letter from Fiona, she is suggesting that Diana might benefit from going to stage school. She says, she's not academic but she is good at the arts. Oh, that is a relief, I was wondering what she had done this time!" he added.

"Well, she's not like Rachel; not as clever," remarked Susan.

Susan didn't know why she was defending Diana, but there had always been something vulnerable about her. She had taken the death of her parents much more deeply than Rachel, and it was probably something that would always be hard for her to cope with.

"I'm not so sure about that. She is more selfish, and only wants to do what she wants to do."

"That's a bit harsh Clive, all teenagers can be selfish, but we would never win any awards for parents of the year."

Clive conceded defeat, money was something they had plenty of, and if Diana wanted to go to stage school, and have a career on the stage, then who was he to stand in her way? It was a damn good idea.

"There's a good one in the city. I'll check it out if that is what she wants."

Karen came into the twins dormitory, full of excitement.

"The fair is over on the heath, we could go over this afternoon and take a look."

"Oh great, how long is it on for?"

"Just this bank holiday weekend, they'll be packing up on Tuesday morning whilst we are busy studying maths and science."

Karen said this in a careless tone, indicating that her attitude to her studies was very similar to that of Diana.

"Thank goodness we live too far to go home at the weekend, and we're sixteen, so what is there to stop us?"

20

Diana's eyes shone with excitement, and Karen reminded her. "There are a couple of really sexy looking blokes over there, dark curly hair and smouldering eyes just like David Essex."

Diana liked the sound of that. Boys were not part of their lives in a girls' boarding school, but at sixteen she was looking forward to finding out what made them tick. She was aware of her own sexuality, and she knew her looks were striking, so it wouldn't be hard to get a man. But she had to keep it quiet from Rachel, her perfect sister would be horrified if she knew what was in her mind.

She sneered to herself when she saw her sister, seated at a desk, dutifully doing her homework, and squashed down any guilt she might feel about not having done hers too.

"Karen and I are going to check out the fair on the green."

Rachel looked up and bit back her words. A fair was where all the teenage girls would be hanging around because of the lads who worked there, but the more she disapproved, the more Diana would want to go, so she tried a different tack.

"Oh great, let me know how you get on later."

Diana was amazed, her sister giving her licence to misbehave, that was a new one. She winked at Karen, and they took the opportunity to go, giggling in eager anticipation of what an exciting afternoon they would have.

Pupils were allowed the freedom to be out all day on a Saturday, but had to report back for dinner at six o'clock. If they wanted to go out in the evening, they had to have an adult that was responsible for them, which both girls thought was ridiculous now they were sixteen, but that was the rule. It was now three o'clock, so they had three hours of freedom.

The girls were both dressed in jeans; so tight they could barely move, with bare midriffs, and silky tops that also clung tight, and no bras, so the contours of their breasts could be clearly seen. It was lucky for them that no one in authority was around when they ran out of the school, because the staid and strict teachers at McArdle House would have made them put on their bras.

As soon as they arrived at the fairground, Diana spotted the young men Karen had described. One had blond hair brushed back, and reminded her of Billy Fury, the rock singer, but the one she really fancied was the one with the tight black curls, a suntanned face, and very penetrating blue eyes. He was very

21

much like David Essex, and he reminded her of a gypsy, which made him more exciting than ever.

He was operating the dodgems, and the blond man was helping him. They had a couple of goes, and she thrilled every time he jumped up and sat on the bonnet to take her money. When his hand touched against hers it felt like an electric shock, then his eyes stared into hers, and she was lost, he was so wickedly handsome, she had to have him.

Jake Maloney knew he had a way with women; at the age of twenty, he had slept with many, and he knew when a girl was throwing herself at him. The girl with the fiery red hair and disturbing green eyes was making a play for him, and he loved it, but first he had to get rid of his mate Bobby, and her blonde friend. He turned to Karen, and said in a low voice.

"Begorra, my friend is so smitten with you, and I can see why. But you see, he's very shy, so you need to go over and chat to him."

Karen was impressed, she liked the look of the blond man, so she jumped out of the bumper car and made her way over to him. Jake turned his attention back to Diana.

"Well to be sure, you are a little beauty," he said with his Irish lilt, and Diana was captivated. This was her first experience with a man, and at that moment she truly believed herself to be in love.

"Will you come for a walk with me?"

She had not said a word, she was totally taken over by his magnetism and charm. He led her gently by the hand, past his friend, who had Karen chatting to him.

"Keep an eye on the cars," he said to him winking, and his friend nodded silently as if used to being given such instructions.

He led Diana over to a clearing. The touch of his hands excited her so much she could feel her naked breasts straining at the flimsy confines of her top, and she felt so brazen, she was hoping he could see her nipples and would be tempted by them. They sat down on a seat, and when his lips found hers, the world stood still for her. His arms tightened around her, and his kiss became even more passionate, and she felt herself responding with the same passion. She was gasping now, and he lifted up her flimsy blouse, admiring her breasts, and kissing her pert nipples. But then suddenly he stopped, and she felt disappointment flood through her.

"It's a bit open here, but my caravan is empty," he whispered, his magnetic eyes bored into hers.

Diana was riding on the crest of a wave. With promise of more passion to come, she grabbed his outstretched hand, and ran across the grass with him to the brightly coloured red and yellow caravan. Inside the curtains were drawn, and he drew her towards the double bed.

It was as though another being had taken her over, as she allowed him to strip her, and she stripped him. She had never touched a man before, but urged on by the feelings that had taken control of her body, all embarrassment was forgotten. He spent some time caressing her with his hands and his lips, and the feelings that he stirred inside her were so deep and meaningful. At the moment when he entered her, she cried out, it felt so tight, but then her muscles started to squeeze him, and the pleasure he evoked inside her was all consuming, and she was begging him for more. He dutifully complied, and their moans mingled together, as he took her to the heights of paradise; then with a big shudder, it was over, and he climbed off her.

Karen had been having a laugh with Bobby, even helping him to operate the big handle that controlled the dodgems. When he had his break, he took her over to buy some candyfloss. Another man had come to relieve him, and she wondered idly where Diana was. Bobby wanted to see her again, a proper date next time, maybe they could go to the pictures, and she happily agreed, forgetting they were moving on, as Bobby sounded so convincing.

Time was passing very quickly, and she realised if she didn't leave him soon she would be late for dinner, and as she didn't want to get hauled up before the head, she decided to go back to school. There was no sign of Diana anywhere, and she felt slightly annoyed that her friend had abandoned her and gone home. She arrived back at school in time to join the throng of girls who were filing into the dining hall, all busy chatting about their day. She scanned them, but could see no sign of Diana, then spotted Rachel making her way towards her.

"Is Diana with you?" she asked.

"I thought she was with you," said Rachel, her voice now

sounding anxious, but Karen was not going to allow herself to be guilt tripped.

"She is sixteen, you know, she can do as she wants," she said defiantly.

"How could you just leave her?" Rachel felt she had good reason to be worried. It was only last year that a girl had been stabbed in a fairground, and even the knowledge that a jealous boyfriend had done it, and was now safely locked up for life, did not stop fear and anxiety running through her mind. Diana might be sixteen, but she was naïve and trusting.

But Karen was not prepared to accept any blame, she just shrugged her shoulders and moved along with the throng.

Rachel had only one thought in her mind, she paid no heed to the consequences of going out; finding her sister safe was far more important. She ran outside and along the drive, her heart was thumping, and she tried to control her senses. Maybe the side gate would be open, it was not usually closed until dusk, so she headed that way, and to her relief it opened at her touch.

She sped along the road until she reached the green where the fair was. It was early evening now, a beautiful late August evening, the sun was shining, and many people had flocked to enjoy all the delights of the fair. Excited screams rent the air as the big dipper lurched its way past, and loud music came from just about everywhere. Rachel was almost sobbing, as she realised how hard it would be to find Diana; and when she did, would she have been raped or murdered?

Chapter Four

Jake opened his eyes and came down to earth. This beautiful girl lay curled in his arms, he had just had amazing sex with her and it had roused feelings he never knew he had! For sure he liked a good shag, but never before had he gone to sleep with his arms around anyone; it had been a case of wham, bam thank you mam, and then they parted, usually never to meet again; but this time it was different. He didn't know what had happened to him, all he knew was that having her in his arms felt right.

Jake had joined the fair when he was only eight years old; well, Bobby's parents had found him roaming the streets of Dublin. He didn't even know his father, and his mother, who was a heavy smoker and an alcoholic, had managed to catch the council flat alight, and Jake had got out and run, just in time to see the fire brigade arrive. His mother had survived, but he was sure she hadn't missed him. After the fair had left Dublin and come to England, no one had ever tried to trace him. Cliff and Mary Slater had given him a home in their caravan, and he had done odd jobs around the camp, and even gone to school occasionally. It was ironic that Jake looked more of a gypsy than his friend Bobby, and yet by blood he wasn't one.

Jake could have done really well at school if he wasn't always getting into fights. He learned to read and write very quickly, but gypsy children were not popular either with teachers or parents of children at school, and even at eight, Jake, with his beautiful tight black curls and very bright blue eyes, coupled with a touch of the

b

blarney, inherited from somewhere in his mother's family, was always liked by girls.

So as he entered his teens, his attendance at school was getting less frequent, and he was now able to help operate the dodgems and the big wheel. All the travelling around didn't help, just going from one school to another, so at fourteen he left, and became a very useful addition in the fairground.

From that age onwards he discovered the delights of sex, having been initiated by a thirty year-old dolly bird with high heels, dyed blonde hair, and a very short mini skirt. She had spent all afternoon on the dodgems, and had made sure that every time he leaped on the bonnet to collect her money, she leaned forward enough for him to see down her low neckline and quivering cleavage. She had not even got as far as the empty caravan; she had been so desperate they had simply lain down in the woods behind a bush, and she had taken complete control of him and shown him what to do. He had never even known her name, and the next day the fair had upped and moved; but he had never forgotten his first experience, and from then onwards pulling girls had been his greatest thrill.

Jake didn't really understand anything about respecting women. If they were willing to sleep with him, and so many women were, then they were in for a good time, but he never asked their name, or gave his. So, many one-offs, but his life was with the fair, and he didn't want any woman complicating it. He had worked well for Cliff and now had his own caravan, not bad at twenty, so he had a bit of independence of a sort.

But all of a sudden, that had all changed. Cradled in his arms was this beautiful young girl. He didn't know her name, but he wanted to, and where she lived, and everything about her. He had met someone he wanted to spend time with. He twined his finger gently through her hair, smoothing a long strand of it.

Diana woke up suddenly with a start. For a moment she wondered where she was, it was dark inside the caravan, and there was someone with their arms around her. As she sat up, she remembered what had happened, and was suddenly covered with guilt and embarrassment. She was with a gypsy boy from the fair, in his caravan, she didn't even know his name, and yet she had allowed him to have sex with her. Whatever had come over her?

26

She felt shame wash over her, as she tried to pull the sheet over her naked body.

Jake could see her awkwardness; he had realised that he had taken her virginity, and now he felt bad. This girl was so special, he should have treated her like a queen and not like an easy lay. He spoke gently to her.

"You are so beautiful, so captivating, please let me see you again. My name is Jake Maloney."

His eyes looked so sincere, and Diana felt strangely comforted by the gentleness of his tone.

"Diana Wilcox, I live in Wimbledon, but am a boarder at McArdle House."

"Diana, to be sure you feel awkward, so I am going outside whilst you get dressed. Please come out when you are ready. I must see you again!"

She was moved by his insistence; surely he didn't just think of her as easy. It was her first time, and it felt really precious and special and she was so drawn to him. She tugged her clothes on quickly, and when she went out onto the steps of the caravan, Jake was sitting there smoking, and there was something about the aroma that was different, making her feel heady.

His blue eyes held hers as she watched him blow a smoke ring, and she felt her heart flip, and the pungent odour, which was strong but addictive, seemed everywhere.

"Here, take a drag, it's very calming."

Diana ignored the voice inside her that was reminding her smoking was bad for you. According to the newspapers, and doctors, it caused cancer and heart disease, and people that already smoked were being urged to give up. At school they had been told not to start in the first place, but right at this moment it seemed a cool thing to do, to prove to Jake just how grown up she was. She laughed, and leaned towards the cigarette; he held it to her lips and she drew deeply on it. Her head started to spin a bit, but she liked the feeling of euphoria it seemed to create inside her. They sat close to each other, enjoying a companionable silence, and Diana forgot everything except the buzz inside her that she was with the most gorgeous man ever, who had said he felt the same way about her. Could life get any better than this?

Jake was desperately trying to hang onto this moment; he was aware that tomorrow they were off again. He had just found Diana, and he didn't want to lose her.

"Can you come here tomorrow before midday, we are moving on in the early afternoon?"

Even as he spoke the words, he realised how hopeless the situation was. He was a wandering fairground attendant, that's all he was, but Diana obviously came from a rich family, she had bearing and class oozing out of her; but even if she hadn't, he would have wanted her. This feeling inside was so new to him that he wanted to nurture and savour it.

Diana felt the same; she didn't want to lose him, her first love, she would remember today for the rest of her life. His dark Romany looks, and casual way of life excited her; always on the move, how great it would be to leave school and go with him. She was risking a lot of trouble if she cut classes and came here to meet him, but something she had no control over propelled her on, she just had to see him again.

"I'll come during the morning, probably before eleven."

She took another puff of his cigarette, slowly blowing the smoke out to get the maximum pleasure from it; but then Jake was alarmed to see her suddenly choking, her eyes were transfixed ahead, and when he followed her gaze, he thought he was dreaming when he saw the figure coming towards them. Apart from wearing different clothes, he felt he was seeing another Diana; there were two Dianas, now how could that be?

Rachel ran towards the brightly coloured gypsy caravan, she could see by the horrified look on her face that Diana had seen her. Her eyes had not deceived her, her stupid twin had been smoking, no doubt egged on by the swarthy looking gypsy who was sitting next to her. As she got close she realised what it was, he was smoking pot, and her sister was mad enough to go along with it! She could feel her anger rising, but she realised that bawling Diana out in front of him wasn't a good idea. Not only would she humiliate her, but it would also put her back up, and make her more defiant. Sometimes Rachel felt more like her mother than her twin sister. She must show relief at finding her, and not appear to judge her.

"Diana, I am so glad to find you, Karen came back without you, and you didn't appear for dinner. Are you OK?"

This took Diana totally by surprise. She knew Rachel had seen her smoking, and that she was out later than she should be; and apart from that, she was with Jake, who was definitely not the sort of boyfriend that Rachel and her aunt and uncle would approve of. All the rebellious answers died on her lips, and she found herself saying:

"I am fine Rachel, just chatting to Jake, who works here. Jake, this is my twin sister Rachel."

Rachel barely gave him a nod; just the sort of boy Diana would find, a travelling gypsy. She fervently hoped her sister hadn't been stupid enough to sleep with him. This was 1996, and Aids was rife, she wouldn't have asked him to use a condom, she might even get herself pregnant, if only she could voice all this to her without Diana taking umbrage. Instead she said coolly.

"Nice to meet you Jake, but now we have to go back to school as we are late for dinner."

Jake could sense her disapproval, although she kept her lips smiling politely at him. Now he understood, they were twins, but this one was more serious than Diana, very matter of fact, and didn't give off the same sexual aura that Diana did. He knew that her disapproval was justified; they were in a different class from him, they lived in houses, had middle class parents, and money, and he was just a wanderer without a stable home. But now he had met Diana, he wanted something more than that from life.

He pushed Diana gently towards her sister, although what he wanted to do was to beg her to stay with him. He was being a fool and he knew it, where had the cool uncomplicated Jake Maloney gone?

"You best go now babe. I'll be seeing you."

Diana didn't want to leave him either, and she had expected Rachel to bawl her out. Being late for dinner didn't worry her at all, even the thought of detention for being late, but it would worry Rachel, as she never usually got detention. She would have liked to kiss him goodbye, but then Rachel would know they were an item, and right now she was not ready to share her first love with anyone, least of all her sister, whom she knew would not approve of Jake, but that only made him even more attractive to her. She said goodbye, and didn't look back to see if he was looking at her as Rachel hurried her away. Once they rounded the corner, out of sight of him, Rachel became much less composed.

"Diana, you know we will get detention for this, and we promised Aunt Susan we would behave!"

"So what, I can't be perfect like you!"

Those last words really inflamed the normally placid Rachel, and even she was surprised at the words that passed her lips totally unheeded.

"When are you going to stop behaving like a spoiled child Diana, and fancy getting talking to a scruffy looking gypsy like him! I know you were smoking pot. You're only sixteen for God's sake, and right in the open where anyone can see. Please don't tell me you've slept with him as well!"

Diana tossed her hair defiantly, an angry look in her eyes; who the hell did Rachel think she was?

"I don't need a keeper thank you, just because I don't prove to be perfect like you. I can choose my own friends."

"Well, did you sleep with him?" demanded Rachel again.

"No, and even if I had, I wouldn't tell you!"

The lie came easily to her lips, she felt it was her secret, so she was justified in protecting that secret, even from her twin. She knew it was her fault that their closeness was fading, but as they got older, they didn't even share the same interests or friends, Rachel was too much of a goody goody to her.

"What did he mean by see you soon?"

Normally Diana would have confessed that they were meeting the next morning, but in this instance she would be missing lessons, and that would involve a punishment, so she just said airily.

"It's just a saying like 'bon voyage' or something; they travel everywhere, as you know."

Being reminded of this calmed Rachel a little. Of course, the Bank Holiday was over, so he would be gone tomorrow, and no doubt Diana would never see him again. She didn't like falling out with her twin, they only had each other. She was grateful that her aunt and uncle had given them a home, and spared them from being taken into care, and maybe even being separated, but no one could ever replace their parents. Ella and Paul Wilcox had been the best parents in the world, and she understood how much Diana missed them too. Her mother would have wanted to try and curb the wild side of Diana, and her dad would have applauded it and called her feisty.

30

There was an awkward silence between them. They were no longer comfortable in each other's company, nor did they feel as if they were a unit, as in the past, as they walked towards the side gate of the school. Dusk was falling now, and they just made it through the gate, but were told curtly by the man who was locking it to report to the secretary's office.

"We don't have to, he might forget to tell her," said Diana airily. Rachel sighed, did she never learn?

"He won't forget, he is a typical jobsworth, but leave it to me. I will go to the office and try and get us off the hook."

Diana didn't argue with that. Rachel had always been there to protect her. She had acted as though she didn't need protecting, but detention was so tiresome. Not only that, Rachel had to get herself off the hook too, and she would have more tact in dealing with the very thorny secretary, who Diana felt had never liked her.

When they arrived at school, they made their way towards the secretary's office, and Rachel told Diana to wait outside whilst she tried to make the peace. She knocked at the door and was asked to enter.

Margaret Wells, the school secretary, looked up impatiently from the letter she was trying to type. How many more interruptions would she get?

"My twin sister and I have just been told by the caretaker to report to you, as we only just came in the gate, but there is a reason."

"It best be a good one!" said Margaret, her jackdaw eyes boring into Rachel's; her raven black hair was shining in the light, and she looked almost satanical. Woe betide anyone who upset her.

Rachel swallowed before speaking. She was not versed in lying, and she kept her face averted.

"My sister and I went shopping, but I wasn't well. She had to take me into a park, and I was sick. We sat on the bench for ages, I just couldn't face coming back, and had no idea what the time was."

Margaret was not impressed by the excuse, and then to her huge annoyance, the telephone rang. This letter would never get typed, it was already seven o'clock, and filling out a form for Rachel to take to her house mistress, who would dish out a punishment, would hold her up even more. Was she never to get finished today?

"Wait!" she said commandingly, then picked up the telephone, and in her polished telephone voice, which was nothing like the one she used towards the pupils, she spoke the school name, and invited the caller to hold the line and she would soon come back to them. She then covered the mouthpiece and in a harsh uncaring voice said:

"Go Rachel Wilcox, take yourself over to the medical centre in case you have anything catching. You won't need any supper tonight if you've been sick, but your sister is probably hungry, so she can go and collect late supper from the kitchen, if she tells them I gave my permission."

That was it, she was dismissed, and once again Rachel would suffer for her sister's behaviour. She was absolutely starving, and thirsty, and tonight she would probably have to spend in the medical centre; the beds in there were hard, and she had to pretend to be ill. She went outside to explain to Diana, who gave her a quick hug, and disappeared off towards the kitchens, where she would sit and eat whilst the staff continued to clear up ready for the next morning. Rachel walked slowly towards the medical centre, trying to ignore her groaning stomach, and comforting herself with the knowledge that they had both escaped punishment.

Chapter Five

Buoyed on by escaping punishment the previous day, after presenting herself at assembly the next morning, Diana slipped away from the throng of girls who were making their way back to the classroom to collect their books. It was a double maths period, which she hated; it might be the subject where Rachel shone, but for Diana it was boring, and she felt, unnecessary. She made her way discreetly towards the side gate; she wouldn't be back for break at eleven, and once more Rachel would be trying to find her, but she didn't care. She was desperate to see Jake again. Today he would be moving on, and she had to stay in touch with him. After finding him, she couldn't bear to lose him.

But this is when her luck ran out, when with dismay, she saw the burly figure of the caretaker approaching as she got near to the gate.

"Where's your letter of authorisation from the secretary?" he snapped.

"I left it behind, in my desk, but it's OK."

Diana tried to put on her most beguiling smile, whilst privately thinking what a horrible bad tempered fat slob he was; very much as Rachel had said – a jobsworth!

"Well you had better go back and get it then."

"But I will be late to the dentist." And then came the tears. If all else failed, Diana had learned with men, just put on the waterworks. But this man was different, he was completely unmoved, and now she was at a loss, how could she get out of the school? Desperation was taking control of her, she had only one

33

more escape route, the main gate; far more risky, but she had to do it. But as if he was reading her mind, the caretaker spoke.

"Don't get any idea about the main gate either, there are two people manning it. If you were going to the dentist, you can get your letter."

They both knew she was lying, so Diana had no choice but to slink away. She was heartbroken, and also very angry, but she was powerless, and all her hatred towards being shut away in this school, and unable to be independent, came to the surface. Even if she wanted to run away, she couldn't. For once in her life, and without the support of Rachel, Diana was not getting her own way.

When she presented herself at Maths she was fifteen minutes late, but a look at her sullen face was enough to stop her teacher from enquiring what was wrong. Just before the lesson ended a prefect came in with a message from the head, after reading it she thanked the girl, and spoke briefly to Diana.

"Diana, can you go to Miss McCoy's office when this lesson ends, please?"

She made it sound more like a question rather than an order. Past experience with Diana had found her to be a volatile young woman, quite dramatic at times, and if she was in trouble for something, then let Fiona deal with it, she was headmistress, after all.

Diana shrugged her shoulders, muttering, "Yes, OK." No doubt that nasty caretaker had reported her, and they had found out that she wasn't going to the dentist, nor did she have a letter; but she was past caring, her heart was broken, her life ruined, so she no longer cared what happened to her.

She made her way slowly towards the study of the headmistress, on the way she saw Rachel and explained she had to report to Miss McCoy.

"Oh no, the secretary must have reported us after all last night. But why is it only you?"

"No idea, and I don't care!"

Diana didn't bother to enlighten her about her failed attempt at leaving school earlier; let her stew! She was already forming a plan in her mind about asking her aunt and uncle if she could leave school and get a job, maybe after Christmas term ended. Then she could leave home and try and find Jake. She didn't really care about money, she felt she could happily live in his caravan with him and travel with the fair.

"Tell me how you get on after," Rachel said, and they parted company. Diana felt no fear as she headed towards the office. First she had to tell that miserable secretary Miss Wells she was here, one look at her face would confirm whether she had been told about Diana's attempt to leave school; that woman wouldn't be able to stop herself from gloating.

But the secretary barely glanced at her, so deeply engrossed was she in reading something. She just buzzed through to Miss McCoy, and then nodded Diana in. When she opened the door, confusion registered on her face, Miss McCoy wasn't looking grim, she had a smile on her face as though Diana had done something to be proud of. Now that was a first, that this old biddy would smile at her!

"Come in Diana, sit down."

She did as she was told, and watched her headmistress shuffling some papers in front of her. Maybe the old crow was going to expel her and she was happy about it. Well, she couldn't wait to go! She studied the headmistress's features, the lines on her face showed more because she just scragged her hair back and wore no make-up. She looked a typical old maid. What was the betting she was still a virgin. She remembered once at home, Pam's brother had said when a virgin died she was returned to God unopened, and they had laughed their heads off about it.

"I have been in contact with your uncle and aunt because we have all noticed just how much you love the arts. You dance and sing with a natural ability, and nobody could play the lead better than you in any of our school plays."

Diana's face was a picture of surprise. She had come in here expecting to be in serious trouble, and instead of that Miss McCoy was praising her to the skies. Perhaps the old girl wasn't so bad after all.

"Yes, I love acting, singing and dancing. I'm not much good academically."

"I have had a letter back from them. Instead of leaving school next summer, your uncle is prepared to fund you going to stage school after Christmas, if it's what you want. They would have discussed it with you if you had been at home, but as you are here until the Christmas holidays, they asked me to find out how you

35

feel, so your Uncle Clive could make the necessary enquiries. You would, of course, be allowed time off from here to go and visit anywhere that seems suitable and has a vacancy for you."

Diana couldn't believe it. Her uncle was going to take her away from this drab school so she could pursue her dreams to be an actress; no more boring maths and science. Of course, she was still broken-hearted about leaving Jake, and she would miss her protective sister Rachel, but what an opportunity this was. For once she was lost for words.

"Thank you, Miss McCoy," she managed to say as she was leaving the room.

"This is your chance in life, good luck!" said Miss McCoy kindly. The situation would benefit them both. Diana was not cut out for sixth form and university, but with her place free, she could now offer it to the daughter of a prominent politician, and she had no doubt he would be so grateful that he would donate a healthy sum to the school fund. What a great result, and everyone was happy.

Jake got up early to pack up for leaving. He had not slept that well, as images of Diana cascaded through his brain. He saw the sun shining through her red-gold hair, those green eyes had totally enslaved him; so much that he couldn't eat his breakfast. He could feel tremors inside him. This young girl had changed his life in an instant, and he yearned to see her again and arrange some way to keep seeing each other. He realised the situation was very difficult, because she was at school in Edinburgh and the fair was moving on to Carlisle, and then even further towards the south of England.

His mind was going in two directions; should he ask her to join the fair, live in his caravan and travel around with him? But wasn't that just a dream? Would a girl from a well to do family, at an exclusive boarding school, jack it all in to be with him? The other alternative was for him to leave his fair family, get a job and a place to live, and stay around close to her, and in time she might leave school and move in with him. Even though his life had been the fair for the last twelve years, he knew that he would leave it all behind him in a heartbeat for Diana.

It was now eleven o'clock, the time she said she would come.

In an hour or so the caravans would move on, along with all the fairground equipment which was now packed up. He was feeling nervous now, he ran his tongue over his dry lips and gulped, however would he cope if she hadn't been able to get away? He walked along the path to the clearing where he had first kissed her. He could never forget her soft lips, and her passion. She had stolen his heart, and he knew whatever happened in the future, he would never forget her.

As the minutes ticked by, and there was no sign of her, he felt the misery building up inside him. He couldn't go and look for her, he might miss her, but when midday came he was resigned to the fact he would probably never see her again. He couldn't even explain to Bobby; he would not understand, just think he was off his head.

Now everyone was springing into action; the vans were moving out, lorries rumbled slowly over the uneven ground, but Jake hung it out as long as he could and his van was the last one to depart. He looked back at the empty field with the flattened grass one last time with tears in his eyes, this woman had entered his life so briefly, and stirred his emotions in a way that had taken complete control of him. He felt lost without her; hope was now gone, his beautiful Diana had either been unable to come, or changed her mind, but whichever it was, he was left with an aching heart, and now he had no choice but to move on.

Rachel was delighted to hear that Diana was going to drama school. Doing something she really liked could be the making of her. She didn't feel even a twinge of jealousy. She had become used to giving her support; Diana was not a bad person, she was insecure.

The only regret she had was a selfish one; she would miss her. During their lives they had never spent a day apart, and she was so used to taking care of Diana and trying to steer her in the right direction. Her mother would have approved, and in some ways, with the absence of their parents, she felt more like her mother than her sister. Only really having each other had forged such a close bond, and even though their personalities were so different, and they fell out just like siblings did, they would always be close. No matter how difficult it was to get on with Diana at times, she would always love her and have her best interests at heart. She accepted all her twin's faults, and she hoped that Diana accepted hers. She knew she was too serious, she always did as she was told, and she didn't get a buzz out of flouting rules unlike her sister. She was probably a boring person, and she would never be as popular as Diana was. She was one of life's plodders; as was expected, she would continue to study maths and the sciences. One day she might become a scientist; maybe an unusual choice of career for a woman, but she wanted to study illnesses and try and find cures. Maybe a bold decision to make at sixteen, but the future would take care of that.

She had not seen Diana so animated for a long time, as she explained that Uncle Clive was making enquiries about a drama school in the city of London. Her eyes were sparkling and she was smiling.

"We are lucky, you know sis. Uncle Clive and Aunt Susan have been so good to us," said Rachel.

"I know we are. Drama school costs a bit, it's not their fault they are not Mum and Dad."

At one time Diana wouldn't have even thought about the cost of drama school let alone remark about it. Rachel was pleased to see she was becoming more unselfish. By the time she got to London, she would have forgotten all about that gypsy boy she met yesterday. Her sister was finally growing up; they could go their separate ways, and make their own way in life, but nothing would ever come between them because they were twins.

Chapter Six

2002

"Congratulations Rachel, you have worked hard and you deserve every bit of success! "

"I am so lucky landing a job like this. I didn't expect to get a job in a laboratory up in London, and get paid so much money!"

"Not lucky Rachel, you have done all the training and this is the result. Clive and I couldn't be more proud."

Susan didn't add the unspoken words, "If we had been your own parents," but it was in her own mind. It might be fourteen years since they lost their parents, but it was sad that Ella and Paul had not seen their lovely girls grow up. Rachel was always going to get on in life, she had the brains and dedication, but it had been harder for Diana, although even without the brains of her sister, she had found her own way in the arts and was thoroughly enjoying her life. After training at drama college, she now had her own flat in London, and had started off modestly by doing television adverts, but was on the list of many agents just waiting for her big break to come. Clive helped her a bit financially; he didn't mind, it was a drop in the ocean to them, and she seemed to be getting on OK with only a little bit of help.

"Well, it's only a little way from Diana's flat, so I thought until I find my feet, I could move in with her and we could share rent and expenses."

"What a good idea, it will help you both," said Susan warmly. Now the girls were growing up and leading their own lives, she felt their work was done. They still had their family ties, but they were ready to embrace independence, and hopefully they would find themselves good reliable husbands in time and have their own families.

It was a few months since Rachel had seen Diana. She had missed her so much at first when they went their separate ways, but gradually she had found throwing herself into her work at Cambridge had kept her mind occupied. They spoke on the phone once a week, so kept up with what each was doing. She knew Diana would love a part in some production, no matter how small, but apparently there were hundreds of other trained actresses that wanted the same thing. In the meantime, Diana was working as a waitress; she said she got good tips and, with a little bit of help from her uncle, that paid the bills. Rachel was sure her twin would welcome her with open arms; she had a regular wage, and her help with the bills would be just what Diana needed.

The one thing that she had to check was Diana's boyfriend situation. It was getting usual now for couples to move in together without being married. Everyone did it, unlike years ago, when girls didn't always leave home until they got married. If she did have a boyfriend living with her, then Rachel would not expect to stay.

"Does Diana speak about a boyfriend at all?"

"Not lately," said Susan. "Whilst she was at drama school there was a young man there, we met him a couple of times, but to be honest he was so full of himself we didn't really like him, not that we said that to her, it's her life. She never speaks about him now. She seems to work most evenings."

"Do you know which restaurant it is?"

"Not really; somewhere near to the flat."

Susan felt a bit guilty as she had never bothered to ask, or take much interest, when Diana had told her. She always knew that should the job go wrong, or Diana get bored with it, she would have Clive to fall back on.

Rachel was looking forward to catching up properly with Diana, maybe even eating at the restaurant herself and have her sister wait on her, that would be fun. They had not lived together for six years, and at the age of twenty-two now, whatever they each did with their lives was up to them. Although she still had the urge to protect her scatty sister, she realised that Diana was her own woman now and she must not interfere.

During her time at Cambridge, Rachel had found friends, all

like herself, anxious to do well in exams, get their degree, and then find a good well paid job. But away from the studying there was a lighter side, although Rachel didn't get caught up with any of the hard partying that some of the other students did. She partied a bit, because she knew that she was a serious type of person and she wanted to show she could have fun too, but she only had the odd glass of wine, smoking did not appeal to her, and if there was any drug taking, she was unaware of it because that was something she never wanted to try. She had never forgotten the time when she caught Diana smoking pot with that gypsy boy; how scared she had been that her beloved and wayward sister might become addicted to it, but luckily he had vanished into the mist, and Diana had gone to drama school.

Later that evening she picked up the phone to ring Diana, but there was no reply. Then she remembered her aunt had said Diana worked in the evening; of course, she would be in the restaurant. She rang back again, leaving a message for Diana to ring her at Aunt Susan's, as she was temporarily there.

Diana returned the call at lunchtime the next day. Her voice came over the phone excited and she was talking so fast. Rachel smiled to herself, Diana had not changed.

"I heard you're coming to work in London sis, you must look me up."

"I'd like to do better than that if I can; lighten your bills by staying with you for a while, until I find my feet."

Whilst those words were sinking in, Diana found herself panicking a bit. She was sure Rachel would not approve of her job, and then there was Clare, Rachel would definitely tell her to steer clear of her, but Diana loved helping lame ducks. Finally she made up her mind; she was a grown woman, it was her flat, and if Rachel didn't like the arrangements, then she probably wouldn't stay.

"You are welcome here sis, of course. I also have my friend Clare staying."

Rachel first felt a little twinge of regret that they couldn't catch up on old times with Diana's friend there, but then she wondered whether Diana actually had room for her.

"If it means you will be overcrowded, just say, I can always stay at a B and B until I find somewhere."

"You have a choice sis, you can either sleep in my room on a fold-up bed, or the sofa. Clare has the little box room, it's so small she stands by the door and jumps into bed. But of course I want to see you!"

"Me too, I can't wait; the fold-up will do nicely. I'll come this afternoon and get settled. Are you at work tonight?"

"Not tonight, I always have Monday off."

"Of course, lots of pubs don't do food on Mondays, I guess restaurants are the same."

Diana grimaced to herself, but continued to chat excitedly. It would be lovely to see her twin again, it had been several months, and those bonds would always be there.

"See you later then sis."

Rachel had lunch with her aunt, and then took a taxi to the station. Living in London would mean getting about by tube or bus, there was no need for a car, although she had passed her driving test whilst she had been in Cambridge. She hadn't bought a car; right now it suited her to live in the city close to work, but when she was more established in her job she might prefer to move out to the suburbs. Whilst she was staying with Diana she intended to look around for her own little place, but there was no rush.

She got off the train then took a tube, which as always was full of people. She was thankful to get out in the air, and as she came up the steps, she saw a row of terraced houses in front of her. Diana lived at number twenty-seven, which was halfway up the road. At least it was handy for the tube to work, but the continual flow of traffic over the years had discoloured the paintwork on most of the houses. She remembered her aunt saying how expensive it was to live right in the city, no matter what the property was, it was the sheer convenience of being close to where you worked. She pulled her case along behind her through the small gate, and before she could reach the door to knock, it was flung open, and her sister ran out and threw her arms around her.

"Great to see you, come in."

"Wow, you look different. It's your hair, how come?"

Diana had a new bouncy look, her long straight locks had been teased into bouncy curls. It shone with vitality as she pulled at it to show just how curly it was.

"I've been doing a shampoo advert, and they styled it with mousse and curled it, but tomorrow it will be just like yours."

Rachel smiled, clearly impressed. "It makes you look older and more mature somehow, and now people can tell us apart."

"I know, but it takes hours to do, so I am going back to the straight look. If you only knew how long it takes to make a twenty second advert; they have to get it right, sometimes it's all day!"

They had walked into the house by now. Rachel let go of her suitcase.

"By the way, we are upstairs; one flight up, so I'll give you a hand with that."

It was a Victorian house, deceptively large inside, and the staircase was wider than modern ones. They were both puffing by the time they reached the next flight, and Rachel noted there was another flight of steps and wondered who was unlucky enough to have to go up there every day. As if reading her thoughts, Diana explained.

"Clare sleeps in the box room up there. Like I said, it's very tiny, but she doesn't mind. She needed somewhere very quickly. She is at work right now, and I'll tell you all about it over a coffee. You do still drink coffee I take it!"

"Of course!" Rachel gave her a playful dig in the ribs. How great it was to be with her sister again, and she was intrigued to hear about Clare. Diana opened the door to a bedroom, which was a fair size; there was a single bed, and a fold-up one already made up. The walls were painted a cream colour to lighten it, the high ceiling was white, and the skirting boards were stained brown wood, which seemed to be in keeping with the age of the house. Rachel left her case there and followed Diana along the hall. The bathroom was the next door along; she peeped inside and noted it had a shower as well. Then at the end, was a large kitchen-cum-diner, which Diana explained had once been another bedroom with a scullery at the end, but the landlord had put in a new kitchen, knocked out the wall in between, and now it was a light, airy room, which was spacious. It had sofas and a TV, and in another corner was a computer and a desk, whilst the kitchen sported a washing machine, microwave, tumble dryer, and everything that one could need. The breakfast bar had tall stools, although Diana confessed that they mainly ate their meals on trays on their laps, especially in the evening. There were wooden floors with rugs everywhere, even the bedroom.

43

Whilst they were drinking their coffee she explained about Clare. She was training to be a midwife at the local hospital. She had been married to a man she had really loved, and after only a few months of marriage she got pregnant. She was so thrilled, but he wasn't, and had tried to make her have an abortion, saying that they were not ready for a baby yet. Clare defied him, and one night he lashed out at her, and realising that he was not only trying to control her, but also had a temper to match, she had left him, and he didn't now know where she was.

"So if she works at the hospital, how did you come to meet her?" enquired Rachel, already feeling sorry for Clare before she had even met her.

"She is the sister of a girl I work with, someone who herself has no home and virtually lives out of a suitcase."

"Why is that?" asked Rachel.

"It's because she gets jobs all over the place. It's not that easy in the entertainment business, you can work for a month, then have nothing for a year. If you can't put enough money by, then you can't buy your own home. So Ruth travels around staying at Premier Inns."

"It must be hard not having your own home, I can't wait to get mine."

"Yes, we are lucky. Uncle Clive is always willing to help out. If I am short on rent he makes it up, but I do so want to be independent and eventually buy my own home. Not that I would buy this flat, I would prefer a top floor one with a roof garden; somewhere to sit out when it's sunny."

"You don't want much. Let's hope something good will come up soon," said Rachel encouragingly, feeling rather awkward because she was earning a comfortable wage in a steady job, and had already made enquiries and found out she could get quite a substantial mortgage. It was a shame that after all the money her uncle had spent on drama school, Diana couldn't get the parts, being just one of many who went for auditions. None of the family had realised that might happen.

Now that Diana had made her point, she decided to drop the bombshell before Rachel started asking her where the restaurant was and if she could dine there. She knew that was exactly what she would do.

"Rachel, I don't work in a restaurant, I work as an escort. I am wined and dined by rich men who are looking for company."

Rachel had never been very good at hiding her feelings, so the look of horror on her face prompted Diana's next words.

"Now don't get hold of the wrong end of the stick. I work for an agency, the money is good, but it would stop immediately if I got a part in a play. I don't sleep with any of them, and they treat me with respect; it's a very reputable and high class agency. I know you are wondering why I told Aunt Susan that I worked in a restaurant, well it was because just like you have, they would assume the worst."

"I haven't assumed the worst, it was a surprise that's all. I know there are escort agencies in London; there seem to be lots of lonely travellers. I can understand why you haven't told our aunt and uncle. The only thing I am sorry about is that I will be at work all day and you will be working in the evening, so we are going to be like ships that pass in the night."

"Well Clare will be here soon. I think you will like her, and she needs all the friends she can get, and at least we can spend Monday evenings together."

Rachel hoped she would like Clare; it didn't sound as though Clare and Ruth had family backing like they did, but stage school fees were expensive, someone must have paid them.

"So when is her baby due, and is her husband likely to turn up in a rage?"

"No, he has a court order forbidding him any contact, and poor Clare miscarried the baby, I blame all the stress he gave her."

"That is sad."

"I know, but I am sure she will have another baby one day. She loves babies, that's why she took that job. At least it breaks his ties with her, but right now she is grieving and doesn't see it that way."

As they were speaking, a key could be heard unlocking the front door, Diana put her fingers over her lips, and Rachel guessed she was about to meet Clare. Her imagination had conjured up a mousey type woman, lacking in confidence after being subjected to bullying from her husband. Clare sounded quite unlike the flamboyant type of friends that Diana had always been drawn to in the past.

"Hi Di. Wow, you must be her twin, if it wasn't for your straight hair, I couldn't tell the difference."

The young woman who entered the room had long straight hair, which was very dark, as were her eyes; right now those eyes were sparkling with humour and she was smiling, showing a perfect set of very white teeth. Her dark hair was piled on top of her head, giving her an air of bearing and sophistication. She looked as if she could easily hold her own, not a cowed down abused wife.

Rachel shook her outstretched hand, her grip was firm, and she smiled back.

"Hi Clare, it's great to meet you. Are you tired from work."

"Not a bit, I have just helped to deliver a beautiful little boy. It's moments like that which make my job so worthwhile." And then Rachel spotted it, very fleetingly, a look of sadness in those eyes, no doubt thinking about what could have been, and instinctively her heart went out to her. How brave to do the job she did in spite of her own heartache. Rachel found herself liking Clare; she seemed down to earth, she admired someone who was a survivor, she didn't seem like the usual friends that Diana attracted, thank goodness. At last her sister was making much better judgements of character, which must mean she was growing up.

Chapter Seven

Although Rachel had not intended to wear out her welcome by staying for too long, it was obvious that the extra money she gave to Diana towards rent and expenses was making life much easier. Clare didn't earn much whilst she was training, but she helped a bit too. Rachel was hoping that Diana might give up her escort job, because however respectable she made it sound, there was always the worry that one of these apparently "nice" strangers she kept company with might turn out not to be so nice. If she decided to leave the flat, there was no chance that Diana would give up that job.

Rachel spent her evenings with Clare, they watched TV together, had the odd takeaway, as they both liked Chinese food, and got on well enough. Clare spoke a lot about the babies she delivered, and her job, and it was clear to Rachel how important it would be for her to be a mother. Her divorce was going through now on the grounds of mental and physical cruelty. Her husband had not contested it, which was a good thing, and Clare hoped that one day she could meet the right person, and become a mother. In a rare moment of closeness she had confided to Rachel her fears about another miscarriage, but now the doctors were aware of it, they had said they could do some sort of stitch to prevent her losing the baby at three months.

Diana had made a slight concession and no longer worked as much, she had trimmed it down to four days, making Sunday, Monday and Thursday her days off. Occasionally the three girls went out together for a meal at the local pub, or a social drink, and

47

it was during one of those evenings that Neil Morris came into their lives.

On this particular Sunday evening, they had opted to go and eat at the local Harvester. Diana and Rachel had enjoyed a nice restful day together, then Clare, who had been doing a weekend shift, arrived home tired and very stressed because one of her mothers had given birth prematurely to a little boy who was now in the special care unit fighting for his life.

"He is such a fragile little boy, his little finger clutched mine, he so wants to live," she said, with tears in her eyes.

Rachel instinctively put her arms round her, saying soothingly, "I am sure he will be OK tomorrow. Try not to worry, doctors are amazing these days, and many premature babies survive."

Diana agreed with her, and then suggested the trip out for dinner.

"A nice meal and a glass of wine to take your mind off it, you've earned it."

"My treat!" added Rachel, knowing she was the one who could most afford a night out.

Clare protested that she wasn't in the right mood to go out, and they should go without her, but the twins were having none of it. Diana opened a bottle of wine whilst Rachel ordered a taxi, and by the time Clare had drunk a glass of it, her colour returned, and she looked more relaxed. She knew what Rachel had said was true, and by tomorrow that little baby boy could even be off the ventilator; his firm grip meant he wanted to survive.

"Let me get out of my uniform. What are you both wearing?" she asked.

"Anything you like, it's quite warm. I am wearing my white trousers with a black and white top, and Diana said she is going in jeans."

"They are new jeans, not ripped or anything, and I've got a peach shirt blouse that goes with them," explained Diana.

Clare also opted for jeans; hers were teamed up with a blue silky blouse, and by the time she was dressed, the taxi had arrived. Rachel knew she was the odd one out, but she had never liked jeans, she always preferred to wear slacks or tailored trousers; long gone were the days since she and Diana had dressed alike. Now it was much easier for everyone to tell them apart simply by what they wore, and Rachel's build was stockier, her legs were not as shapely and slim as Diana's. But facially they were still very much alike. The way they dressed was in keeping with their characters, Diana was casual and free and easy, whereas Rachel was more serious, hence the tailored look.

They sat in the bar sipping their wine. Tonight it was quite full, it had been a pleasant spring day, warm enough to tempt families to take a day trip, then stop off for a meal on the way home. Families with children were already seated eating, but the girls were in no rush, the waiter had said there was a corner table becoming free soon, it was by the window with a nice view of the small courtyard which boasted lots of pots with spring flowers, golden daffodils and white crocuses and there was a tree laden with pink blossom, reminding everyone that spring had truly arrived.

By the time they reached their table, they were all feeling ready to eat, as the wine was making them feel a bit light headed. Rachel was pleased to see that Clare was much brighter now, and when the waiter came over, he took their order, then invited them to go up and help themselves to salad. They had all ordered chicken, so they went up to get a roll and butter, then fill their little bowls with as much salad as they would hold.

"That man over there is staring at us," said Diana in what she hoped was a stage whisper, whilst they were eating their crusty rolls.

"What man?" asked Rachel, not even looking up from her salad; eating seemed more important to her right now.

"Oh, do you mean that one with the fair hair? There are two other men with him too," said Clare.

"Yes, that one, the other two look ordinary, but he has very expressive eyes, and right now, those eyes are watching our every move."

"Watching your every move you mean," said Rachel lightly. It was bound to be Diana whom he was watching. She put down her fork and glanced over. Diana was right, he did have very expressive eyes, and was a very handsome man. She guessed his age to be about twenty-five.

"He's not my type, I prefer dark haired men," said Diana, and fleetingly her memory went back to Jake with his amazing blue eyes and tight black curls. In the last six years, none of her dates had touched her heart the way he did. She guessed she would always remember her first love.

49

c

"Don't look, you will encourage him!" said Rachel starchily, but only because the way he looked had caused her heart to miss a beat. This man with the penetrating eyes was having an effect on her, she had no idea why, but she wanted to stop it right now.

But it was too late, he got up from his chair and walked slowly towards them, and although she didn't want to catch his eye, Rachel found herself looking at him. His eyes were grey, and his brownish blond hair was inclined to flop forward a bit, which only added to his charm. There was something about him that reminded her of the American actor Leonardo DiCaprio who always had women dropping at his feet in adoration, not that she would, of course! He was probably only average height, but it was those eyes that right now showed warmth and friendliness, that were so hard to resist.

"Good evening ladies, I hope you don't mind me coming right over like this, but I am new in London, right now staying at The Hilton, but looking for somewhere more permanent. My name is Neil Morris."

Rachel studied him with suspicion. So he was American, but he wasn't Leonardo DiCaprio? He was obviously very wealthy if he was staying at the Hilton. Maybe this explained why he was dressed in a suit, and not casually as they were. So what on earth was he doing at a Harvester? He looked out of place, as did his two companions, all dressed in suits, who now wandered over to join in the conversation.

"Hi Neil, pleased to meet you. My name is Diana, this is my twin Rachel and our friend Clare."

Diana was impressed that he was a rich man, it might be useful to have him as a friend, and there was a certain charisma about him that she liked, as well as his American accent. His two companions were like mere shadows to him, it was just like they had only come along for the ride.

So far Rachel had said nothing, and only politeness caused her to grip his outstretched hand, but she marvelled at the sensation that shot through her, just like an electric current when they touched. She had always been too busy working and studying to ever have a serious relationship with any man, and she certainly wasn't looking for romance right now. She needed time to settle into her job and find herself a home, it was just too early, but her heart wasn't listening to anything that was in her head. She told

50

herself to stop feeling this way, he was simply being friendly. Diana and Clare seemed to like him, so they invited him and his companions to join them. The men brought their chairs over and pushed an empty table nearby up to the corner, much to the amazement of the waiter, but Neil gave him a tip of twenty pounds, which totally disarmed him, and so he left them to continue their conversation.

Neil introduced his two friends, and explained that they had come over from America for two years, and they were scientists working at a laboratory in London. They specialised in genetic studies. When she heard this, Rachel was amazed, and with her defences now down, she became very much a part of the conversation.

"Now that is amazing. I am also a scientist, studying the causes and prevention of cancer, and my laboratory is very close to yours."

"Wow really? That means you and I will have plenty to talk about."

She blushed, quickly moving the conversation away from herself. "Clare is a midwife, and she works at the local hospital. . . "

Not to be outdone, Diana cut in. "I am an actress." She knew that wasn't strictly true, but she had trained hard for it, and she would be when she got a part.

"Gee that's interesting, what shows have you done?"

Diana did not look at Rachel or Clare, she knew they wouldn't shop her to him.

"Well right now I am doing shampoo adverts, but I have a top secret part that is coming up very shortly."

To her disappointment Neil turned his attention back to Rachel, and they started a conversation about stuff that she knew nothing about, so she had to be content with chatting to the other two men, who also seemed to be scientists but were content not to talk shop all evening. By the time they left and went home, it was obvious that Rachel and Neil were on the same wave length, they had so much in common.

Chapter Eight

Neil Morris was delighted at how the evening had panned out. Ever since he had heard about Rachel Wilcox, how clever at her job she was, he had been intrigued to meet her. He hadn't realised quite how beautiful she would be, those green eyes were to die for, and her twin sister was cute too. As soon as he met her, he felt it, such a strong attraction for her. She wasn't as bold or confident as her sister, and yet by all accounts, she was a very successful business woman. He was very grateful to Barry for finding out so much for him.

He smiled to himself as he lay in bed; the little lady didn't know it yet, but he planned to marry her. With her beauty and brains, they would make a great couple, and could enjoy a happy life together. But he sensed she could not be rushed, he had to take his time and woo her, maybe a bit of old fashioned charm would win her over, but they had plenty of time to get to know each other.

He turned over, plumped up the pillow, then stretched out contentedly, maybe this time next year they would be sharing, not only their home together, but also the marital bed.

Rachel was also deep in thought as she lay in bed. During her time at work, most of the people she had met were older than herself and settled in life. There were very wise professors, men dedicated to discovering cures for so many illnesses, women who somehow combined family life and working life, and all of them were dedicated to doing their very best for medical science.

But she had never met anyone like Neil, at only twenty-five she assumed he had recently left his student days behind. With his eye-popping good looks, he looked more like a film star than a scientist, he just didn't fit into the image she had, but then she reasoned with herself, ever since she had been in her job, her youth was often commented on, and she obviously didn't look like a scientist either.

She liked the idea that they both shared a desire to discover answers to such important questions, which could make people's lives better, and in some cases prolong lives and give people with serious illnesses some hope. Neil had asked to meet up with her again, but she reminded herself that they were only friends, he was just in England for a couple of years then he would go back to America. There was no future for them so friendship was the best option. When she was ready to fall in love, she would find someone in England. So why was it her heart argued back, and her skin prickled every time she thought about him? Physical attraction was a powerful thing, but she was not looking for an affair; when she found the right person it would be a lifetime commitment.

She could hear the even breathing of her sister in the other bed. For the last few months she had endured this fold-up bed, with a mattress that had virtually no support, and most mornings she woke up with a backache. It was silly really, she had enough money to get her own place, and the only thing stopping her was the knowledge that Diana wouldn't manage without the extra money she gave her. All her life she had put her sister first, but she knew that she really wanted to experience her own home comforts, and she wouldn't be that far away from Diana and Clare. She had even thought of giving Diana a monthly allowance; she could easily afford it, but it might seem like she was patronising her. She was always careful not to say too much about what good money she earned, being conscious of the fact that Diana envied her, but could she blame her for that? They had all wrongfully assumed that once she left drama school there would be plenty of work for her.

When she got up the next morning, she went into the kitchen to see Diana with a look of jubilation on her face, and the telephone receiver laying carelessly next to her. She jumped up from the table and hugged Rachel.

"I've done it sis, the audition I went to last week, I got the job! It's a TV drama in six parts. I am acting alongside some big names, and it's quite a big part. They are paying me good money for it and expecting it to do very well, with a possibility of a sequel in the autumn. Finally I can call myself an actress!"

Rachel hugged her back; she was genuinely pleased for Diana, and she knew her aunt and uncle would be too.

"Oh well done sis, do you have to travel for it?"

"No, that's the good thing about it, it's all filmed in London, right on my doorstep, so I can come back here every night. Of course, I will have to pack in the escort agency, but that was only a stop gap anyway."

Rachel could not hide her relief, not only would Diana stop being an escort, she could justify moving into her own flat without leaving them both in the lurch. Oh how wonderful this had all come at just the right time!

"It's time I moved on now Di, that fold-up is doing my back in and you will be OK now."

"I know, it's been great having you, and now you have Neil in your life you don't need to be here with us cramping your style."

"Oh, it's not that. Neil is only a friend you know. He's not going to be in the UK for long, but obviously with our jobs we have so much in common."

She hoped she sounded convincing, but she wasn't sure that Diana was convinced. Although her decision to move out was certainly nothing to do with Neil. She had simply been waiting for the right time.

"He likes you, anyone can see that." If Diana's tone was a little disgruntled, it was at the knowledge that not only did her sister earn more money than her, she had also attracted the best looking man around last night.

Rachel shrugged off her attitude, nobody understood Diana more than she did, there was always a need to be the centre of attention, and unwittingly Rachel had robbed her of that. Even she was surprised that Neil had noticed her first, because Diana's vibrant personality always got her noticed. Deep down, if she cared to admit it to herself, it had been quite a boost to her morale.

She left Diana to ring her aunt and uncle and tell them the good news, and went out to the local estate agent. She wasn't going to be bothered with renting; why throw good money away every month when she could easily get a mortgage and also had quite a substantial sum to put down on a deposit. The prices around Chelsea, and even further into the city, were astronomical, and she realised she would be paying for the area rather than the property; she wouldn't be content with some of the poky little studio flats on offer. Places like Tooting, Balham, and Wandsworth were only a short tube journey away from where she worked, and in those areas she could get so much more for her money.

When she went to view the properties, she was dismayed about the condition of some of them. She could certainly get someone in to smarten them up, but how nice it would be to move into somewhere new, with everything modern and bright.

"Well Miss Wilcox, what do you think?" asked Jeremy Bryce hopefully, after he had spent the whole afternoon showing her just about every flat on his books.

To Rachel he looked a typical estate agent with his city suit, blue shirt and shiny shoes. Even his dark hair was immaculately groomed without a single lock out of place, and he reeked of aftershave.

"I will know it when I see it, but nothing yet attracts me," she said kindly but firmly, and his hopes were temporarily dashed. Didn't these customers realise he worked on commission, and had bills to pay? Nevertheless he managed her a polite smile when he shook her hand, and promised to let her know when something more suitable did come up.

After doing quite a bit of thinking, Rachel came up with a different plan. She liked the Clapham Common area; most of the houses there were Victorian with sash windows, high ceilings and wide staircases. What she liked most about them was they were spacious, the rooms were big, and the accommodation was set out on three floors. The gardens were not much more than a courtyard, but that suited Rachel, they were easy to care for with still enough room to sit out on a pleasant day.

Her plan was to get one converted into three separate flats, so she could get an income from letting out the other two floors. She would live on the ground floor, where there were normally two big rooms, one would be her lounge, with a sofa bed in case anyone came to stay, the other would be her bedroom, next to that would be a bathroom, and the end room, which generally led onto the garden, would be her kitchen/diner after a builder had knocked out the old fashioned walk-in larder and totally modernised the kitchen.

There was a very neglected property in which an old lady had lived for many years before she died. It had not been decorated or modernised since about 1950, and the wall paper had turned brown and was peeling, but she could see the potential. It was overlooking the common, which at this time of the year with the blossoms on the trees and a carpet of daffodils glinting in the sunshine, looked particularly attractive.

The relatives lived abroad and all they wanted was their inheritance. It was still full of old and very dusty furniture, which had put off a lot of would-be buyers, but Rachel agreed to dispose of it all, and in return she negotiated a price much lower than that which they were asking. After a couple of weeks of telephone calls back and forth, the price was agreed.

She had taken Diana to see it, and even suggested that if she wanted one of the flats, it was hers, and the same applied to Clare. After giving it some thought, they had both decided against it as their current flat was so close to where they worked.

When she had organised the builders and set them to work, she asked Neil if he wanted to see it. He had been searching around the city for somewhere to rent without success. His two friends apparently had found somewhere, but he explained that it was too small for him and he didn't really want to share.

Neil was a great companion; he made her laugh, and everywhere they went he seemed to get on with everyone. He was a perfect gentleman too, he never tried to get too close to her, so she assumed he also only wanted a friendship. She squashed down any feelings of disappointment that he didn't find her attractive; was there no pleasing her, and wasn't that exactly what she wanted?

"I have lots of plans for this house," she explained as they were walking around. Since she had found a furniture clearance company to take away all the old furniture, she could appreciate even more the size of the rooms.

"Which floor are you having?" enquired Neil. He liked this quaint Victorian house with such a sunny outlook. He wondered whether she would let him stay there. The location would suit him perfectly.

"I am having the ground floor. Come and take a look at the kitchen that is almost fitted."

Neil enthused about it. Keeping her at arm's length was becoming difficult. Her beauty shone out of her, and he wanted to take her in his arms, but he wasn't sure how she would react to that. Three months seemed a long time to spend with someone so lovely, who stirred his senses so much, and yet keep their relationship platonic. Maybe if she let him stay here they could become closer. He took a chance, she could only say no.

"Rachel, how about letting the second floor to me? You know me already, I am a clean and tidy guy, and I don't make much noise."

She looked into his grey eyes, they looked so pleading, and the thought of having him here made her feel safe. She clasped his hand, and she felt it, that tingle at his touch, and suddenly she found herself tilting her face up to his and stroking his cheek, and before she even had time to draw breath, his lips met hers. His kiss was gentle, but as her lips clung to him, she felt such passion flare through her, it totally took over her senses, and time stood still for her. When he eventually released her, she was trembling, and his words were overwhelming.

"Rachel, I love you, from the moment I saw you, I knew, and I think you feel the same way. I don't want to just be friends, please tell me you feel the same."

Rachel snuggled into the warmth of his arms. Having Neil around felt so right, all her barriers were down now, and she realised she couldn't choose who to fall in love with, or when. It had already happened, and she had never felt happier.

"Yes, I love you too," she whispered.

Chapter Nine

"Well Barry, we are finally a couple. Just in time too, as I had asked her to rent a floor out to me but no way could I pay for it."

"Have you moved in with her?"

"Of course, and right now she thinks I am hard at work in the laboratory," smiled Neil, lifting up his pint of beer. "Thanks for the ale, when we get married I can pay you back your dues."

"I just don't know how you get away with it; women are so trusting."

"Well, it's so easy with her; she's in love with me, and I must admit I fancy her too, so it's no hardship sharing her bed. But as you know, I need money to survive, and so do you, so once I've got her under my control, let's say her money will be spread out more evenly."

"But how have you kept her believing you are a scientist rather than a fraudster? You know as much as I do about genetics, which is nothing."

"Ah, well, I am a good listener, I let her talk about her job and I tell her mine is top secret, and she is very impressed."

They had finished their drinks now, so they left the pub to walk along the embankment to the small flat that Barry now shared with Colin. It was fairly shabby, but all they could hope to have as dole money didn't stretch that far, and they had been lucky that Neil had charmed the landlord's daughter into letting them have it, as she believed that Colin was starting a new job the following week. They both walked down the cracked and rickety steps to the dark basement flat, and Neil once again marvelled at his good fortune. This place was not for him; once he had lived in San Diego, California, a home near the sea with sunshine all year round. At least Rachel's house was grand, and in a nice setting, he truly had fallen on his feet.

"Neil, you crack me up, I can't believe you told her we were staying at the Hilton and she believed you."

They both chortled at the memory. Neil always had expensive tastes and a plausible line, he had perfected the art of using his eyes to convince people of his sincerity. He always believed in making use of whatever nature was kind enough to give you, and his expressive eyes and good clean cut looks had so far proved to be his fortune.

Rachel was truly in love for the first time in her life. It had hit her with a bang, Neil meant more to her even than her job. She still relived that first night when they had both realised they wanted the same thing. She couldn't have taken him back to Diana's flat, and there were builders wandering around the house in Clapham. She remembered how Neil had suggested booking a hotel room for the night, and how annoyed he had been when he realised he had left his wallet with his credit cards behind. But that had only been a hiccup, as she always carried her cards in her handbag.

Neil had said he had left The Hilton, and after only one night with his friends, he realised he needed his own space. Knowing what he was used to meant Rachel chose a very upmarket hotel in Knightsbridge for that night.

It was four in the afternoon when they arrived there, but when they were finally alone, his kisses sent her dizzy with excitement, and driven on by such passion, they undressed each other and his hands explored every inch of her body. At the age of twenty-two, and with no sexual experience, Rachel had endured being teased at University, but until now no man had ever reached her heart and made her feel like this. Any shyness was now forgotten, as lust and a need to experience sex now took control of her body. His hands and his mouth were teasing her, she could feel orgasms ripping through her, and she found herself begging him to take her properly; she was using language she never had before, and it was so erotic.

When he finally entered her, she felt all her muscles tightening around his penis. It was the first time she had ever touched a man, but she felt no shame or embarrassment, this was what love was all about, the joining of two people together in mind and body. They were both groaning as he pumped away inside her, and when she felt that final orgasm erupt, she knew she had finally experienced heaven; this was true love.

Being in love she felt, had mellowed her as a person. Suddenly the world seemed a wonderful place, and everyone in it too. The contentment that she felt at finding the right person, who loved her as much as she loved him, was so gratifying. She even thought briefly about Diana's first love Jake, and she felt sad for her, that she had been so young. After all, time would have shown whether their love would have lasted. She had never known whether it had just been teenage innocence, Diana had never told her, but over the last six years there really hadn't been any relationships, so she hoped her twin had moved on. Now she was happy, she wanted everyone to be happy.

So when Rachel took up residence in the house, Neil came with her. They moved in together, and after a very short time they were making plans to get married in 2003. Her uncle and aunt had met Neil and thoroughly approved of him, and were so happy for Rachel. Uncle Clive was going to give her away, and Barry had agreed to be best man. Her uncle and aunt had always thought that Rachel had a wise head on her shoulders, and they would certainly make a very beautiful couple, so it was pleasing to know that one of their nieces had sorted out her own future. Indeed it appeared that instead of going back to America after his two years was up, Neil was going to make a new life with Rachel in England, that was how strong his love for her was.

Diana heard the news with mixed feelings. Part of her wanted Rachel to be happy; being married and having children would provide her with the love and stability they had both lost when their parents died. But another part of her felt very jealous of her sister, and because she knew she was jealous, she couldn't be sure whether it was this jealousy which made her mistrust Neil.

There was no foundation for it except a feeling deep inside her that he might not have her sister's best interests at heart. Usually, in the past, Rachel had been the one with common sense, the one who could detect when something was not quite right; but love was blind, and Rachel had fallen heavily for Neil, so she knew she would only put her sister's concern down to jealousy. And maybe it was, even Diana herself wasn't sure.

She considered the facts: Neil had no family to invite to the wedding. He had said that his parents had also been killed in a car crash before he came to England. He was an only child and stood to inherit a lot of money, but unfortunately there was a court case going on right now with regards to the accident, and this was holding up the release of his inheritance. Apparently it had been like this for two years, since their death.

This might well be true, but she knew that her sister was paying out for everything, willingly it had to be said, but Neil was a scientist too, so what was he doing with his money? She hoped he wasn't a compulsive gambler; after all what did they really know about him? The other thing that made her feel uncomfortable about him was the way his eyes followed her around. He was marrying her sister, and once she knew they were an item she stopped entertaining any thoughts about him, he was off limits, soon to be Rachel's husband. But it didn't stop him from looking at her. On more than one occasion she sensed him admiring her cleavage, so she made sure when he was around to only wear high necked tops and dresses, but she knew she really shouldn't need to go to those lengths. He had been such a gentleman to them both when they first met, but she now decided she thought he was a conceited oversexed man; which was sad, because keeping that from her sister would be hard, they were so close.

Rachel had chosen a beautiful white wedding dress, it had a scalloped neck, and the bodice had tiny flowers etched into it. It was shaped to her tiny waist, then the very full skirt flowed out in front, also etched with flowers, and the long train flowed behind her, which as chief bridesmaid, Diana would be responsible for, making sure it didn't get caught up in any way. Rachel had been very generous, and said Diana could choose her own colour for her dress, and the two young female cousins who were also bridesmaids, would also have dresses that colour and the two page boys would be matching too, with shirts of the same colour. Being a strawberry blonde meant that not all colours suited her. Coffee would have been a good compromise, but Diana thought it quite a dull colour, so in the end she decided on tango orange; that was a colour that would make her stand out.

Rachel didn't bat an eyelid when she told her. She wanted Diana to be as happy as she was, and if the two little boys had a problem with tango orange shirts then she would simply find someone else to replace them. Her sister's well being and happiness was very important to her.

Uncle Clive would not allow Rachel to put a single penny towards her wedding. He ignored all her protests, and those of Neil, he felt this was the biggest thing he could do for her in the absence of her parents. Money was no problem to him, and he intended to treat Diana the same way when she found herself a husband.

The wedding was booked at the little local church where Clive and Susan had married some thirty years earlier, and then afterwards Clive had hired the local golf club where a very nice sit-down meal would be served, followed by dancing to a band that had been recommended to him. During the evening, the newly-weds would slip off and leave everyone enjoying themselves whilst they flew to the Maldives for their honeymoon. No expense was spared, and he even took the strain off Rachel and Susan by hiring a wedding planner.

Diana had tried to speak to her uncle and aunt about her fears, but they were having none of it. Diana had always been very dramatic, she still loved to be the centre of attention, and was often jealous of her sister. She didn't mention that Neil often ogled her, but she spoke about his lack of family.

"Don't you think it's strange, Aunt Susan, that he has no other family to invite, just his two friends in England?"

Susan thought it was a shame that Diana envied her sister's happiness. Being in love with Neil had totally brought Rachel out of her shell; she was far less serious, and no longer married to her job. She put Diana's misgivings down to the shock of losing her sister, but it had been bound to happen one day.

"Well Diana, his parents are gone, and from what I can gather, the little bit of family left are only a couple of cousins, and they are fighting for part of the inheritance, which is why it's taking so long."

"But why would his cousins imagine they stood to inherit anyway?" persisted Diana.

"Oh, I don't know all the details," said Susan. "But I believe his parents brought them up for a number of years because their own mother had a breakdown. So sadly for poor Neil, there is some bad feelings in the family."

Diana could see that her theories were not going to be taken seriously, so later that evening, she spoke to Clare about it.

"Clare, do you think Neil is genuine, and will make my sister happy?"

Clare looked up from the magazine she had been reading. It had been a very busy day, and here was Diana, as dramatic as ever, getting all heavy with her.

"I think he adores Rachel, they were made for each other!" she said very firmly, hoping there was not going to be a post mortem. As far as she was concerned, it was her friend's sister getting married, and it was her own life, not really her business. She had an invite to the wedding, so would go along and enjoy the day with everyone else and wish them both well. But whatever happened after that, would happen, and it was nothing to do with her.

Well, it seemed that everyone else liked Neil and thought he was the right person for Rachel, so maybe she, Diana, was seeing things that weren't there. One thing she knew, there was no way she could put her suspicions to Rachel. The glow of being in love positively shone out of Rachel. Her sister was besotted with Neil and would not take her reservations seriously. Not only that, it would cause a rift between them, and Diana never wanted that to happen. They loved each other, warts and all. They were twins, and she didn't want to think any man could come between them.

Chapter Ten

The wedding was set for April. A spring wedding whilst there was blossom on the trees and daffodils in bloom. It was exactly a year since they had first become a couple, and Rachel couldn't wait to be married. She worked long hours, so to come home to Neil at the end of a day, and sit down and have dinner with him, whilst discussing how her day had gone, was still a novelty. During that year he changed so little, that she was convinced they knew everything they needed to know about each other.

He spoke about how his father had run so many businesses in California, and his mother had looked after his cousins as well as himself. They had grown up like brothers together, so he found it particularly nauseating that they should challenge his parents' will and try to deprive him of his inheritance.

Rachel had assured him many times that it wasn't an issue with her. They could start again; they had their own home, and both had good jobs. Rachel really didn't worry about money, she was careful, and she saved whatever she didn't need. In the past she explained that she had helped Diana, but now her twin was getting more regular work and was able to stand on her own two feet. She had done TV work, and now had a small part in a film. She had gone to Yorkshire to shoot the scenes, but would be back in time for the wedding.

For Neil it had been a year of keeping up his gentlemanly behaviour, and it was a strain sometimes; holding open doors, walking nearest the road, none of this came naturally to him, but to be convincing, and not a fraudster, especially where women were concerned, these were the tricks of the trade. Even when he felt angry, he never showed it, he kept his volatile temper under control, he had to, because they were not married yet and he had no power over her.

In March, Rachel realised she was pregnant. She told Neil, but no one else. With a bit of luck in the next month she wouldn't fill out enough to need having her dress altered. It was obviously not the best time, right on top of her wedding, but that didn't stop her feeling excited and happy. To have a child by the man she loved had been her dearest wish; to start their own family, and be a mother, and what an amazing father Neil would make. He swung her up in the air with joy when she told him, he hadn't realised it would be so quick. Obviously having a child between them gave him even more power and access to her money. She had wanted for a while to have a joint bank account, but he realised she would be very suspicious if he didn't have any wages paid into it, so he had suggested that they do it later, after his money came through, and that way he would have much more money to add to the pot.

"It's kinda freaky for me babe, that my inheritance is taking so long," he complained.

Sensing his embarrassment, Rachel quickly squeezed his hand and changed the subject. She knew her husband to be was proud, and the last thing she wanted to do was make him feel a lesser person than herself over money.

Rachel told Diana during their night out before the wedding. They decided to go out for a meal rather than having a party in the local pub. A couple of friends from school came with them and Clare as well. It was an old fashioned restaurant overlooking the River Thames, with white linen tablecloths and crystal glasses. At one end there were sofas to sink into and have a drink before going to the table, and there was a rich burgundy carpet, unlike most of the modern eating places which had opted for hard floors.

Along the walls were black and white photographs of stars of 1950s and later, Audrey Hepburn with her elfin face, James Stewart puffing on a pipe, and Marilyn Monroe in a slinky dress pouting. Further along was Cliff Richard curling his lip, with his famous quiff, and Rod Stewart in teddy boy garb looking mean and moody. Rachel liked this restaurant, they had been there with her aunt and uncle many times, and she had done her best to persuade them to come this evening, but they had thanked her and said no, she should enjoy the evening with friends of her own age, because they had tomorrow to look forward to.

She was suffering with morning sickness, but was hoping the nausea would not come back to plague her tonight. Usually she spent the evening quietly at home with Neil, but Diana had talked her into this get together on her final night of being single. Neil had gone out celebrating with Barry and Colin.

There were bottles of champagne on the table to accompany the meal, and Rachel wondered how she was going to get away with not drinking without Diana noticing. The waiter hovered politely waiting to be told when to pour. They made their way to the table, Rachel was at the head, and she indicated she wanted water by picking up the small tumbler. Diana seated herself on one side, explaining the other three girls had gone to the ladies' room.

"Good!" said Rachel. "Then I can explain to you; no champagne or anything alcoholic tonight, as I am pregnant."

Diana looked dumbfounded, but quickly composed herself. It wasn't that surprising really when she thought about it, this marriage was about to take place, and maybe she was wrong to think it wouldn't work. A baby should bring them very close.

"Oh, well done sis. When are you due?"

"I think it is mid-November according to the dates I have worked out, though we haven't told anyone else. Right now I am suffering from morning sickness."

"Oh nasty. If you want to keep it a secret from the girls, let the waiter pour your champers, we'll toast you, and we can swap glasses."

They hugged briefly, as they saw the others coming towards them. Rachel was so grateful for Diana's support. Lately her sister had shown such maturity and loyalty, she didn't know how she would manage without her.

The evening passed very well, she allowed herself a sip of champagne, when toasted, but Diana had the rest of it whilst the others were busy talking. She wasn't ready to share her news with her other friends yet, it was only fair that her uncle and aunt should know first, but after the wedding would be time enough. The only one she had misgivings about telling was Clare. It was clear that she still wanted to be a mother, she was now even talking about having her own baby by a sperm donor, as after her ill fated marriage, she had lost all faith in men. During their time together before she bought the house, Rachel had come to realise having a baby was a bit of an obsession with Clare, and they had both told her not to judge all men by one bad one, and most men would make a great husband and father, but she wasn't sure Clare was listening to them.

When the evening was over, and they were in the taxi heading home, Rachel hugged Diana and whispered, "Thanks sis, for all your support." Diana squashed down her misgivings; within a few months she was going to be an auntie, and Rachel was positively glowing with happiness. She was truly in love, it wasn't her place to interfere, and she wished them happiness from the bottom of her heart.

Neil was enjoying his supposed last night of freedom. What a laugh that was, he would enjoy freedom whenever he wanted to, it's just that Rachel wouldn't know about it. Even tonight he was being eyed by a sexy looking blonde on the other side of the bar. She might not be as striking as his green eyed beauty and her cute sister, but she would do for tonight.

Barry hadn't missed what was happening. He was used to all the women lusting after Neil, and he knew he couldn't keep it in his trousers, and he wouldn't after he was married, but tonight was their stag night, not Neil's shag night.

"Keep your eyes off her bruv, we need to sink a few pints tonight."

"No harm in looking," said Neil very lightly. He wasn't that bothered really, he was sure that he could have a lot of fun with the new credit card he now had. Rachel had encouraged him to get one. It was linked to her bank account, she said money didn't matter when you were in love, and he just knew he was in for a life of wealth and comfort; that is if he stayed with her long enough, but that depended on how soon he could get his hands on her money.

Barry envied Neil his looks and charm, and whatever else he had that attracted women, but he was also wary of his temper. Neil became a different person at those times, and when it happened he made sure to keep out of his way. But tonight everything was going his way, and he was in great humour. The drink would flow, and the wedding would not be mentioned. Tomorrow the deed would be done, and very shortly Neil would be rewarding him for manipulating the meeting with Rachel. Very shortly he would be in credit. It had been a while, and he was looking forward to having money again.

Colin wasn't saying much. He had always been the quiet one of the three. He was easily forgettable, with his mousy brown hair, which always looked greasy, his ill fitting clothes, which hung on his small thin frame. He was a listener rather than a talker, but no doubt Neil would see him all right too when he came into the money, as Colin was the odd job man; he did all the dirty work. He was quiet and often not noticed, which could be very handy at times.

Whilst wishing he had Neil's looks and charm, Barry knew he himself was ordinary and no oil painting, and he could do with losing a bit of weight; his fondness for pizza and takeaways was to blame for that. But his dark hair was always kept neat and short, and right now he had it short at the sides with a quiff at the top, which he frequently brushed back. He wished he could make sincerity shine out of his eyes the way Neil did. Of course, there was nothing sincere about Neil, but as far as women went, it worked every time.

Over the next couple of hours they did themselves proud, and when they got up to stagger home from the pub, Barry was talking about stopping off at the fish shop to buy a kebab; whereas, through his drunken stupor, Neil noticed the blonde was still there, with another girl, who was not as tall and slim, but had brown hair with golden lights in it, so he thought, or was it a light from behind her; he couldn't be sure, but she had a doll-like face and tiny hands and feet.

Neil lurched towards them.

"Hello ladies, can we escort you home?"

The blonde seemed amused by that.

"I don't think you'll make it without falling over," she retorted.

Neil liked her, she had attitude, he loved those sort of women. But maybe she was right, he might not even be able to walk a straight line, let alone shag her. But he wasn't about to find out, as Barry intervened.

"We need to get you home Neil, otherwise you won't make it to the church tomorrow."

"Don't tell me you are getting married," laughed the blonde, not appearing to mind at all.

But although Neil's mind was lusting after either of those two, they both looked good through the haze that was assaulting him, his body was not going to comply. He collapsed onto the floor in front of them, vomiting violently and passing out.

"Very classy!" said the blonde, and they moved away from him rapidly.

Now Barry was worried. They could not afford for anything to go wrong, they had to get him back to the house, sober him up and ensure he was fit for tomorrow. Luckily Rachel would not be there, as she was setting out from her uncle and aunt's house, as was tradition with her uncle giving her away.

The landlord had come over by now, shouting angrily for them to get him out of there. The bar man was ready with a bucket of hot water to clear up, and the whole of the pub was alight with interest as to what was going on.

"Come on Colin, help me move him!" ordered Barry, and together they lifted Neil's prostrate body to the outside of the pub.

They were both puffing now, and although it wasn't that far to walk to the house, they weren't sure they could carry him between them.

"I don't understand why he's so ill!" wailed Barry in frustration. "He only had pints like us."

Colin grinned inwardly. He had spiked the bastard's beer with vodka. After all, the pratt owed him money. But as usual his face was inscrutable to Barry. He only said:

"He can't take his drink!"

"Well they won't let him in a taxi like this!"

Maybe that wasn't Colin's finest move after all. He didn't like the idea of having to carry him home. But Barry was doing his best to rouse Neil by shouting in his ear, and finally he came round, much to Barry's relief. They had no choice but to support his weight between them, and walk him home slowly. Two streets felt like a hundred miles, and all the mocking comments from other less inebriated drinkers, who were also on their way home, made them both feel ridiculous. If Colin had his way, they would leave him in a heap on the floor, but Barry knew Neil was their meal ticket for the future, so one way or another, he was determined to get him home.

When they finally arrived at the flat and opened the door, they simply dumped Neil on a sofa in the lounge, found a blanket to put over him, and then went to bed themselves, choosing a bedroom each, with a proper bed in it. It was doubtful whether Neil would be aware of anything, let alone where he slept that night, so Barry fell into a troubled sleep, resolving to make sure that Neil would make it to the wedding tomorrow in one piece.

The next day they all had bad headaches, but Neil's was worse. He didn't want to eat any breakfast, and his face was pale and wan. As the wedding was at midday, Barry realised he didn't have that long to get Neil organised; it was now ten o'clock, and he was just sitting there complaining about his head.

"You're not the only one, and if it wasn't for Colin and I, you wouldn't have made it home last night," Barry reminded him. "We all need to have a shower and get our suits on shortly, and in the meantime Neil, I have made some scrambled egg and toast, you need to line your stomach."

"OK," said Neil wearily. He felt like shit, but the plan was falling into place. He just had to get through today, because tomorrow he would be a married man, sunning himself in the Maldives.

Chapter Eleven

"Rachel, you look stunning!"

Susan was not an emotional person, but when she saw her niece gliding downstairs, helped by Diana, who was holding the train of her dress up so her sister would not trip, she could feel tears pricking at her eyelids, and she hastily blinked them away. It had been the same when Rachel had graduated; the day they went to see her, even after all these years, the thought of just how proud her parents would have been was always there, and unspoken. Both the girls had grown up to be daughters their parents would have been proud of. Even Diana seemed less self-centred these days, and her bond with her sister would always remain. They seemed so far removed from the bewildered and scared little girls who had been orphaned so suddenly at eight years old.

Rachel's dress fitted perfectly; her nipped in waist still held the secret of her pregnancy, but there was a glow about her which only enhanced her beauty. Not having been a mother herself, Susan had not realised it was the glow a woman gets when she is pregnant. Her red gold hair was piled on top of her head in a neat chignon style which accentuated just how big her green eyes were. There was a slight flush to her cheeks, and she only needed light make-up. Her headdress and veil were kept simple and radiance shone out of her. If she was nervous, it didn't show, she was smiling happily, and had declared that she couldn't wait to get married.

"Thank you, Aunt Susan, the hairdresser and Diana have worked hard on me."

"Not that hard. You started off looking good, and I even had time to get dressed myself," said Diana generously, with maybe a tinge of jealousy; after all, she hoped she looked good in her tango orange dress.

"Well sis, everyone can tell us apart today, me in white and you in orange, my hair up on top and yours loose. That tango colour really suits you, doesn't it, aunt Susan?"

"Yes, they both look lovely, don't they Clive?" said Susan pointedly, as Clive was flicking through the newspaper, so he obediently paid attention and agreed with her.

"The car is here," said Diana, spotting it drawing up in the driveway, resplendent with its satin white ribbon. "I'm supposed to be there before you anyway," she added.

"It's ok, we are not going yet, there is another car for you and the bridesmaids and pageboys."

Diana felt quite panicky inside. After all, she was losing her sister a bit today; but Rachel remained calm and in control. This felt reassuring to her as, together with her aunt, she made her way outside to their car. Her uncle remained behind with Rachel, as they were going in another car.

"Don't forget to help her with her dress, and I will be waiting at the entrance when you arrive," she reminded her uncle as they passed him, and Susan patted her hand, and told her not to worry because she had already given Clive full instructions.

Rachel was in her own bubble of happiness today and nothing could penetrate it. She was marrying the man she loved with all her heart, and the father of her baby. She could not wait to meet him at the church and say her wedding vows, and she marvelled at how he had come into her life and swept her off her feet. She felt beautiful, and she knew being in love made her that way. Her husband to be was so handsome, he could have chosen anyone, but he had chosen her. Everyone remarked what a handsome couple they were, and what beautiful babies they would have. She hugged her tummy silently, revelling in her precious secret that only Diana knew about.

She was aware of her uncle guiding her into the car, helping her to arrange the vast folds of her dress. As the car left the long driveway and glided along the road, there were neighbours outside waving, and she felt like a princess going to a ball.

It was a beautiful sunny April day, trees with pink and white blossoms were glinting in the sun, crocus's had pushed their way out of the ground, and carpets of daffodils were everywhere. Outside the church was a big tree, with branches spreading over the archway, and birds were chirping as they walked underneath it. Rachel drank it all in, it felt like the whole world was celebrating what she was about to do, and it made her special day feel even more right.

Diana and the other bridesmaids and page boys were waiting at the entrance of the church for her. She knew her aunt would be seated inside with the other guests, and now her calmness was deserting her; she was about to lose her twin, and become a wife and mother. Inside that church, the man of her dreams was patiently waiting for her. For some unknown reason, which scared her, she wasn't sure she could go through with it.

All through their lives, Rachel and Diana had often sensed each other's thoughts and feelings. They knew it was because they were twins, and although Diana had a fixed smile on her face at that moment, Rachel could feel vibes coming from her and she knew her sister was unhappy. She drew her to one side, and whispered:

"Diana, what's wrong? I don't want to lose you because I am getting married; you will always be important to me."

Diana knew her emotions were all over the place. She still wished she hadn't lost Jake. No man she had met since had even come close to how she still felt about him. Even though it was seven years ago now, she knew the only way she could know if it had just been a childhood first love, was to meet him again; but he had vanished forever. Rachel had her love and was marrying him, and that made Diana feel alone. And how would she cope with being second best? Because obviously Neil would take precedence over her. She was selfish, she knew she was being selfish, and she thought that maybe this selfishness was making her feel that Neil was not right for her sister, and she told herself angrily to butt out of it! She would be honest, because Rachel would know if she was lying.

"I am sorry sis. It's your day, and I am being selfish. I will miss you so much!"

"I am not leaving you. Neil knows how important you are. Be happy for me, and one day it will be your turn."

Rachel knew Diana so well; her insecurities, which would

d

probably never go, and her need to be loved, and she vowed that even though she was entering a new phase of her life, she would not turn her back on her sister; Diana would always be her best friend.

They embraced, and even Clive was moved to see how much love these girls had for each other. Rachel's moment of doubt had passed, and once again she was in control. Diana had the bridesmaids and page boys lined up behind her, as Rachel linked her arm through her uncle's.

"Right everyone, let's walk slowly in."

Neil, with the help of Barry and Colin, had finally got his act together. After the food had gone down, he took a hot shower and was starting to feel more human. He wondered why a few beers had given him such a hangover. He really couldn't remember much about last night. He vaguely recalled a blonde up at the bar; had he shagged her? He really didn't know. If he had, it had hardly been memorable.

"What happened with that blonde last night?" he asked Barry whilst he was towelling himself off.

"Nothing, you were sick right in front of her, collapsed on the floor, and we had to walk you home." Barry actually felt quite peeved about it; all that hard work last night, and Neil wouldn't even thank them for their help. Neil only thought about himself, and if it wasn't for the money he had been promised, Barry decided he would have walked by now.

"I don't know why a few beers made me like that," remarked Neil, as he put on his suit, brushing off an imaginary speck of dust. Colin had come into the room now to get dressed, in time to hear the last remark, and he smirked to himself; he could have told him why.

Barry had also been wondering the same thing, but had noticed Colin's face twitch as though he wanted to laugh. Then it all fell into place. Of course, Colin was even more sick of Neil than he was, so he had laced his drink with something. He cursed the bloody idiot for what he had done, which had made his job so much harder in making sure Neil got to the church today. But this was not the time to show anger, as he had to keep everything on an even keel. If Neil had found out what Colin had done, he would erupt; he was very unstable. Colin was definitely not the sharpest tool in the box, and Barry made up his mind that at a later date Colin would find out just how angry he was with him for being so stupid.

"Maybe it was that scotch egg you had. If you remember Colin and I had fish and chips. I had a dodgy one once."

Neil seemed to be content with that.

After they had all got ready, the car arrived to take them to the church. As they sat next to each other, Barry marvelled that here were the three of them, not really friends, more associates, and the only thing that held them together was money; they all wanted money. He pitied that lovely young woman, but not enough to enlighten her. She honestly thought the sun shone out of Neil, and she was in for such a shock when she found out the truth.

Susan watched with pride as Rachel glided down the aisle on Clive's arm. As she reached Neil, he turned towards her, and she noticed how smart he looked in his suit. He had an air of innocence about him, and that lock of brown hair that normally flopped over his brow had been tamed today; it was slicked back. He gave Rachel such a beguiling smile, it would be enough to melt the coldest heart. She was so pleased that Rachel had found such a likeable young man.

Rachel's heart swelled with love as she reached her husband to be. He looked so handsome; his grey eyes, so very sincere, never failed to melt her heart. The lady vicar welcomed everyone and the marriage ceremony began. When they had finally exchanged rings, they were proclaimed man and wife, and her heart felt like it was bursting with pride.

Neil was then invited to kiss the bride, and he was conscious that everyone's eyes were on him, so he made a great display of kissing her long and tenderly which received rapturous applause. But whilst he kissed his new wife, his thoughts were already straying towards his sister-in-law. What a shame Diana was the poor one, as she was the sexy and provocative one, and if he could have married her, he could have had an exciting sex life. He had sensed that she didn't quite trust him, so he had stopped admiring her boobs. For a while she had hidden them away, but today the pert little mounds were on display, and he longed for the time when he could get his hands on them. All his life Neil had found he could have any woman he wanted; his looks were such that they all found him irresistible. He was certain that he could give Diana a good time, and no matter how close they were, that was something she would never tell her sister. He liked the idea of this marriage already; with the twins it was buy one and get one free, the perfect scenario for his voracious sexual appetite.

After all the photographs had been taken outside the church, the photographer suggested that he could take more at the golf club where there would be a very picturesque back drop, so Neil and Rachel should get into the car. Diana was busy bending down and helping her sister with her voluminous skirt, which gave Neil another opportunity to appraise her cleavage, and he only stopped when she glared at him as she straightened up, so he met that glare head on with a most disarming smile, which he was sure would charm the birds from the trees.

Diana felt that cold finger of fear clutching at her heart again. He was up to his old tricks, and Rachel was so trusting and so in love with him, she had not noticed a thing. If he could be like that with her, then it was obvious there would be others. He would not be faithful to Rachel, and her heart ached for her poor unsuspecting sister. Diana vowed to keep him at arm's length at all times, because his attitude unsettled her, he clearly had no morals or loyalty to Rachel, but she knew if she told anyone they would just think she was jealous.

When they arrived at the golf club, more pictures were taken, and then Rachel and Neil stood at the door greeting everyone as they all filed in to sit down for the meal. Diana watched him charming everyone as they arrived, and it sickened her to see how convincing he was, but she now realised that her fears were not unfounded, her sister had married a cheat and he was unlikely to change. Then it suddenly hit her; he didn't seem to love Rachel, so of course, it was her money, he was after a comfortable life.

Diana was not that impressed by his two friends either. Barry seemed a bit like a wide boy; even with his suit, his tie looked loud, and he had that way of speaking. He had made a glowing speech about all Neil's attributes, and Diana didn't believe a word of it. He could not have known Neil all his life, as he was East London born and bred, yet Neil had by all accounts grown up in

California. That is the only thing she did believe about him, as his strong American drawl did seem to endorse the fact.

Now that the meal was over, the band struck up, and Diana watched Neil lead Rachel onto the floor for the first dance. Her aunt and uncle sat at the table with her, looking proudly on.

"What a beautiful couple they are," smiled Susan, captivated by what she saw as a loving union, and Diana had to check back her retort. In her mind she was thinking the words, handsome is as handsome does; an old fashioned saying, which very much fitted Neil.

Barry approached her now for a dance, and she knew as chief bridesmaid, it was expected for her to dance with the best man. She smiled politely at him. He smelt quite strongly of beer, so she had better get this dance over and done with. Because it was a slow song, he had his arms around her, and it was hard for her to relax. He squashed her close to him, which she didn't like, especially as she could feel his hardness against her. She made some excuse about going to the ladies' room and escaped, and when she got there, she leaned against the basin panting; that had not been a nice experience. After she came out she noticed that the dance floor was very crowded, so she decided to slip outside for some air.

Neil thought he had done really well today, acting the attentive husband, but it was now getting just a bit boring. Diana excited him, she had a provocative look about her, but he could see she had the measure of him and she wasn't fooled like everyone else. But that didn't matter, he had plans for her, and once he had slept with her, she would be just like all the other women he had known; willing and compliant.

It was whilst he was dancing that first waltz with Rachel, that he spotted Barry, he was all over Diana like a rash. How dare that trashy east end villain paw her like that! Jealousy took hold of him and he could feel a red mist coming over him, and there were times when he let that mist take control. He could see that Diana didn't like that oaf pawing her, of course she wouldn't. He, Neil, could make her feel so amazing that she would never look at another man. He had the power.

She had run off now, and Barry was just standing there, but

77

then as he watched, he saw him go after her. It was time to bring him back in line, he was not going to have first pickings of that little lady. He hesitated momentarily whilst another male guest asked permission to dance with Rachel, and he accepted gratefully. Never mind Rachel, he had to find Diana.

When he reached the outside, there in the far corner he saw them, by a tree, and the bastard was trying it on with her again. He didn't stop to think or ask anything, his fist came out and he hit Barry square in the jaw, and down he went. But not content with that, as Barry was spluttering with blood pouring from his mouth, he bent down and drew his face up to him, and then he just kept smashing it; he wanted to make him unrecognisable.

"Leave him alone!" screamed Diana. "You will kill him!" She could see that Barry's face was just a mass of blood, and Neil was clearly out of control. He seemed like a madman.

"Don't you know a lady when you see one? Leave her alone," said Neil.

"He wasn't doing anything," wailed Diana, "just talking to me, that's all. We need to get an ambulance. His face, just look at it!"

Suddenly there seemed to be people everywhere. Diana was crying hysterically, lost for words, so Neil had to quickly control the situation. He explained that Barry had been coming on rather strongly towards Diana, so he felt it was up to him to defend his new sister-in-law, he hadn't realised that he had hit Barry so hard. The ambulance had arrived by then, and Barry was taken off to hospital. One thing he knew for sure was that Barry would never report him to the police; they had too much history, and when his face was back to normal, not only would he realise he should never cross Neil, it would also make sure he was back in control again.

Diana was just beginning to realise what a dangerous man her new brother-in-law was. She had seen the way his eyes changed, that manic look on his face, and she was scared to cross him, so she said nothing and she didn't dispute the lies that Neil told. She was realising that for him to react like that, he must have some sort of obsession about her, and this was all so wrong as he was her sister's husband. She wept with frustration because it seemed the only thing she could do was get right out of their lives forever, and when he showed his true self to Rachel, and broke her heart, Diana vowed that she would be there to pick up the pieces.

Colin had arrived on the scene now; it was his job to support Neil, so by the time the story about the attack reached Rachel, and the others who were dancing, the version that she heard was that Barry had tried it on with her sister outside, Neil had seen him, and pushed him away from her, but in falling he had knocked his face on the concrete and was now on his way to hospital to be treated. Neil went up even more in Rachel's estimation, and that of the other guests too, for defending her beloved twin sister.

Diana wanted to tell Rachel the true story, but she knew she would not be believed. It seemed to her that Rachel had married a monster, and she truly feared for her sister's safety although she felt powerless to do anything about it. However heartless it sounded, Rachel really had to find out for herself.

The rest of the afternoon passed without incident, and halfway through the celebrations Rachel and Neil slipped away to go on their honeymoon. Diana was now battling with not only the loss of her twin, but also the fear that her unbalanced new husband might harm her. She said a silent prayer for her sister's safety, and wished that Neil would stay right out of her way. She felt that her relationship with Rachel was about to disintegrate, and all her fears and insecurities came back to haunt her. If only Rachel had never met him!

Chapter Twelve

After a truly perfect day, Rachel leant against her husband in the taxi with a sigh of contentment. It was five o'clock, their flight was at seven, and then they would be on their way to a sun filled holiday. Suddenly, a pain ripped through her stomach causing her to catch her breath. Whatever could be wrong, what had she eaten to upset her insides so much?

"Neil I have a bad tummy ache. I need to find a toilet."

Neil hid his irritation. He was looking forward to getting on that plane, and just like a woman, Rachel wanted to stop.

"What's wrong babe, something you ate disagreed with you?"

"Maybe." Rachel didn't even want to speculate, she just wanted five minutes to herself.

"Hey buddy, could you pull in at the next services, my wife needs to make a stop."

The taxi driver did as he was asked, and Rachel made her way towards the public toilets. Once inside, her worst fears were realised when she found a show of blood. She cried out in anguish: "My baby, I am losing my baby!"

A woman who was washing her hands heard her, and realising she was inside the cubicle, asked her if she could manage to open the door. Rachel drew back the bolt and walked slowly out. She was sobbing and clearly very distressed, so the woman helped her to sit on a chair. Her daughter was with her, and after finding out that Neil was outside in a taxi, she told her to stay with Rachel whilst she went and explained to him what was happening.

Neil wondered what was taking her so long, he tapped his feet impatiently, and then his attention was caught when he saw a middle-aged woman running towards him. She shouted in her agitation.

"Your wife is unwell. You need to call an ambulance, she is worried she might be losing her baby."

His heart sank; not only would he have to get her pregnant again if she lost this one, but there wouldn't be any holiday in the sun. He felt cheated, but he hid it and allowed an expression of concern to cross his face. He took out his mobile phone and rang for an ambulance. Then the woman took it from him and explained to the operator just where they were, and they promised to send an ambulance as quickly as they could.

Neil paid off the taxi, there was no point in the man waiting any more, and then he realised he must act the concerned husband. So he rushed over to the toilets and went in to find Rachel sitting on a chair clutching her stomach. She was totally distraught, so he cradled her head in his hands beseeching her not to cry because the ambulance was on its way. The woman was standing the other side of her, trying to pacify her too, and he made sure that she got the impression that he was a very caring husband.

When the ambulance arrived they didn't waste much time. Rachel was put in a wheelchair and wrapped in a blanket, then lifted into the vehicle. Neil thanked the woman for her help, and then went with Rachel, holding her hand all the way there. She had stopped crying by now, and sat silently whilst the paramedic was trying to cheer her up, saying it might not be as bad as she thought, and to keep positive.

She was taken straight into the casualty department, and someone asked Neil to wait outside whilst they examined her. He walked up and down for a while; hospitals gave him the creeps, and he wished he didn't have to be here. He didn't feel the loss because until it was born, to him it wasn't a baby.

To his surprise, who should come along the corridor but Barry. He had forgotten that Barry had also been taken to this hospital. Barry was sporting a couple of black eyes and facial bruises, but then what could he expect for making a pass at someone who was off limits to him. Neil felt he had done what any man would have done when he saw that asshole trying to make out with his wife's sister. Even he now believed his own tale, that Barry had fallen on concrete and damaged his face.

Barry was very wary when he saw Neil. Had he come to meet him? He wouldn't have thought so, Neil wouldn't be that generous. Ever since the attack, which he knew would have been covered up by Colin, because this is the way they worked, he had cursed himself for not realising that Neil had a thing about Diana. She was the one he really wanted, but it was all going to end in tears, and there was no way Barry would ever approach her again. He had only spoken to her outside to apologise for dancing too close to her. She was in a different class to him, and he had realised when she left him, that he had been too familiar with her. It had never entered his head that newly married Neil had set his sights on her. If he was honest with himself, he didn't need Neil in his life, only the money, and now he was even beginning to wonder if it was all worth it, or was it better to be poor and unhurt? Should he get out now, because there was not going to be a happy ending?

Neil smiled at him as though nothing had happened, then put on a most sympathetic voice.

"How are you Barry? Such a nasty fall you had on the concrete; and now Rachel is in here too, with a threatened miscarriage."

"Yes it was. I am sorry to hear about Rachel, that is awful. So the honeymoon is off then?"

"Yes, but we can do it later, when she feels up to it."

Neil was just about to ask him if Colin was picking him up, then they could all ride together, when a white coated doctor appeared.

"Mr Morris, your wife is now sedated and resting, we are hoping that she won't lose the baby. The problem is, she did not go to the doctor to get it confirmed, and if she had we would have told her that flying within the first three months is not a good idea; that in itself can cause a miscarriage. I am afraid your plans for a honeymoon will now have to be put on hold until after the baby is born. It's far too risky, even when she is better, for her to fly."

"We were busy planning our wedding. She was going to the doctor soon, but she knew herself that she was pregnant."

"I get that, but you were just about to board a plane. It's a real risk, so please heed my words, the health of your wife is the most important factor here."

"Of course doctor, we have the rest of our lives ahead of us, and I will make sure she doesn't fly whilst she is pregnant. Can I see her now?"

He had made it sound good. He could see the doctor was satisfied that he was a concerned husband, but inwardly he was seething at Rachel's difficulties. She had messed up the holiday totally; after the kid was born was such a long time to wait.

Barry had been hoping to slip away. He had put up with more than enough from Neil today, but it would look uncaring if he didn't go and see Rachel. None of this was the poor cow's fault. Coming from East London, he knew how much family meant, and he hoped she would not lose her baby.

"I will just come in and wish her well, I hope the sight of my black eyes won't unnerve her."

"No way," said Neil. "She will be glad to know you are all right and going home."

The doctor led the way, and when they saw her she was leaning against her pillows, her green eyes had dark rims and her face was very pale. She was so far removed from the sparkling beautiful girl who had walked down the aisle earlier, and Barry felt a wave of pity towards her, knowing that her callous husband would not be wasting much emotion on her. But Rachel forgot her own misery when she saw him.

"Barry, I am so sorry to hear about your face. I am sure Diana would not have wanted you to be injured like that."

"It's better now. It looks bad, but when my black eyes go, it will all heal up."

"Well buddy, you now know that Diana is off limits," said Neil with a steely glance at him, daring him to say anything different.

Barry hid his anger. What he knew about this unbalanced fraudster would fill a book, but he was here to comfort Rachel, so he ignored the comment, and turned towards her.

"Rachel, you must rest and take care, for your baby's sake."

"Tell me about it!" she sighed, "I am staying in hospital until I reach three months, and am not allowed out of bed! But I will do anything to keep this baby, nothing else matters!"

Neil reached out for her hand and squeezed it. He actually felt like throttling her. Another month in hospital; that meant he would have to cook his own meals and do his own washing. Rachel usually did it all.

"You rest honey, I'll be fine."

Barry excused himself; he didn't want to listen to Neil pretending to care about her. It had been a long day, and right now he wanted to put as much distance between them as he could. But Neil was having none of it. He kissed Rachel good bye, urging her to rest, and then followed Barry out, suggesting they should get a cab home, or ring Colin. Neil got his mobile out and rang Colin, who said he could be there in fifteen minutes. He then remembered that Rachel's aunt and uncle didn't know anything about this; they thought they were on a flight, as did Diana. So he rang them and explained that Rachel was pregnant, which was a shock to Susan, as they didn't know, and was going to spend the next month in hospital to try and protect her pregnancy, and by the time he had passed on that distressing news, Colin arrived to take them both home.

Diana was still at the Golf Club celebrating when her mobile rang. She had felt more relaxed since Neil had gone, but had wondered how Barry was; it was amazing that he was so loyal to Neil when he had such a manic temper. She didn't really want to speak to Neil, and the first thing that sprung to her mind when she heard about Rachel was fear that he might have had something to do with it. The more she got to know this man, the more he scared her.

But Neil explained about how she was taken ill in the toilet, and gone to hospital, and he then went on to explain that Barry had now been released to go home; apart from a couple of black eyes, he was fine. Diana wondered if her imagination was playing tricks on her. Neil sounded really concerned about Rachel, and it was certainly good news about Barry, she had been convinced he would need an operation to restore his features, but maybe she had overreacted; that dramatic part of her character might have gone a bit overboard. She couldn't be sure, but her overriding concern was for Rachel and her baby. Her first thought was that she should leave right now and go to the hospital, but when he explained the doctor had given Rachel a sedative so she could sleep, she told him she would be going to see her at the hospital tomorrow. If he had done anything towards her, Diana would know, she could tell.

84

*   *   *   *

Colin dropped Neil off at the house, which was standing tall and silent. Rachel's idea to turn it into separate flats had never materialised, because Neil had suggested that with a baby coming, it might be good to keep it as a family home. So she had put it on hold right now. Neil didn't want to share this house with strangers; Rachel was not short of money, so there was no need for it.

It had been quite a day, and he had so many thoughts on his mind, but his overriding thought was his obsession about Diana, and he was still angry about the way Barry had tried to muscle in. Well he had taught him a lesson today, he wouldn't mind betting that Barry would leave her alone in the future.

Maybe it was a good thing that Rachel was not here right now, because the plan had been for Colin to contact him whilst on honeymoon, to tell him that he had an official letter from his company; then he was going to ask him to open it, and it would be to say his contract had now ended, as the investigation into genetics was completed. So when Rachel found out he had no wages coming in, she would not be surprised. He could make Rachel believe anything, she was such a pushover. Colin had produced a very good fake letter, so in a few days, all he had to do was look a bit down, then take it in and show it to her.

Then there was Diana, she was like a very bad itch that had to be scratched and, after downing a couple of whiskies, he decided there was no time like the present. He guessed she would stay until midnight at the golf club. It was now eleven o'clock, so he called a taxi to take him there, where he intended to collect her and take her home. But there was still Clare to think about, she lived there too, so he picked up his mobile and rang Colin again, who had just arrived back at the flat, and asked him to go back to the golf club and pick up Clare and take her home. Colin agreed, and told Barry what he was doing. His face was inscrutable, whatever Neil was up to, he didn't care, he just did as he was told and got paid for it, although right now it was a long time coming, and if Neil didn't hurry up and give him what he was owed, he might be looking for another dogsbody soon.

But Neil's plan back-fired, as when Colin arrived with the car, Diana and Clare both got in to come home. When a half drunk

Neil arrived in the taxi to find Diana gone, he was angry, and this only fuelled his desire for her even more. But he realised going to her flat was not an option that night. Clare was there, and when he bedded the beautiful and tempestuous Diana, he would make sure they were alone. He jumped back into the taxi and ordered the driver to take him home. He made up his mind that tomorrow he would find a way to get Diana alone. The harder it seemed to get her, the more he wanted her, and he wouldn't stop until he had succeeded.

Rachel had passed a restful night, thanks to the medication, but now she was awake and she felt so sad that her wedding day had ended like this. She had been so looking forward to her honeymoon with Neil, he must have been disappointed too, even though he had not shown it to her. It was hard to believe that staying in bed might save her baby's life; that show of blood and severe stomach pains had really scared her, but today her stomach felt all right, and there had not been any more blood.

Aunt Susan and Diana had arrived as soon as they were allowed to see her. She knew her aunt would scold her for doing too much, and say how glad she was that she was in hospital and taking a rest. Diana said very little, she just sat holding her hand, asking her if she was OK. It was unusual for her normally chatty sister to be so quiet, but she was clearly traumatised by what had happened to her. Whilst they were sitting round her bed, with Aunt Susan trying to keep the conversation light, Neil arrived with a holdall packed with the things that he had been told by the nurse last night Rachel would need. He had also bought her some magazines and a bunch of flowers, which prompted Diana to jump up and seek out a nurse to get a vase to put them in.

Diana was shocked to see her normally so in control sister propped up on her pillows, trying to do all the right things to protect her pregnancy. She knew it was her time to step up and be a rock for her; after all, during their lives up until now, Rachel had been her rock. She was truly hoping that this stressful experience had made Neil realise just what a wonderful wife he had. He certainly seemed very concerned and loving towards her today, and Diana didn't want to think anything bad about him.

She was all mixed up inside about him; was he really the rogue she had thought he was yesterday? But how could she forget his out of control rage towards Barry, or had her imagination made it worse, as by all accounts, Barry was now home with nothing worse than a couple of black eyes. She really wasn't sure, but Neil was well versed in deception, he had practised it all his life, and this morning he made sure to act the very concerned husband, and to keep his eyes on his wife, even though he was very aware of Diana's presence.

After an hour it was time for Rachel to have lunch and another rest, so they took their leave of her. Susan had shared the taxi there with Diana, but Neil suggested rather than the driver take such a roundabout route, he could drive her home as Colin had lent him his car.

It seemed a reasonable suggestion, especially as Neil had asked Diana to stop off at their home and help him find Rachel's dressing gown because she didn't want to wear a hospital gown and he'd been unable to find it. Neil hardly looked at her today, so she wondered if she had been wrong about him lusting after her yesterday. It was so confusing, as he seemed very changeable. Her trust in him had been restored, so when they arrived back at the house, she went inside to help him find the dressing gown.

As they entered the house, he went into the kitchen to put the kettle on, and Rachel went upstairs to look in all the places where she thought Rachel would have put her dressing gown. When she entered the bedroom she noticed that the bed was unmade, and when she opened the wardrobe door, hanging on a hook just inside it was the 'missing' dressing gown. Just as she was wondering why Neil hadn't spotted it, as it could not have been more obvious, she heard a sound behind her.

Fear coursed through her as she turned to see his face; his eyes were glittering and strange, and in that instant she knew she had been tricked, she was caught like a rat in a trap with this frightening and unpredictable man.

She licked her dry lips. She could see lust gleaming in his eyes, but maybe she should humour him, getting angry and showing fear was what he wanted her to do, and at that moment, even though the drama queen inside her wanted to scream and shout, she was wary of his temper; she had seen it first hand yesterday, so she said calmly:

"Neil, I have the dressing gown, I am going to take it downstairs, and put it in a bag for you to take to Rachel."

Neil wondered if she was for real, had she not got it? He had her upstairs for one reason only, and her indifference made him angry, he needed to prove to her that she was under his control. He stepped towards her, roughly pushing her down on the bed, and he could see then she had got the message. The terror in her eyes was what he wanted to see; he had the power, and she knew it.

Diana fell back onto the rumpled bed, and as she opened her mouth to scream, his hand clamped fiercely over it; his eyes were menacing, she had never been more terrified in her life. Her chest heaved as she tried to breathe, and his voice, now low and threatening, unnerved her.

"No you don't my pretty little lady, no shouting, the only shouting you will do is when I make you glad you are a woman."

She could not believe this was happening to her; her sister's husband, it could not be true, one false move and she had no doubt he would hit her, but she had to fight back, he couldn't have it all his own way. She brought her knee up in an effort to kick him in the groin, but Neil was too quick for her. He seemed to have superhuman strength as he batted her knee away with one hand, and then she felt his hands round her throat, and she was convinced that she was done for; he was going to strangle her.

"If you value your life little lady, you won't make a sound, and if you do try to, you are done for!"

He ignored her sobbing; she was compliant now, just as he wanted her to be, so he ordered her to remove her jeans; he didn't care how traumatised she was, and how badly her hands were trembling. He ripped off her panties himself, but his own urges were so strong, he didn't stop to check whether her body was responding to him, he just released his penis from his trousers, and entered her with a gasp of pure pleasure. She was still sobbing, so he slapped her face, and told her she should be enjoying it, as he was a super stud to all women.

Diana was filled with revulsion at his advances; her body was stiff, and when he entered her, it really hurt, as her internal passage was dry. She closed her eyes so she didn't have to see his evil face above her, and turned her head away when he tried to kiss her. She barely felt him slap her, she was so used and abused, but she wanted to live, so when she felt him withdraw and explode, inwardly she wept with relief when he rolled off her.

Neil was so full of his own self gratification, he barely noticed her lack of response. She didn't shout or scream at him; she was in the bathroom now, putting herself to rights, and babbling that she needed to get home. He wasn't worried about her telling anyone, how could she possibly? They wouldn't believe her. Rachel certainly wouldn't, and next time he felt she would be more willing, he wouldn't have to force it, she had a naturally sexy aura about her, and he intended to make sure there were going to be many more times.

When Diana exited the bathroom, she was squashing down all her fear and terror of this man, trying to appear normal to him. She needed to get out of there. She felt unclean, and now his character was fully exposed to her, she knew, that for her own protection, Rachel had to be told. Her sister had married a monster; he was a madman, and she could not possibly stay in this marriage.

Chapter Thirteen

If anyone had asked Diana how she had got home that day, she would not have been able to answer them. Her journey on the tube was a time she had forgotten, as the only thought in her mind was utter disbelief that she had been raped by her sister's husband. It was the sort of thing you might see in a Hollywood movie, but you never expected in real life.

She felt unclean; the thought of his invasion into her body made her retch, it was so unreal. And the question of how this man had become a part of her family hung unanswered, but heavily, in the air. Her sister was so madly in love with him, would she even believe her? Until now it had always been Rachel who was a good judge of character, it was Diana that often got taken in, but this time it seemed that Rachel was so blinded by love she saw him as a good person. Diana knew that she had to make sure, when Rachel left hospital, that she knew exactly what he had done. What scared her most of all was, by telling her sister, not only would it break her heart, but also it could finish their relationship if she didn't believe her, and Diana couldn't bear to think of how she would cope without her sister in her life.

She got in the shower and scrubbed her body vigorously, desperately trying to wash away anything of him that might be on her. He had pulled out of her when he ejaculated, so she scrubbed at her legs just in case there was any trace of him there. The thought of what he had done welled up again, and she knew she was going to vomit, so she rushed towards the toilet, regardless of the water dripping off her and collecting on the floor. Luckily

Clare was at work so could not see her bizarre behaviour. Whatever had this monster done to her?

After some considerable time, she hoped that she had washed off any trace of that ogre on her, then she washed her hair, and put on her towelling robe. Her anger had subsided now; she felt completely drained, so she lay down on the bed and fell into an exhausted sleep.

When she woke up, it was late afternoon. Visiting times at the hospital were until eight, and as it was now five o'clock, a time when most people didn't visit because patients would be eating their dinner, she was hoping Neil would not come until later. She didn't think she could bear to see him, but this was weighing so heavily on her mind that she had to tell her twin. Then it occurred to her that she should report him to the police, but she owed it to Rachel to tell her first.

When she arrived, Rachel was sitting up in bed; she had more colour than the day before, and she was just finishing off a bowl of soup and a roll. Diana's heart ached so much about what she had to tell her, but it was something that she had to know immediately.

Rachel was feeling a bit better today. There had been no more pains or shows of blood, she had rested, and also found an interesting book to read. Also one of the nurses had given her a book of crosswords, and that had kept her occupied for an hour or so. She had accepted that no matter how boring it was, for the next month or so she had to stay in bed and, if it meant saving her baby, then she would do everything she was told.

As soon as Diana came in, Rachel knew something was wrong, her face was pale, her eyes had dark rims, and she looked as though she had been crying. She immediately forgot about her own plight, and when she bent to hug her, she grabbed her hand.

"Diana, who has upset you? I can see you have been crying."

"I don't know how to tell you. I can't tell you."

She was trying to hold back the tears; the ward was not that private, even though Rachel's bed was at the end of it. She came close to the bed and sat in the chair, and drew a deep breath.

Then it all came tumbling out; the way Neil had made her feel uncomfortable for a while, then his request to her about finding the dressing gown, then how violent he had been earlier today, and how scared she had been. Finally she said that he had raped her, but in order to spare Rachel even more distress, she did not go into details.

As Rachel sat listening to Diana, she truly thought her sister had gone mad, and by the time she had finished, Rachel had covered her ears and refused to listen. The man she was describing was not her Neil. He was kind, loving and gentle. She refused to even listen to this nonsense, and the anger she felt towards her sister for trying to burst her bubble of happiness, and ruin her marriage, was immense. There could be only one reason she had made up this fantastic story; she was jealous, she was trying to break them up because she wanted Neil for herself.

Diana was dabbing at her eyes now; her shoulders were hunched in an attitude of defeat, and they heaved as she quietly sobbed. Well, her play acting did not fool Rachel this time, she had always been a drama queen, but this time it wouldn't work. Rachel clung fiercely to her belief that it wasn't true, because she knew if she had any doubt about Neil, that would be the end, and she loved him with all her heart.

"I am sorry I had to tell you, but he's a dangerous man, you can't stay with him. You should have seen the way he attacked Barry yesterday."

Rachel didn't want to think about yesterday. It was her wedding, she had married the man she loved so much, but now all the attention was on Diana. The drama outside had all been about Diana; her selfish sister had been so desperate to be the centre of attention that she had gone to such huge lengths to achieve it.

But her love was not too blind for her to realise that none of this added up. If Neil had attacked Barry because he was making advances towards Diana, then why would he do that? Jealousy usually caused tempers to flare, but why would Neil be jealous unless, of course, it was the unthinkable, he fancied her sister? And then an even worse thought struck her. She was a wealthy woman, had he married her for her money but really wanted her sister? Probably Diana had encouraged him, and now it had gone so far she was panicking and shouting rape.

Rachel would never have called herself a jealous person, she had always felt content with her life, and when Neil had come along, to her it had all been perfect, he was the love of her life, and the father of her baby. So the powerful emotion that was raging away inside her right now, the thought that her sister had got her husband, the man who was the focal point of her whole life, was a pain that she couldn't bear. The love she had always felt towards her sister, at that moment, turned to hate, a burning hate that wished her all manner of harm. So they had slept together, they had both betrayed her. She felt so sick, and at that moment, the nurse came in to take her empty tray away. So Rachel finally spoke, coldly and calmly, to the nurse.

"Can you please ask my sister to leave, and don't let her come back again, ever! As for my husband, don't let him in at all. I don't want to see either of them again!"

The bewildered nurse did as she was told. Diana had tried to beg and plead with Rachel, but she had simply laid down in her bed, closed her eyes, and ignored her. The nurse thought that whatever had happened in that family had obviously hurt Rachel very deeply, and she was supposed to be resting so they could save her pregnancy. She did so hope they could patch it up soon, if only for the sake of the baby Rachel was carrying.

Diana felt like she had been crying forever when she arrived home. She had been oblivious of the stares of people on the way, as she was so wrapped up in her own grief. Surely when Rachel had time to think about it, she would realise that she would never have gone after Neil, and that he must have raped her.

Clare was there, having just returned from a Sunday shift at the hospital, and she was concerned to see Diana's tear-streaked face and obvious distress. Diana poured out everything, including the brutal way that Neil had raped her, but no matter how badly that had affected her, it was obvious that the most distressing happening was that Rachel had turned against her. She knew the twins had always been close, and when she heard the details of the way Neil had behaved, her face went pale, as she realised what an ordeal Diana had suffered.

"I am going to the police now, to tell them everything, he's not getting away with this!" said Diana angrily reliving it in her mind. "He's a monster, and it might stop someone else having to suffer at his hands."

"I can imagine how you feel, but it's even worse when it goes to court, women are often treated as though it's their fault, very few rape cases actually get proved."

Diana was taken aback, as she had expected Clare to vehemently agree with her.

"I had to come home and wash all trace of him off me, he made me feel unclean!" she protested. "Surely you don't want him to get away with it?"

"I certainly don't," said Clare, putting her arm kindly round her, "but if you have washed yourself since he did it, then you have washed away the proof, and no one will believe you."

Suddenly Diana realised how true those words were. What a fool she had been; getting in the shower had been her first thought, washing away anything connected with evil Neil. Now it looked like he was going to get away with it.

Clare tried to focus on the most important aspect of Diana's life.

"If I were in your place, I would forget about reporting it. Even though Rachel has banished him, I am sure that sort of publicity about her husband won't please her. Spend your time trying to make it up with her."

"She told the nurse to stop me from ever visiting again."

"Well give her time to get used to the shock of finding out what Neil did. She may realise that you are telling the truth in time, don't just give up on her."

Diana pondered her words; they made sense, she had just given Rachel the worst possible news ever, and she needed time to digest it. She vowed she would keep trying to break down Rachel's defences, but she knew, that even if Rachel did forgive Neil for what he had done, there would not be room for both of them in Rachel's life, and it was more than likely she would be the one who had to go. The thought of being without her sister in her life was almost as painful as the death of her parents had been.

Clare felt relief that she had managed to talk Diana round from reporting Neil's rape of her to the police. Clare had no doubt that Diana was speaking the truth. She did not imagine for one minute that Diana had tried to seduce him. She felt so angry with him, why couldn't he control that temper of his? First of all he'd gone for Barry, and managed to put him in hospital, and now violently raped his wife's twin sister. His out of control behaviour was getting to be a liability, and the last thing they needed was for the police to be involved. She resolved that when she next spoke to Neil she would remind him of all this, otherwise they would all be sunk.

*   *   *   *

Neil was flabbergasted that in spite of his threats, Diana had told Rachel about this morning. In his mind it was not rape, he had just been showing her what she was missing. He had been let in to see Rachel, but she had kicked up such a fuss, that in the end he had been removed, as they said his presence was not helping her to rest and get well.

He was tired of his new wife already, just laying in bed like the queen, giving orders to ban him. He had used all his charm to try and convince her there was no affair, it was just Diana being her usual dramatic self. He said he had known she had a thing about him for a while, but had no idea she was going to cause all this trouble. But it seemed that Rachel didn't want to think her sister had initiated it, she truly believed that he had seduced her. His violence towards Barry had triggered off that thought, and she was now regretting meeting a man who had come between herself and her twin.

The only thing that bothered Neil was that it was just a bit too early. He had no intention of spending his life with boring scientist Rachel. He had not reckoned on her having such a sexy twin sister, and he found it really kinky to shag two women who looked so alike. He would have liked to have more encounters with Diana, but none of this situation was going as planned, so he might have to move on. It was a shame that he had not managed to get his hands on any money, although the credit card might provide him with a bit. Barry and Colin were not going to be pleased that they were going empty handed; he had kept promising them, but now it was unlikely to happen.

When he got out of the hospital to head home, he saw there was a voice mail on his mobile phone, it was Clare, and she sounded really angry. He supposed Diana had been blabbing to her about him. She was ordering him to call her. Neil didn't take orders from anyone, he gave all the orders, but this time, by the sound of her voice, he guessed that he should call her.

When his phone connected to her, Clare was able to give him a piece of her mind. Diana had gone into her room for an early night, and to watch her TV in bed, desperately trying to focus on anything other than what had happened today. Clare raised her voice in anger when she heard his smooth voice on the other end; what did he care about anything?

"Neil, you crazy idiot, I had to stop Diana reporting you to the police for raping her, and don't bother to deny it. I have seen you eyeing her so many times. You just can't keep it in your trousers can you!"

"Well, she's messed up all our plans. Rachel won't listen to me, and I'm tired of all this anyway. I think we should move on."

"You try telling that to Barry and Colin, they want money; we all need money. You are going to have to try and win her back again. Deny raping Diana, say it was a fling you regret now. Once the baby is born, then you have paternal rights, and more chance of money."

"Maybe, we'll see."

It was easier to just agree with Clare. He made up his mind that he was not going to keep crawling round Rachel, and anyway, it looked like she had seen through him, and then there was her closeness to her twin. It was more than likely she would eventually forgive her sister, and even believe he had raped her, and then he would stand no chance of ever being forgiven. There was always the risk, as Clare had pointed out, that they might involve the police, which is the last thing that he wanted. He would talk to the others and see what they thought.

The next day, when Susan came to visit Rachel, she could not contain her grief, and poured out the whole story to her aunt. Susan had always felt closer to Rachel when they were growing up. Her sensible nature and calm attitude had endeared her to Susan, and her strength towards her sister when their parents had died had been so endearing. Susan had not understood Diana so well; her instability, and dramatic nature had not helped, as sometimes Susan was not sure whether she always spoke the truth, or whether everything was exaggerated for effect. When Rachel had told her that Diana had said that Neil had raped her, it sounded such a tall story, that she also agreed with Rachel; he had more than likely seduced her, and Diana's guilty conscience about how she had betrayed her sister, had caused her to shout rape.

Susan wasn't sure she ever wanted Diana in her life after what she had done, and it didn't look as though Rachel would ever forgive Neil. Susan was so disappointed in him, she had been

96

totally taken in by his charm. But how could anyone blame Rachel for wanting to end this marriage that had barely started? If Clive had done that to her, she wouldn't have been able to forgive him either.

She stayed with Rachel for about an hour. She was in a bad place emotionally. She had loved Neil so much, and she confided in Susan that she believed he had been after her because she was wealthy, but it was Diana he truly wanted. It hurt her to say that, but it all fitted in, so she had stepped back so they could have each other, and she didn't want either of them in her life any more.

Susan felt bad leaving Rachel in such distress, but she vowed that when her baby was born, she would get support from both herself and Clive, she wouldn't have to bring it up on her own. She also vowed that she would cut Diana out of her life, because after stealing her sister's husband, there was no way their relationship could survive.

Later that night Rachel lost her baby. When the hospital called Susan to tell her, she found herself with mixed emotions. Sad for Rachel that she had miscarried, but deep down she felt relief that nothing would now link Rachel with that man, and maybe in time her heart would heal, and she would move on.

e

Chapter Fourteen

When Rachel left hospital, she made some big decisions about her future. It was her way of coping with the heartbreaking loss of her baby. She had so wanted to be a mother, but in just one day, her perfect life had ended up in ruins. She now believed that Neil was with Diana. As far as she was concerned they were welcome to each other.

All through her life she had shielded and protected Diana, sometimes even taking the blame for the things she had done, but it seemed her sister had been so jealous of her happiness that she had destroyed it. Rachel had always tried to be kind to people, and forgive them, her nature had been generous enough to realise that everyone makes mistakes, but what they had done to her had changed her. She felt such hatred towards them both, and the strength of this hatred even surprised her. She refused to dwell on the fact that as sisters they had been so close; those memories were gone now, and the only way she could possibly survive was to move on.

She had seen Neil only once, and he had tried to lay the blame at Diana's door. That made him even worse in her eyes. Her love had turned to hate, and she saw him as a weak man with no morals or values, and was amazed that she could have so easily been taken in by him. It was difficult to know which hurt her the most, being betrayed by her twin, whom she had loved all of her life, or by Neil, the man she thought she would spend the rest of her life with.

The loss of her baby was devastating; it was no matter to her that its father was a huge let-down, she would have loved that baby so much, and the thought of having her arms full of that tiny life would have given her a reason to carry on, but even that had been denied her.

Her aunt had invited her to stay for a while, as with the depression she was now suffering, Susan did not think that Rachel should be on her own. Whilst she was with her aunt and uncle, she made up her mind she was going to sell the house because she could not run the risk of meeting up with either Neil or Diana. She told Susan her London contract was due to end soon, and she was going to start afresh as there were opportunities abroad for scientists.

Susan hoped that she was doing the right thing, but Rachel was a grown woman, and a strong one, and absolutely determined to move on, so all she could do was remind her that Clive and herself would always be there to support her, and to make sure she kept in touch.

Rachel had become a much harder woman, she had to, so she could survive emotionally. She refused to waste any tears on either of them, even when she heard from Clare, her only contact, that Neil had returned to the States. As far as he was concerned, it was good riddance to bad rubbish, and if there was a pang of regret, it was only that she had made a bad choice. The sooner her house was sold, the sooner she could move on and start again. Hopefully a divorce would follow later.

Diana felt so wronged that Rachel did not believe she had been raped. They were so close, she thought her sister would have known she was telling the truth. She had not been allowed near to Rachel, no matter how much she pleaded, and the shock of seeing her warm caring sister turn into a cold heartless person was more than she could bear.

Nobody seemed to believe her; she was desperate. Her uncle and aunt had made it clear she was not welcome, the only person left in the world it seemed to her, was Clare and she wondered how long that would be for. She felt sick and ill, and shut herself away from everyone, just lying in bed all day, feeling like her whole world had fallen apart.

When Clare tried to encourage her, she said she felt ill, she had a tummy bug, and she couldn't eat. As time went on, she became more stressed, and after she missed her second period, she announced her dreaded fears.

"Clare, I think I am pregnant, God only knows how, 'cos he pulled out of me, but what other reason could I be late?"

"Stress maybe," suggested Clare, "but maybe go and see the doctor, I will come with you."

When they came back after her pregnancy was confirmed, Diana announced she was going to have an abortion. She shuddered with distaste when she explained the reason.

"I couldn't bear to have anything of his growing inside me. That man is pure evil, and he must not find out I am pregnant."

"No need to worry about him, he's gone back to the States."

That piece of news was a relief to Diana, because she was so scared of him, he haunted her dreams, and she could not forget his staring eyes, but she still had no desire to be the mother of his child. She felt every time she looked at it, she would be reminded of the violent rape she had endured.

Clare had been planning to leave soon as well. She didn't really know whether Neil had left the country, but what she did know was all three of the men had cleared off out of it, as Neil's plan to get money from Rachel had back-fired, and he had made himself scarce at the mention of the word "police". They might not stick together, as there was no love lost between them, and she had no desire to see them again. The only thought in Clare's mind was her own future. She was now a qualified midwife, but delivering babies only made her want her own child even more. She craved the love her own mother had never given her, so she made the decision to go out to Uganda. There were so many babies out there needing a home and love, and as a qualified midwife, she would be in great demand.

Neither Rachel nor Diana had found out that she knew the three men, and she wanted to keep it that way. It was because of her, that Neil had come into Rachel's life, as she had told Barry about her, and her wealthy lifestyle. Once Neil got a sniff about money there was no holding him back, but he had messed it up big time. He wouldn't care that Diana was pregnant, but suddenly Clare saw it as a way out for her.

After Diana had announced she was having an abortion, Clare

knew she had to put the fear of God into her, to achieve what she wanted.

"Diana, abortion is so risky; if it goes wrong, you can be left unable to have another baby when you do want one, or even worse, you could die!"

Diana looked at her in horror, hospitals had always scared her, and her vivid imagination made her envisage her own life ending at just twenty-three. Seeing her distress, Clare continued.

"Diana, we can make some good come out of this whole sorry mess if you agree. If you carry the baby and give birth to it, I will support you all the way, then afterwards I will adopt it, and go and live somewhere where you never need to see it again."

Diana pondered her words. She was now too scared to risk an abortion, and she certainly didn't want Neil's child growing up and forever reminding her of what he had done. Clare's idea was a good one, she had no desire to go back to work or see anyone whilst she was carrying, and the knowledge that Clare would take care of her was comforting. She needed to have someone in her life who cared about her. After Clare and the baby had gone, then she would go back to work.

"Yes Clare, you can adopt my baby," and when she saw the look of happiness on Clare's face she felt a glow inside her; she had made someone happy, not everyone hated her. It was at that moment Diana realised she must be a stronger person, and she vowed that when Clare moved on, she would work hard to rebuild her life and make new friends, and maybe one day Rachel would realise how much she had misjudged her.

When Rachel heard about Diana's pregnancy, there was a pang of jealousy because that should have been her. She knew Neil had deserted Diana, but it was no more than she deserved. Rachel felt God was paying Diana back for her sins. At one time she would have forgiven her sister, and stood by her, but all she could feel now was hatred; not only had Diana ruined her marriage, but also she was having a baby by Neil. Well she hoped for Diana's sake that the child would not turn out to be as bad as its father. Or did she care? Not really! That man had used the credit card to syphon a few thousand pounds out of her account as a parting gesture. How stupid she had been to trust him. She had even thought of telling the police, but she wasn't sure whether Diana would jump on the band wagon and say she had been raped, and before they knew it, the whole of their private lives would be splashed all over the newspapers, and she would be a laughing stock, so she decided not to as she could soon make up the money.

Clare had not told Rachel about the adoption because she was worried that she might reconcile with her sister now that Neil had gone, and try and put a stop to it. So telling her Diana was pregnant would probably make her jealous, and bring all that had happened back to her. She needed to keep them apart until she was gone, so she told her Diana was so looking forward to the baby, as now Neil was gone, it was all she had left of him.

During the next few months Diana became a bit of a recluse. She wasn't proud or excited about the baby she was carrying, so if she went out and anyone commented about it, she would have to explain she was giving it up. No legal arrangements had been made, she had not given that part of it any thought, she would just hand over the baby to Clare as soon as she left hospital. She wasn't even going to ask Clare which country she was going to; as far as she was concerned, it was out of sight, and out of mind.

She could feel no love towards what she believed was a parasite growing inside her. Her fear of doctors and hospitals had convinced her to see her pregnancy through, then give her baby to Clare. Maybe after that she could pick up the tattered pieces of her life and start again. She knew she had to be strong, and she did try, but depression hung over her like a black cloud. She had lost the love of her sister and her uncle and aunt, so she clung to Clare and relied on her.

Clare left Diana every day to go to work. Diana usually spent the day in her dressing gown. She had stopped going out, the only time she did was for check-ups, and Clare always came with her. Clare had felt the baby move, and been there with Diana as she had promised, and it felt to Clare, like someone else was carrying her baby.

She knew Diana was depressed, and assumed once the baby had gone out of her life, Diana would then get better. But whether she did or not, Clare would not be around to see. She actually had told herself that hormones had caused such a depression, and afterwards Diana would be OK, and it was highly likely that in time the twins would reunite. Not that she had much of a conscience, because the sort of world she lived in, it was dog eat dog, and each looks after his own, although she did have sympathy for Diana because she believed that Neil, with his violent ways, had raped her.

Each evening she encouraged Diana to eat, making sure she had nutritious meals. She was steadily putting on weight, and Clare was thrilled to see her baby bump growing. Diana grumbled about feeling uncomfortable and the loss of her figure, and Clare smiled and applauded her for being stoic, reminding her frequently it was not forever.

By the time Diana had reached eight months, her bump was very noticeable. She wore loose tops to hide it, and she felt no pride in showing it off; not that she went out, but sometimes she had to open the door to the postman, or whoever might be calling. She was adamant she did not want anyone noticing it, it was almost as if she was trying to pretend she was not pregnant.

One morning, after Clare had gone to work, Diana heard the intercom buzz whilst she was dressing. She knew that the postman would want to leave mail in the bottom hall of the flats, but Clare was expecting a parcel, so she would want her to take it in. She spoke to him on the intercom, then released the catch so he could come in.

"I will be down in a minute, I expect you want me to sign for it."

"Yes please," confirmed the postman.

Diana came down the stairs to greet him but, in her haste, she missed the last step. She fell forwards with a loud scream, and tried to put out her hands to save herself, twisting her arm underneath her. She could feel pains everywhere, and she saw the postman's anxious face, as he bent down to try and encourage her to stand up.

"My arm, my arm, it hurts!" she was wailing. Then the door of another flat opened, and a lady came out to help her. The lady kept her cool, whilst urging the postman to phone for an ambulance.

The lady wrapped a coat around Diana, who was still sobbing and asking someone to take the pain away. She continued speaking calmly to Diana, explaining that when the paramedics arrived, they would free her trapped arm and give her some pain relief. She also explained that she couldn't move her, as it might make things worse. She had by now noticed Diana's bump, so realised she had to be handled with great care.

When the paramedics arrived, they were able to free Diana's arm, but it was swollen and puffy, and would need a doctor to look at it. Her face was very pale, and she was very distressed, and kept asking for someone to let Clare know about her fall. The neighbour told her she would tell Clare, and the last she saw of Diana was the paramedics putting her into the ambulance and taking her to the hospital to be checked over.

Clare did not find out about Diana's fall until the afternoon, as she was busy with a delivery in the morning, but when she returned to the staffroom to have her lunch, she was given the message. As much as she loved her job, adopting the baby was even more important to her, so she explained that it was an emergency situation, and was granted permission to leave that day. She wasted no time in getting to the hospital, and during the journey, rolling all through her mind, was the worry that this accident might have affected her baby. By now, as far as she was concerned, this was her baby, and Diana was merely the vessel that carried it.

She was left waiting outside the ward for what seemed like hours to her, but was only a few minutes. All sorts of images flashed through her mind; the baby might be still born, or be harmed by the fall. She couldn't lose this baby now, after all her hopes and dreams appeared to have been granted.

When the nurse finally came out to call her in, she was told that Diana was sleepy as she had been given pain killers that made her drowsy but would not harm the baby. Relief flooded through her at these words.

"So the baby is OK then?"

"As far as we can see, but Diana is bruised and uncomfortable, and in shock too."

"Of course, poor Diana. How long will she be here?"

The nurse was cautious, it wouldn't do to tell her that Diana had started premature labour. The doctor thought the baby was small, so they had given her an injection to stop the labour, but

104

right now, they didn't know if it would work. Just to confuse the situation another doctor felt the baby was big enough to survive, so they should let nature take its course. She answered the question as diplomatically as she could.

"She will be as long as is necessary, but we hope she can be back home as soon as possible. Does she have any other family?"

"No, she only has me."

"What about the father, will he be involved?"

Clare drew a deep breath; now was the time to explain the situation, otherwise after the baby was born, there would be social workers and goodness knows who else buzzing round Diana, trying to tell her what to do, and even working to convince her to keep the baby. She could be economical with the truth, and then explain to Diana how she had paved the way for her when the baby did arrive.

"The father won't be involved at all, and Diana is allowing me to adopt the baby as soon as she leaves hospital. All the legal papers have been sorted now, so the most important thing is for her to get well, and then give birth to a healthy baby."

Nurse Peggy Owen paused at the door before entering the ward. It was not really her business, of course, but sometimes mothers changed their minds when they held their baby; Diana might still want it. So she said briskly:

"That all sounds fine, as long as you know Diana can change her mind afterwards, when the baby is born, and if that is the case, you have to accept it, no matter what legal documents have been drawn up."

"Of course." Clare smiled at her through gritted teeth. What did that busybody know about it anyway? But she realised she had to lay the foundations just so the hospital knew what to expect. Hopefully when Diana did give birth, she would be back home within a day or so, then Clare would take off with the baby, and by the time all the do-gooders came round to see Diana, it would be too late.

As she entered the ward, she fixed a wide smile on her face, sitting on the chair and taking Diana's hand. She noted how pale she looked, and sleepy too.

"What have you been up to? I am so glad the baby is all right."

Diana had been in a dreamy sleep; the pain was subdued now, and the whole experience had exhausted her. She opened her eyes to see Clare sitting there holding her hand, but even with that gesture of affection, somehow deep down, she knew that Clare's concern was more for the baby than for herself. She had been feeling this for a while, but without anyone else in her life who actually cared about her, Diana clung to Clare, she felt like her saviour. She knew that if she was not pregnant, Clare would have left for Uganda by now, and when the baby was born, she was going anyway, but right now she had one friend left, and she was here.

"I missed the step and fell, but the baby is OK," she said wearily. She watched Clare's face light up.

"Well that is good news, isn't it?"

She felt like saying, for you, yes. But that sounded all bitter and twisted, and right now she felt so drowsy, she just wanted to go back to sleep, so she just murmured her agreement. She slipped back to sleep, and Clare could see there was no point in staying, so she went home.

Diana woke again in the middle of the night, she was dreaming she was in the water, and to her amazement, when she felt around her, the sheets were soaking. Had she wet the bed maybe? She called for a nurse to come quickly, and then all hell was let loose; her waters had broken.

Chapter Fifteen

Neil was unhappy that he had not been told about Diana's pregnancy until now. Clare had told Barry, and it had slipped out accidentally last night. Not only was she eight months gone, but also she was in hospital right now. By all accounts, Clare was hovering around her just waiting for the kid to be born, and then she was going to adopt it. Every time he thought about it he was disgusted, it was his kid and no one had told him anything. It was risking a lot if he went to see her, but in his own way, he did care about Diana, and he wondered what right Clare thought she had in adopting his kid without any permission. After all, it took two to tango, and he felt quite proud to think he was having a kid, especially after Rachel had miscarried the other one.

Barry was regretting his slip up; if Clare knew that Neil had found out, she would be livid with him. She was scared that he might put his oar in. Neil always thought he owned everyone and everything, but he was an idiot if he ever went anywhere near Diana again. Barry had no doubt he had raped the poor cow; he had got away with that, and now there was a baby, no wonder Diana wanted it adopted, how could she stomach a mini Neil growing up and reminding her just what a brute its father was. Knowing Clare as they all did, and how desperate she was to be a mother, he knew she would take that child as far away from all of them as she could; she would not want to share it. But he didn't blame her for that, Neil wouldn't know how to be a good father, it was just the prestige of knowing he had fathered a child, he would leave all the taking care of it to others. Knowing Neil as he did, he might even coerce Anna into getting involved, but he did hope that wouldn't happen. Barry had tried to start a new life away from Neil and his violence, but here they were again, starting another life in Cornwall where it was far from London, and it hadn't taken Neil long to ensnare Anna, another deluded cow who thought he loved her and was going to marry her.

Neil had found Anna living in a studio flat in Bodmin. It was a quiet place, near the moors, and as usual, it had not taken him long to get to know her. She was an artist, living in such an area of beauty it inspired her to paint it. She wore long skirts, was a tall girl, and her long blonde hair was almost down to her waist. She frequently put it in a ponytail, which made her look like a teenager, but she was in fact twenty-four years old. Her face was captivating, with enormous blue eyes and a pert nose. He liked her as soon as he met her whilst she was painting a local scene one day. After only a month he had moved into the studio with her, and Barry now had the small cottage that they were renting together all to himself. Neil had used the money he had managed to get through Rachel's credit card before she had cancelled it, but as always, he knew he had to find a meal ticket to keep them going. Colin had done a runner and Neil no longer cared where he was, as it was one less hanger on to pay when he got lucky.

It had been so easy to persuade Anna she was something special; he just admired her paintings and pretended to be interested. She had a rich daddy who was giving her a generous allowance until such time as her career took off. She was besotted with Neil, her eyes followed him around like a little puppy dog and she drank in every word he said, so now he had plenty to tell her.

When he arrived back from his meeting with Barry, she was just finishing off her latest creation. To him it was just a painting of some hills and a meadow, but he praised it to the skies as always, and her face lit up with happiness.

"Anna I have something I need to share with you. I need you to sit down and listen."

Anna smiled with happiness, not only did she have the best looking man on the planet, he was also baring his soul to her, complete honesty, and she liked it.

108

"I am all yours," she laughed. "Now what is so pressing that you need to tell me before I put the kettle on?"

"I was in a relationship with a girl called Diana, we broke up just before we moved here and, to be honest, until I met you, I was pretty cut up about losing her, but of course it doesn't matter now."

"Go on," she urged, noting how sincerity positively radiated from Neil.

"I have just heard she is carrying my child. It's due next month, but now I am worried, because I don't think she will make a fit mother. She has spoken about having it adopted, but as you and I plan to get married, how about we adopt it?"

"Well I need to think about that," said Anna. She wasn't sure how she felt about taking on another woman's child; but one look at Neil's eyes, and her heart melted. It would make him happy, and he was everything to her.

Neil came over and put his arms around her, holding her close, he kissed her and then murmured in her ear, which sent her heart racing.

"Of course, I can't show my face at the hospital, whereas you can, but we'll talk about that later," he said, putting his hands onto her breasts, which were showing over the top of her blouse, and deftly undoing the button to expose them. He was glad she didn't wear a bra, and as he felt her nipples hardening when his fingers touched them, he knew he had got her just where he wanted her, and she would be willing and compliant to anything. So when he needed her to get his kid, Anna would.

Susan had been glad to have Rachel staying for the last few months. She still shuddered inwardly when she thought about everything that had happened to her. Being married one day, then to find out that her husband had cheated with her sister the next, and then the biggest shock of all, to lose the baby, which Susan had not realised she was carrying.

At the time Rachel and Clive had both found themselves unable to forgive Diana for wrecking her sister's life. It seemed to be such a selfish act towards the one person who had loved Diana so much, and always looked out for her. They had since found out that Neil was not the sincere person they had thought he was, and it seemed since his rapid departure, he had only been after Rachel for her money. He had even managed to get some few thousand pounds out of her account before he vanished.

Since Susan had heard that Diana was now pregnant by Neil, and in hospital, she felt a deep sorrow inside her at just how lonely she must be, and although Clive remained firm in his mind about disowning her, as did Rachel, she could feel herself wavering. There was a doubt in her mind now, had Diana been misjudged? Had she been raped by him? He had already proved himself to be a fraudulent person, so why wouldn't he also be capable of rape?

But she had not dared to share this with Rachel, who had become much harder since it had all happened, and never even mentioned Diana's name. It had really affected her mentally, but Susan was hoping, after the baby was born, Rachel might change. After all, the baby would be her niece. But it seemed Rachel had no plans to stay around. She had said that her company were sending her worldwide to do more work on the causes and prevention of cancer. Rachel said she would not have a permanent address, just moving from one hotel to another, but would keep in touch via her mobile phone. It was not an ideal situation for Susan to accept, because she seriously believed that Rachel was very emotionally damaged by her experiences, but she also realised that having a complete change like this was her way of trying to put it behind her.

Clare was the bridge between the twins, friend to both of them, so Susan had also got to know her so she could keep up with all the happenings. Clare had telephoned and told her that Diana was eight months gone, and now in hospital after a fall down the stairs. Susan's heart went out to Diana; if her baby was born early, it had a chance to survive, but was the birth of that child going to cause even more trouble in the family? Only time would tell.

Rachel was all packed and ready to go in a few days. She deliberately kept any thought of Diana out of her mind; their relationship was over. Inside her a voice was arguing with her, trying to soften her up by suggesting that maybe her lying cheating husband had raped her sister. But she pushed these thoughts right out of her mind. Her jealousy that Diana was having the baby she so desperately wanted was more than she could bear.

There was no longer a place here for her. No doubt, with a new baby in the family, eventually her aunt and uncle would reconcile with Diana, and she couldn't bear to be around to see that. Going away and starting a new life was the only answer. She was doing her best to stay strong, because even now, eight months after her sham marriage, although she appeared positive to everyone else, inside her heart was truly broken, she was a mess!

Clare wasn't sure about anything now. Would Diana give birth early, or would she go full term? The thought that she might soon have her new baby was overwhelming to Clare, but she knew she had to stay calm.

It had been a good idea to tell them that she was going to Uganda, because it made her seem so caring, but she wanted her own child, not to spend her life delivering babies for other women. It was amazing how easy it was to fool people; that story she had come up with about being an abused wife was great, and it had persuaded Diana to offer her a home. The only truth she had told was about her miscarriage. She had loved that man, but she had known he was already married, and she was one of many of his dalliances. The pregnancy had been real, and saying he was violent had made herself feel better about when he left her.

She had never known love from her own mother, as she had been taken away and put in a foster home. Well, in fact, a series of foster homes, and the need to have her own child to love had become so strong. Her brothers didn't show her love either, they had grown up all wrong, so having her own baby was what she desperately craved.

It would work out well if the baby was born now. She knew she would have to change her name. A false passport was now being arranged, and the baby would be added to it when it was born so she could travel without raising any suspicions. She had everything in place. Once she had left England, no one would know where she was, or be able to trace her, and together with her new baby, she could start a new life.

Chapter Sixteen

"Come on Diana, cut the histrionics, it's time to push!"

Betty Miller was a midwife with a no-nonsense approach to delivering babies. She believed in getting on with the job. She originally lived in Yorkshire, and true to the area, she always spoke her mind. She was a big woman with a florid complexion. Her grey hair belied her age, which was forty, and she had no time for vanity, so she wore it short and straight. Never having been married or had children herself, made her feel these were all her children as soon as they left their mother's womb. This was her domain, and woe betide anyone who tried to take over from her.

She had not taken kindly to the woman Clare, who also said she was a midwife, and had wanted to come in and help. Strictly speaking patients were allowed a birthing partner, but this one had dared to question her, saying that after eight hours of labour, if there was something wrong, maybe Diana should have a caesarean. So she had demanded she wait outside because she was upsetting her patient, and very few people argued with Betty. She had a loud voice and a bossy manner, but she knew how to safely deliver a baby, and in this case there was no need for an operation, they were nearly there.

She had the measure of Diana straight away; a beautiful young woman, and very melodramatic, but then she was an actress by profession, so what could one expect? Of course childbirth hurt, it was no picnic, but she had been given pain relief, and now she needed to shape up and get on with the job. Although only eight months, the baby seemed a normal size, and apart from a touch of jaundice, Betty was confident it would be all right.

"I am pushing! God knows I am pushing, it will rip me in half!"

Nurse Peggy wiped some of the sweat off Diana's face, pushing was the hard part, and Betty barked back at her.

"Don't be so silly. You won't rip apart, women were made to bear children."

Peggy remembered that Diana wasn't keeping the baby, and she marvelled at all the pain she was going through to then just hand her baby over to someone else to bring up.

Diana had been given quite a lot of pain relief, and she felt unreal. One minute she was floating, the next pain was ripping through her body, taking over her senses, making her shout, although she could not remember what she was saying because her voice seemed so far away to her, she could barely hear it.

That woman, the midwife, was so harsh with her, and she had not allowed Clare to stay. Clare was her only rock right now, and she needed her because she no longer had Rachel. This was a time in her life when the support of her sister would have made it so much easier, but all she had was a harsh midwife and a nurse.

She heard them telling her to push, and then they shouted that the baby was coming. The pain intensified so much, and she was panting; she had no idea childbirth would be like this! The sweat was pouring off her, and once again she was engulfed with pain, but this time she felt she wanted to give up, she could not bear this pain, she wanted to die, and her screams of agony rent the air.

Suddenly the pain subsided briefly, and they were exclaiming that the head was there, and she could feel it, like a huge hard rock inside her. She was finally going to rid her body of this parasite. She could feel them gently easing the baby from her, and then there was a silence. Weren't babies meant to cry when they were born? This one wasn't, and then they were helping her to deliver the afterbirth.

Diana had a feeling of loss, which she could not understand, now that her baby had left her body. She was trying to focus through the haze which hung over her. "My baby, where is my baby?"

"Diana, you have a little girl, but she has not cried yet, we think she is choked up with mucous. Just to be safe, we have taken her to special care, where she can have some help."

Suddenly her parasite became a baby; an innocent little baby, who was fighting for its life. The baby she had wished so many times she was not having. Maybe God was punishing her for her wickedness, and her baby would die. At that moment she prayed so hard for it to live, it did not deserve to die!

She was vaguely aware of a doctor in the room. He said she was going to have some stitches. She did not remember feeling anything, except a numbness inside, wondering and worrying if her little daughter would be all right. She had not even thought of a name. She had assumed that Clare would name her; but could they wait that long? If her baby didn't make it, she would be unnamed, that wasn't right.

The haze was beginning to wear off now, and she was put into a side room and offered a cup of tea. Diana shook her head, and addressed Peggy, who had come with her.

"No tea, and I want to name my daughter, just in case. . ." the rest of her sentence was drowned when she sobbed. "I want to call her Ella, after my mother."

"Try not to worry. They have said she is stable, and although she has not been weighed yet, she seems a good size," said Peggy encouragingly. "They have to make sure her airways are clear."

Diana lay back on her pillow, totally exhausted, there was nothing more she could do except wait. She felt a complete and utter failure; first she had ruined her sister's life, and now she couldn't even give birth properly like other women, without endangering her baby's life.

Clare was furious with that midwife. She had only made a suggestion, and then they threw her out. She was standing out in the corridor now wondering what was happening. Diana's cries were muffled, but she could still hear them, and then it went silent so she guessed the baby was born.

She wondered how long it would be before they let her in. Maybe they had the upper hand right now, but after tomorrow, they would not be able to control her, she would be gone. That was a comforting thought, so she sat down on the seat; but as she did, someone ran past, it was quick, but she did spot a baby. Fear clutched at her heart. The baby made no sound, and the midwife was in a hurry, surely there was nothing wrong with her baby?

She couldn't bear it if there was, because this baby was what her future was all about.

Clare paced up and down the corridor; if only someone would tell her what was going on. She felt her world was crashing in on her. How long would it be before they allowed her to see Diana? She had a glimmer of sympathy for her, but what overwhelmed her most of all was the feeling that her baby might not make it. Was she being melodramatic? She wasn't sure, but the silence scared her.

Peggy saw her standing for a long time and took pity on her. Betty had gone now and would only be interested in the babies, she left the nurses to take care of the mothers, and Peggy had not told her that Diana was having her baby adopted. Betty would raise the roof, even though it wasn't her business. She couldn't say too much, but it was clear that this young woman seemed Diana's only visitor, no family or father of the baby had come, and Diana would need her support.

"I have seen you waiting. Diana is not quite ready for visitors, but if you go and get yourself a coffee, and come back in about half an hour, then she may be ready for a visitor."

"Is she all right, and the baby, how about the baby? It has been born now, hasn't it?"

Peggy adopted a soothing voice that she reserved for all distressed relatives, and managed to sidestep the question.

"Diana is tired right now, but she is OK. We can tell you more later."

Clare found this remark even more bewildering, but she did go and get herself a coffee, and then presented herself exactly thirty minutes later. There was a different nurse on duty, no sign of Peggy, but she was allowed in to see Diana, who was propped up on pillows dozing. Clare pulled gently at her arm.

"What's happened? Where is the baby?"

Diana looked wearily at her. She had let Clare down, and she would be upset, she didn't know what to say to her, but then mercifully Betty came bustling in. Totally ignoring Clare, Betty addressed Diana.

"Your daughter is fine now. We have cleared all the mucous, she has been weighed, and six pounds is an acceptable weight for an eight month baby. At eight months our babies have jaundice for a couple of days, it's quite normal and will wear off. Just as a precaution we are keeping her in special care for tonight, but we expect that you both can go home tomorrow."

Diana saw Clare's face relax, and the tightness that she had felt around her own chest had gone. Her baby was going to live, she felt elated about it. Clare turned her back on Betty, and addressed Clare directly.

"Well done you. A little girl, that is amazing!" and she bent down to hug her.

Betty left, but not without her parting shot.

"Don't forget to put her to your breast in the morning. Your baby needs the colostrum to clear all the mucous from her bowels. This will also encourage the milk to come."

Diana nodded her agreement, as Betty was not to be argued with, but she knew she could not breastfeed her baby because Clare would have her little Ella. She didn't really understand why she felt empty inside, but she knew deep down that she really did want to feed her baby and help her to get strong.

Clare spoke when the whirlwind that was Betty had thundered out of the room.

"You know you must ask them to give you tablets to dry up your milk so you don't feel uncomfortable. Don't worry about bossy Betty."

"Yes, I know."

Clare was only allowed to stay for a few more minutes, as they wanted to move Diana back into the ward with other mothers who had also given birth. Diana felt so tired that she was glad they would just wheel her bed back. She was aching a bit from her stitches, but the relief that baby Ella was alive caused her tears to flow. The young nurse picked up on it, guessing she was suffering from the baby blues, then gave her some surprising news.

"You haven't seen your baby yet. If you feel up to it, we can take you to special care in a wheelchair to meet her. Have you got a name for her yet?"

"Her name is Ella."

Diana had told herself she just wanted to see her baby once, and then she would hand her over, but she had not reckoned on the fact that she already had a bond with baby Ella. Her baby had ceased to be a monster in her thoughts. Just as Diana was innocent of consenting to Neil when she was conceived, so was little Ella innocent too. She had not asked to be born out of such

116

a violent happening. She was just a helpless baby, and it was impossible for Diana to hate her.

When Diana was wheeled into the special care unit, she had to put a mask on and wash her hands. Somehow in her mind, the one thing that had worried her was, as Neil was her father, would Ella look like him and act like him when she was older? But when she saw her lying in the special cot, the first thing she noticed was her red gold hair, just like herself and Rachel. Her eyes were closed, but the nurse said they were blue but might change later.

When she saw the vulnerability of this little baby, something happened to Diana that even she did not understand, she felt a very fierce and powerful feeling of love sweep over her. It totally took control of her. This was her daughter, no matter how she had come into the world; the past must be put behind her now. She had an overwhelming desire to keep the baby and bring her up herself. She wanted to make sure that she didn't grow up like Neil, and as her mother, she could guide her on the right path through life.

"You can hold her now. Just wait whilst I lift her out," urged the nurse.

Diana was trembling with apprehension; she had never held a new born baby before, and this one was hers! But when the nurse handed the warm little bundle to her, it seemed the most natural thing in the world. She stroked her fine downy hair, and the baby stirred, opening her eyes briefly, with a little murmur, and Diana marvelled at her tiny fingers and toes. She gently touched those fingers, and instinctively she felt the baby grasp her own finger tightly. It almost felt to Diana like Ella was saying: "I am here Mummy." She could feel the tears running down her face because against all the odds, she had fallen in love with her beautiful daughter, and she knew she didn't want to share her with anyone. She would be letting Clare down, of course, and she would have to go it alone because no one else cared about her, and she had no idea where Rachel was anyway; but still so powerful was her mother instinct, it would be her and Ella against the world. She was going to make some good come out of this whole sorry mess by bringing up her daughter as a woman to be proud of.

The nurse spotted her tears. Poor girl, all that worry, and now all this was overwhelming but, following a proper rest over night, she would be all right tomorrow.

"I think that is enough for today. I bet you are proud of Ella, she is so beautiful."

Diana nodded her agreement, she was not usually lost for words, but she felt emotionally shattered. They wheeled her back to the ward, and she enjoyed the cosseting. She was given a small amount of scrambled egg on toast, which she realised she needed, as she had not eaten for many hours. Diana also felt very thirsty and drank most of the jug of water on her trolley. This was quickly replenished, and she was also supplied with a bottle of orange to dilute into it.

Diana was praised for drinking so much by Betty, who had returned briefly, and reminded her:

"You need to drink plenty to make milk for your baby."

"I know."

She ignored the voice inside her, reminding her that Clare had asked her to get some pills to dry up her milk. Right now she didn't feel she could cope with any of this, all she wanted was to sleep.

Peggy returned to do the night shift just before Diana went to sleep. She had been warned by the other nurse that Diana was prone to tears, so she went up to her bed to check if she was all right.

"I want to keep my baby. Is it too late?"

Judging by her red swollen eyes, she was not all right, and Peggy hastened to assure her:

"Of course it's not too late! Normally it takes six weeks to adopt. A mother leaves hospital without her baby, but then has more time to make her decision. It's a life changing decision, and your friend must accept that now Ella is born, you have had a change of heart."

"I feel guilty about all the months she took care of me; and now it's all been for nothing, she will be devastated."

"Right now Diana, all we care about is your welfare, and Ella's. There will be other babies that your friend can adopt, but Ella only has one mother, and that is you."

This all made sense to Diana. Clare would be hurt, but there were other babies. So she took the sleeping pill she was offered, as she was reminded once she got home and did night feeds, a good night's sleep would not happen any more for quite a while.

After a peaceful sleep she felt more in control, and when they brought her sleepy little baby to her, she put her to her breast, just as she had been asked to. Already Ella was showing a strong will to live as she sucked hungrily. It might only be colostrum, but it was keeping her alive, which made Diana feel she was a proper mother like everyone else, and she would bring up Ella herself.

She knew that the easy way out would be to bar Clare from visiting and then text her and say she was keeping Ella, but that was the cowards way out, and she owed it to Clare to explain properly. So after Clare had arrived, and held Ella she tried to explain as kindly as she could, why she had changed her mind. She had expected tears and recriminations from Clare, but there were none, she just went very quiet and wished her well. Diana explained that later today, after the doctor had signed her off, she would be going home. Most likely after lunch.

When Clare left Diana, she felt like her whole world was in ruins. It was even worse meeting Ella, as she was such a perfect little girl, but she didn't want to arouse Diana's suspicions because she already knew what she was going to do. Back at home was a nurse's uniform, which would give her much freer access to this hospital. So she hugged Diana for the last time and left, feeling sad inside that it had to end this way just because Diana was unable to keep her word.

Chapter Seventeen

Now that Diana had made up her mind to keep Ella, she felt at peace. Clare had not been as upset as she had expected, but now she realised she was on her own, it was just her and Ella. She longed to ring her aunt and tell her about her baby; she was so proud of her beautiful little girl, but would her aunt put the phone down on her? She really wasn't sure, so she sent her a text. "My daughter Ella arrived yesterday weighing six pounds. We would love to see you."

Susan was not expecting anyone to text her. She had not had her mobile for long, and modern technology was a bit confusing. Luckily Rachel was there when it bleeped. She was packed and ready to go, and was just having a quick coffee before her taxi arrived.

"Oh, what is that funny bleep?" exclaimed Susan.

"You have a text come in," said Rachel.

"Oh bother. Can you read it for me dear, I haven't got my glasses on."

Rachel read out the words, and her face crumpled, she had not wanted to know this. Her sole reason for going away was because Diana had the child that she had so desperately wanted.

Susan saw her face change as she spoke the words, and moved to take the offending mobile from her.

"So sorry, Rachel. I had no idea Diana was going to contact me."

Rachel hardened her heart and composed her face.

"It doesn't bother me now, none of it, but after I have gone, you must have Diana back in your life, and her baby daughter."

Those words bewildered Susan, but the anger she had felt towards Diana had mellowed somewhat over the last few months. Now that Neil was exposed as a trickster, it was possible he was also a rapist. If she had misjudged Diana, and she had not encouraged him, then there was one thing she must do; she must put it right. That text message was like a plea from Diana to be allowed back into their lives. She could not ignore it, and now there was a baby to consider too.

Rachel had virtually given her blessing, and she wondered if there was any chance of the girls reconciling, even if it was only by letter. She decided to find out more.

"Are you still angry with Diana?"

"Not any more, but I still can't stay here. My sister wrecked my marriage and I can't forgive that."

Susan wanted to ask her if she was sure about that, or did she think Diana had been raped? But she might not see Rachel for a long time when she went travelling, so there was no way she wanted to part with animosity. So she said what she thought might make the parting easier.

"Rachel we will miss you, and don't forget, there will always be a place for you here with us if you ever want to come back."

Rachel hugged her warmly. Aunt Susan was the nearest to a mother they had had since they were eight, and Uncle Clive too had been amazing. Parting from them was difficult. Nobody would need to know that she was going to stop off at the hospital and see her new niece, and certainly not Diana. She would tuck her hair out of the way, in a ponytail, and then see Ella. Something was drawing her towards the one thing that was stopping her from staying around, and even she didn't know why she had this compulsion to see the baby. But it was so strong, she had to do it.

Clare had decided on a plan, because she knew she did not have long. She was on her way back to the hospital, and to begin with she had thought that Neil wouldn't need to know about Ella because he would never see her anyway, as Clare planned to take her so far away that he would never find her.

But then again she did not want to fall foul of his temper, and when he found out she had kept the birth from him, there would

121

f

be hell to pay. He was never going to shape up as a father, so all she had to do was text him the news, and then by the time he had got his act together, she and Ella would be long gone, and if he ever did catch up with them, because after all for years she had been trying to escape him, but somehow both Neil and Barry seemed to end up back in her life, then at least he would remember that she had told him about Ella's birth. Whilst she was in the taxi she texted him, it was her last parting gesture to him before she put her plan into action.

Curiosity about Diana being in hospital had brought Neil back to London from Cornwall. He had a plan in his mind about taking his kid back to Cornwall after it was born. Anna's father had coughed up some money, and they were currently staying in a hotel near to the hospital. He had told Anna exactly what she had to do, even to the point of hiring a nurse's uniform for her to wear. He realised they might have to wait for another month, as Clare had said she had a month to go, so when the text came through, it took him totally by surprise. His daughter was born, a month early, but a satisfactory weight, and due to leave hospital later today.

He realised there was no time to lose if they were going to put the plan into action. He felt excited that he was now a father, and he wanted his kid in Cornwall with him. Anna could help him take care of it.

"Quick baby, you need to get that uniform on and go get the baby, she's been born. Here is a photo of her mother, and the baby should be by the bed. You know I am relying on you."

Anna looked into those eyes. They looked so sincere, he truly wanted to care for his baby daughter, and all because she had an unfit mother. But a part of her was scared. What if she got caught? It was a serious crime and she could go to prison. She wavered.

"I am not sure Neil, I might get caught."

"Honey, you won't get caught. Now would I ask you to do anything that put you at risk? She needs to be taken away from her bad mother."

Then he wrapped her in his arms and kissed her until she felt dizzy. Neil truly was the love of her life, and she could not refuse him anything. There was another reason too. If they were going to get married, it was obvious Neil would want a family. She hadn't told him about her ectopic pregnancy last year. The man had ran away when she got pregnant. Her parents had lent their support, as they really wanted their grandchild, but it wasn't to be, she had lost it at three months, after it developed outside the womb and could not survive. The doctor had warned her she might never be able to have a normal pregnancy, and she certainly did not want to go through all that pain again.

Daddy had been amazing, paying out for her studio flat; and painting was soothing, it helped with her grief. Then unbelievably, because she certainly wasn't looking for love after the last man had ditched her, along had come Neil, admiring her work and restoring her confidence. It felt like she owed him a lot, and bringing up his daughter was the least thing she could do for him. By a strange coincidence, the hospital where Diana was Anna knew very well, as that was where she had lost her baby. She lived in London before she upped and went to Cornwall, and although she had not been in the maternity ward, she had visited the surgeon there, and knew the location of the maternity ward.

"OK, I will do it."

Diana had never been the most patient person, out of the two of them it had always been Rachel who was calm and collected. She still missed her so much, with her calmness and sensible attitude. But now she was a mother, she knew she had to change because of that precious little life that so depended on her. She had already fed Ella twice, and it was going well. She found breastfeeding somewhat comforting, as she didn't feel quite so alone. Little Ella depended on her for her survival, and she had roused such fierce feelings of protectiveness inside Diana, the force of which she had never realised would be so strong.

But right now, her feelings of impatience were all about getting home with Ella. Of course, she was not prepared for this because she had not thought she would keep her baby. She needed a cot, push chair, baby clothes; just about everything. However, all Ella needed was her mother's love, and she had that. It was nearly midday, and although she had been told the doctor was doing his rounds, he had not reached them yet, and so she could not leave until he said so. It would be so nice to get home away from all these people who seemed to be in charge of her, and be her own person. Betty made her feel like a little girl at school; she acted like a bossy headmistress. She had insisted that Diana always tied her hair back from her face when feeding her baby, saying her hair was full of germs no matter how often she washed it. Diana did not dare to argue with her. She had breakfast so early that now she felt starving again, and so was relieved to see a trolley with hot lunches coming round. Maybe after she had eaten that, the doctor would come and then she could dress. Clare had brought her clothes in earlier and it was easy to get a taxi; they hovered about near to the main entrance, waiting for fares.

So she ate the chicken casserole and drank her orange squash, as she had been told that food and drink makes milk. When they took the tray away she realised she was feeling sleepy. Ella was sleeping peacefully in her cot at the end of the bed, and that seemed a good idea, a little nap before the doctor came. So she lay back with a sigh, pulling the sheet up. Soon they would be home.

Chapter Eighteen

She was falling, down, down, down, into a bottomless pit, it was pitch dark and she wanted to save herself, but she couldn't. Panic rushed through her shaking body, and she heard the screams. She wondered briefly if they were coming from her own mouth, then bump!

She woke up with a start. The taxi driver was eyeing her with surprise, how had she managed to doze off at such a time, and why was she having such frightening dreams? Maybe it was because of what she was doing and, of course, last night she had not slept at all. It did feel wrong to her, and it left her mind feeling troubled.

There was perspiration pouring off her trembling body, even though it was a cold December day, and she tried not to think about how she had felt when he left her. Her bedroom had been dark and silent. Oh why was she still weeping for the baby she had lost, and the man who had deserted her even before it was born? Maybe it was because she was about to return to the very place where she had lost her baby.

Why had she fought against that pit? Surely no matter what she did, her life was over now? She had been so brave and determined when they parted. She felt she could cope with being a single mother. He had thrown her love back in her face, and moved on to another trusting soul, but she had vowed to love her little child, and give it the best life that she could, because she had someone to love.

She tried not to think about when she had lost the baby. He

wasn't there to hold her hand and tell her not to worry, because he was out of her life. She had kept her grief inside. So much pain, which she had no wish to share with anyone. He had not come to see her after, but she wanted it that way. He had another life now, and he had proved himself to be no good anyway, and the last bond that would have connected them had been broken. She left hospital very quickly afterwards. Her body had recovered, but her heart never would, and being near to a ward of other mothers with newborn babies was just too much to bear. She told them she was going to stay with family. Having connections with the medial profession, as she did, came in useful, as she knew they would not allow her to go home in such distress otherwise. She agreed to the counselling, it would all be arranged. She would agree to anything just to get back in her own home. But after, she had realised it was a huge mistake, returning to the home they had shared, with all the memories of before he had found someone else.

All her life she had bounced back, even when she had suffered the most traumatic of losses, because she was a survivor. It made her angry when she thought that some people were just not fit to be a mother. Take Diana, for example, always wanted a good time in life, then got pregnant by her sister's husband. What sort of mother would she make? There wasn't a maternal bone in her body. She didn't even love the man.

The more she thought about it, the more determined she became. Diana was not the right person to bring this baby up, but she was, and in the long run the child would thank her for caring enough to rescue her from such a situation. It was solely down to her because no one else cared.

They were at the hospital now, so she paid the man and exited the taxi with a strong sense of purpose. He drove off, no longer interested in her, so she took the holdall with her into the ladies' toilet. There was just one person in there drying her hands, who barely noticed her, so she slipped quietly into the cubicle.

Out came the nurse's uniform, and into the bag went her skirt and top. Suddenly she panicked. She hadn't thought about the bag; it had her DNA all over it. She ran out of the back entrance to where the bins were. But she needn't have worried, he was there already, waiting for her. She slung the bag through the open car door and he nodded to her. There was no time for words right now, he had been paid a lot of money to do this job, and then dispose of the car afterwards, and there was no reason why he would ever be linked with her again. She needed her arms free to hold the baby, and he knew what to do, he was experienced at this sort of thing, and would destroy it all in a blazing bonfire. She returned through the back door, having kept back the grey wig. The bouffant 1960s style transformed her, and the glasses with the black frames, adding at least twenty years to her age. When she glanced in the mirror, even she didn't recognise herself. She was also wearing comfortable flat shoes, because it was quite a long walk down the hospital corridor to the maternity ward.

As she took the walk towards the maternity wing, she was glad that no one could see her heart pounding so hard with anticipation it felt like it would burst through her chest. But nobody spared a glance at the nurse who was walking with such purposefulness, she was in the right environment. She even made time to slip into the toilet to make sure her wig was on properly, and to study her face with the big glasses on, then felt satisfied that she looked about mid-forties. She could feel such a dryness in her mouth, as the maternity ward was just next door.

When she first entered the ward, there was not another nurse in sight, which was not unusual because of the cutbacks. But then, at the far end, she spotted Peggy, and her heart missed a beat, she was holding Ella, and that had not been a part of her plan. Then she saw Diana, her red gold hair was unmistakable, even though she had it in a ponytail.

Diana was trying to take a lunchtime nap, but her little daughter was having none of it. Peggy was rocking the baby and doing her best to soothe her.

"Nurse, I feel so tired, and she's very fussy today," Diana moaned. Suddenly the enormous task of being a mother felt overwhelming.

"I'll take her to the nursery and change her. You've fed her, so she might have some wind," said Peggy comfortingly. As she moved towards the door, one of the other patients pressed their bell, so she hesitated, trying to decide what to do. Then she saw the grey-haired nurse standing there. Wonderful, the agency had finally sent someone, and the maturer ones were always the best, because they had experienced it all with their own children and had more patience.

127

She reacted quickly, this was her chance. "Shall I take her to the nursery like you suggested?"

"Yes please," replied Peggy. "I am so glad to have you here, you can see how short staffed we are, and I must answer the bell."

It couldn't have been easier. Diana had turned over with a satisfied sigh. She tenderly gathered Ella into her arms; she had now stopped crying, and it was such a poignant moment for her to finally hold this baby. A baby in her arms felt wonderful, and already Ella felt really special to her; she actually felt like she was her own child.

With Peggy now gone to answer the call, she took the long walk down the corridor again. Her instinct made her want to hurry, but she must not attract attention, so she walked at an even pace, pulling the light cotton sheet around Ella to protect her. The impulse to flee was strong, but she ignored it, and forced herself to remain calm. Her precious bundle was nestling in her arms so this must be the right thing to do.

After what seemed like an eternity to her, she reached the side door that led to the bins and the back of the hospital. She glanced round quickly before she went through it, but no one much came up here, and the corridor was empty. She had bought all the things needed. Little Ella was going to want for nothing, and thanks to this man, they were ready to make a getaway.

Her conscience made one last bid to stop her moment of madness, but she squashed it down firmly. She had just seen Diana ask someone else to take her baby. Diana didn't want that child, so her intervention was a good thing for everyone, and unlike Diana, she would be a good mother.

"Thanks, we can go now!" she said to him. His face was totally inscrutable.

"Right," he said, "don't worry about the clothes and bag, I will take care of them."

And she knew he would. There was so much money at stake, and he was a master at this. Soon they would be parting, and he would conveniently forget that he had ever met her.

When Peggy had helped her patient, who was having a bad day, she looked at the clock, and it was one o'clock. Nobody had yet brought the trolley round with tea and coffee. They were short

128

staffed in the kitchen too. As she passed Diana's bed she saw she was sleeping, and the cot was still empty, so Ella must still be in the nursery. She went along to make sure the agency nurse was not having any problems, because she had been thrown in at the deep end, but when she opened the door, the cot they used for Ella was empty and there was no sign of the nurse. Betty was presiding over all the babies, barking orders at another nurse, on her way through to the delivery room. It was well known that Betty considered the babies to be her property all the while they were in hospital.

"Has Ella gone back to the ward? Did you take her?" She addressed both Betty and the nurse, as the empty cot was a bit alarming.

"She's been with her mother all morning," volunteered the nurse.

"What's wrong with you, woman?" boomed Betty, and without answering her, Peggy ran back to the ward. Diana was waking up now, but the cot at the foot of her bed was empty. Betty had followed her out now, and Peggy told her:

"The grey-haired agency nurse took Ella because Diana wanted to get some sleep." And Diana nodded agreement at this, because she vaguely remembered a grey-haired nurse at the door, who had carried Ella out.

"What grey-haired nurse? We don't have any agency nurses today!" thundered Betty, always totally lacking in tact.

Diana looked from one to the other of them. Surely they couldn't be saying they had lost her baby? She felt the hand of fear clutching at her heart. She needed her baby here with her. What had they done?

Betty's next words left her in no doubt.

"We need to ring the police, and broadcast everywhere. All exits must be staffed. A baby has gone missing, possibly even been stolen. It is in grave danger, as anyone doing that is not right in their mind. Hurry girl!"

Diana screamed with anguish. It came right from the very depths of her soul. But was it her? She didn't know, all she knew was her baby had gone, and then merciful blackness enveloped her.

129

PART TWO

Chapter Nineteen

Victoria Road Hospital had now gained itself world-wide interest for all the wrong reasons. The newspapers soon got hold of the story of the missing baby, and it was all the staff could do to keep over zealous reporters away from Diana. She was not in a fit state to see anyone. Her aunt had been summoned to be with her, and when she heard the circumstances, Susan dropped everything and came to her.

But Diana's grief was so profound it was almost like her baby had died. She spent her time pacing up and down, and didn't appear to recognise anyone who spoke to her. The police came to interview her, but it was pointless; she was grieving for her baby, so cruelly snatched from her, and she just kept repeating, "Where is my Ella, I need my baby!"

Susan's heart went out to Diana. Who could have done such a cruel thing to her so soon after Ella's birth? What was even more worrying; was that tiny baby safe? Because baby snatching was usually only done by someone whose balance of mind had been disturbed? Her mind flashed to Rachel, who was clearly suffering from depression, but she dismissed that thought. Not only had she herself seen Rachel into the taxi that was taking her to a new life abroad earlier today, but also she had gone because of Ella. Seeing a baby fathered by her own husband was too much to bear, she surely would hardly want to take that baby with her.

The realisation that she felt responsible for the abduction of Ella had distressed Peggy so much she had been sent home from work. The police had been round to interview her, and they showed her various pictures of grey-haired women, but she hadn't recognised any of them as being the woman she had mistaken for being an agency nurse.

Because Diana could not keep still, or relate to anyone, eventually the doctor had given her a strong sedative in injection form, in the hopes that after a proper sleep she might be able to function properly. The police were now being kept away from her by doctor's orders, but it was obvious, that because of the severity of the crime, soon she would have to face an interrogation, and they would also have to persuade her to give a television appearance, as it was hoped that in her distressed state, it might prompt the culprit to return the baby.

Diana was in a world of her own right now, pacing up and down, pining for the baby that she had willed to live when she was born, and that someone had now so cruelly snatched from her. She couldn't hear anything and she was not aware of anyone. Her mind was totally fixed on Ella. Even as she was thinking about her, her breasts filled up with milk and hardened. Her body was crying out for her baby, and then the milk leaked out of her nursing bra and onto her cotton nightie. She sobbed with the mental agony she was going through. She couldn't bear the thought that her baby might be in danger.

The doctor was filled with compassion when he saw her. This poor woman could drive herself out of her mind with grief, and it took himself and a nurse to hold her down whilst he gave her an injection. They also had to administer a pill to stop her milk; she looked such a pitiful sight with her milk dripping out onto her nightie. Eventually the injection worked, they felt her relax, and she was then put to bed and moved to a side room. He ordered the nurse to keep an eye on her, and then all they could do was hope that after a sleep, when she woke up again, Diana would be coherent enough to be interviewed.

Susan was completely out of her depth, and wished that Clive was with her right now. She knew that he would forget the past now that Diana was in such distress. But he had not been at home when the hospital had telephoned her. She had stayed close to Diana for the past hour, trying to reach her by talking to her, but she could not get through to her. Her niece was a tragic sight, with her haunted face, eyes wide with fear, and milk dripping from her engorged breasts.

She had watched the doctor and nurse trying to restrain Diana, and was worried that she might be tipping over the edge. If only she knew what to do. She felt so useless; even her presence here was of no use because Diana didn't seem to be aware of her. She looked down at the now sleeping girl, saying prayers inside herself that she would be all right and her baby would be safely returned to her. The nurse spoke kindly to Susan.

"We are hoping she will wake up less confused tomorrow, and then can give the police a statement."

"Yes, I know. I wish I could have helped today."

"You did help; you were here," said the nurse warmly, as this appeared to be the only person who was interested in Diana. "She will really need your support tomorrow if she can be persuaded to do a nationwide appeal on the news."

"Yes I know, I have seen it done before."

"The best thing to do is go home now, then hopefully after a good night's sleep, Diana will be a bit better. Today has been a huge shock to her, but with your help, if we can make her realise how important it is to publicise Ella's disappearance, we have a better chance of reuniting them. Can you get back here about ten tomorrow?"

"I certainly can, and my husband will be with me then," Susan said firmly. Right now she needed Clive, his down to earth attitude would be balm to her anxiety, and together they would stand by Diana. They had to put the past behind them now, and give her all the love and support that she needed.

Diana woke up the next morning, her head feeling a little woolly, and she tried to remember the day before. Then she felt the fear and despair rush through her again; where was her baby, and who had taken her?

But although she was full of despair, and wanted to weep, she could not. She felt numbed, the pain was still there inside her, but it all seemed unreal. So she lay back on her pillows, and when the trolley came in, she obediently drank a cup of tea and ate the bowl of porridge that was offered to her. The milk was not escaping from her breasts today; to her it was like her body knew there was no baby to feed, so it didn't really matter if she ate or drank, the baby was not there.

Her aunt and uncle arrived, and after a quick discussion with the nurse, they both came over to hug her. Susan was relieved that there was recognition in Diana's eyes, even if she did seem to be a bit doped up. Susan spoke gently to her.

"Diana, the police want to interview you, they are trying to find baby Ella. Can you cope with it today?"

Diana stared at them wonderingly. Had they forgiven her, and was she now back in the family fold? Clare had now deserted her to go to Uganda, but she was not alone, she had some of her family back.

Susan's conscience was really troubling her. Although this might not be the best time, she knew what she had to say; she had seen the look of confusion on Diana's face, so she had to explain. She bent towards her, whispering gently.

"Diana, we are so sorry. We do believe that you were raped, and we also believe that you love little Ella. It's not her fault the way she was conceived. So anything you can tell the police would be helpful."

Something flashed through Diana's mind. How could she have forgotten; Clare wanted to adopt Ella, and she had decided to keep her. Maybe it was Clare?

"Oh, my God! It might be Clare, she might have taken Ella to Uganda."

Susan and Clive exchanged puzzled glances, not sure of what she meant, but at that moment DCI Dave Wilson and his female companion arrived to conduct the interview.

Dave was a burly man in his middle forties. He had a kind face, and a nice manner, but he also had a tough side to him, and he could usually tell whether someone was telling the truth or not. His brown hair was worn short, and his penetrating blue eyes were used to boring into suspects' faces whilst trying to sum them up. Right now his eyes looked kindly, as it was impossible to be unaffected by this tragic case. When he saw the young woman, her green eyes huge and filled with sadness, he thought of his own two little girls at home; as a parent, all you wanted to do was protect them.

Chloe Martin, his accompanying WPC was tall and thin, with mid brown hair, and inquisitive brown eyes. She had been briefed about the situation, and because she was keen on performing well in her job, she was hoping that Diana would open up to them today. She seemed calmer than the day before, but obviously devastated, and although at twenty-five Chloe was not yet married, she was engaged, and hoped to be a mother one day, and the thought of a tiny baby being abducted, and being in danger, was horrifying.

Clive and Susan got up to leave them, but Dave asked them to stay for the interview. If Diana wasn't able to say much, at least they would be of some help. He knew how important it was to recover this baby as soon as possible. He fixed his eyes earnestly on Diana and spoke gently but firmly.

"I hope you are feeling better today Miss Wilcox. May I call you Diana?"

Diana nodded assent, and then repeated her thoughts again:

"Clare wanted to adopt her, but I changed my mind. She was going to Uganda yesterday."

"Well, we've had all the ports and air terminals covered world-wide, I doubt she could have got through unnoticed. Can you tell us in your own words exactly what happened before you realised that Ella was missing?"

"Yes, Ella was crying and Peggy said she would take her to the nursery, then someone rang the bell, and I saw her hand Ella to a grey-haired nurse; and that was it, I never saw my baby again."

Her eyes filled with tears, and her body was racked with sobs, so her aunt moved quickly to comfort her.

"She is still very upset; this is hard for her," remarked Susan, wiping Diana's eyes with a tissue.

"Yes, the sooner we can get some leads to get your baby back, the better," said Dave.

Chloe poured some water into the plastic beaker and handed it to Diana, who was now trying to compose herself.

"Can you tell me about Clare?" asked Dave.

Diana spoke falteringly, doing her best not to weep. All she wanted was Ella back. She explained about her arrangement with Clare, and then her change of heart, and her belief that Clare might have taken her out of the country.

"Forgive me for asking, what about the baby's father? Is he likely to have arranged for someone to pose as a nurse to get access to Ella?"

"I don't even know if he knew that Ella was born, as I wasn't due for another month."

134

"I see, and your twin sister; I understand you used to be very close, but not now?"

Dave looked at her quizzically. Susan had said the twins were now estranged, but had not said why, and he could see quite clearly that his questions were making Diana feel very uncomfortable.

"Well you might as well know everything. My sister's husband raped me and I became pregnant. My sister did not believe I was raped; she turned against me, and because she couldn't bear to see Ella, she went abroad."

Diana now felt relieved that it was all out; no more secrets or pretences. She hoped the police would go after Neil, it's what he deserved, and maybe one day Rachel would know she was innocent, and come back to England.

It took a lot to surprise Dave. He met all sorts in his job, and many families harboured secrets for years, but this frank speech from Diana took him totally by surprise. Not that he could do anything about the rape so long afterwards. He was here to question her about the abduction.

"Thank you for being so honest Diana. Now do you think that, later today, you could attend a televised Press Conference and make a nationwide plea for the safe return of Ella? It might help to give us more information, and when people can see how much you want your baby back, it might help."

"I would do anything to get my baby back."

She could not put into words how empty her arms felt. How devastating it was to lose the child she had been breastfeeding; to suddenly have that closeness taken away from her, and so soon after giving birth and finding out just how much she did want to keep her baby.

Chloe saw her distress, and moved to reassure her.

"Don't worry, we will give you every support."

"Thank you. I was hoping it won't be too soon before I can go home."

"I don't think it's a good idea for you to be on your own. Why don't you come and stay with us until you get back on your feet?" said Susan hastily. She was sure that going back to an empty flat without her baby was not a good idea, and probably the hospital staff would not allow Diana to go home unless they knew she was going to get some sort of support.

Diana knew she was right, going back to the flat without Ella, and with Clare gone was a very depressing thought, and rolling round in her head was the fear that Clare had ignored her wishes and taken Ella to Uganda. She voiced her fears again.

"It must be Clare. She couldn't accept that I wanted to keep Ella. You must find her please."

"Don't worry Diana, we will do our utmost to reunite you with Ella as soon as we can, and in the meantime, when you are discharged, I think we would all feel relieved to know you are going to stay with your aunt."

"Yes I will, thank you," said Diana, flashing the glimmer of a smile at Susan and Clive.

Realising that they had all the information possible right now, Dave and Chloe left the hospital, after promising to be in touch for Diana to do the appeal later that day. She still had to be passed by a doctor as being fit to leave, but it was not long before that happened.

Nobody wanted Diana to leave the maternity hospital under such circumstances, but when Susan and Clive assured them that she would be looked after and supported emotionally, it was agreed she could go with them. Beds were always in short supply, and Diana's would soon be taken by another mother who had also given birth. Life continued on no matter what personal tragedy befell her, and Diana was anxious to get back with her aunt and uncle; they were her family, they had not judged her, and they did care, and right now she desperately needed someone to lean on.

When Dave got back to the police station with Chloe, he called a meeting to discuss the information that they had been given. It had been recorded, and when they played the tape back, everyone listened with rapt attention until it was finished. Then Dave spoke.

"We interviewed Diana today, and it was clear from her very emotional state, that she wants the safe return of her daughter, even though previously she had agreed to let her friend adopt her baby. She is convinced that Clare, her flat mate, has taken her to Uganda, so we need to step up our enquiries at all ports and air terminals. She could not have got through without a passport which also included the baby."

He paused as a cup of tea was put in front of him, and then took a couple of sips before continuing.

"Other suspects include the baby's father, who is apparently married to her sister, but they are now obviously living apart. Then there is her twin sister, who we were told recently miscarried her own baby, so may have snatched Ella because she is suffering from her own depression. Finally, it could be a complete stranger, a woman who has lost her own child recently, so we need to get that checked out too."

"Her flatmate Clare seems the most likely," volunteered Chloe.

"She does," agreed Dave, "but sometimes it's the least obvious person. Now what we need to do is get this TV appeal sorted, and as many members of the press there as possible. The more publicity we give this case, the harder it will be for a woman and baby to remain unseen."

Chapter Twenty

Jake Maloney was enjoying his day off today, having spent the whole of the week before in Brighton, helping to expose a drugs ring. He always felt so sorry for the women who were controlled by these men, who just exploited them for their own ends. The poor souls would sell their bodies just for a bit of cocaine, and these drug barons took away all their dignity, and kept them well supplied until some of them, sadly, ended up having a very short life.

Maybe it was because of his own beginnings, with a father unknown and a mother who was so controlled by cigarettes and drink that she didn't know how to be a mother, that Jake had been spurred on in life. He would always be grateful to the Slaters for rescuing him from the streets and making him one of their own, and until he had met Diana that fateful day, he had been quite happy as he was, but she had changed everything.

Over the last seven years, he had come to realise that, if he could have turned the clock back to that day, he would have treated her like the lady she was. There was no doubt that he had taken the virginity of the innocent little sixteen-year-old, and it always haunted him, and he wondered if that was why he never saw her the next day. He had fallen in love with the girl with the red gold hair and beautiful green eyes, but then her sister had come along, and maybe reality had hit home, because that day to him had remained so magical in his heart. He felt he was truly in love for the first time ever, and she was so far above him in class, he knew he had set his sights very high. Why would a girl from a very middle class family want to be seen with a gypsy boy who was just a fairground attendant?

So he had done something about it. He was not really a gypsy, so he had sold his caravan and joined the army. The Slaters and Bobby gave him their blessing, although they would miss him. He was twenty years old now; a young man, and he could make his own decisions. He spent three years in the army and it taught him a lot. Honesty for a start, loyalty, patience and perseverance. He was super fit and went on many endurance courses. He turned his back on the life that had seen him smoke pot. In fact, he didn't even smoke a cigarette now. He still enjoyed a drink, but not to excess, because he still had memories of his mother vomiting all over the place and then lying on the floor in a drunken stupor.

After three years, he saw an advertisement to join the police force. He liked the idea of that, as he could put some of the skills he had learned in the army to good use. He had by now passed the exams needed, so he then took himself off to police training school.

Jake proved to be very bright, and a quick learner, so by the time he was twenty-four, he was no longer a PC, he had become an inspector. But he had set his sights much higher than that. In Jake's mind the driving force had always been Diana. He hoped that one day they would meet again, and the higher he rose in the police force, the more chance that Diana and her family might accept him.

He remembered that she had told him she lived in Wimbledon with her aunt and uncle, so when a chance to work at a local police station there came up, he applied and was accepted. It was there he met Dave, and he had huge respect for his DCI, and was hoping one day to rise as high as he had.

They had worked on a few cases together, but Jake had been given a free rein with the Brighton drugs ring, and he felt proud that he had finally busted that one and earned himself new respect. He really enjoyed the challenge of being in the police force; it was such a varied job and presented new situations every day.

He had managed to buy himself a nice flat in Wimbledon, not far from the famous tennis courts. He liked living in the area. London was only a tube journey away, and there was countryside to enjoy not far away as well. People seemed to warm to Jake and his Irish lilt. He knew how to flatter people and joke with them. He could have been a real hit with women, just as he had been before, with his very blue eyes and tight black curls, which gave him an air of innocence, but in the last seven years there had been no serious relationships, just a couple of casual ones that had fizzled out, and that was because he had lost interest. Nobody seemed to be able to touch his heart the way Diana had.

Today he was dressed very casually in jeans and a check shirt. It was warm in the flat, but cold outside, so he clicked the control button on the central heating, switched on the TV to watch the news, and sat down to eat his bacon sandwich.

When he watched the news, and heard about the abduction of a new born baby, he didn't really take proper notice until the name of the mother was revealed as Diana Wilcox. What a co-incidence, so there were two women in Wimbledon with the same name. But his mouth dropped open with amazement when the cameras zoomed in to show her; this was the Diana he remembered, her red gold hair was tied back in a ponytail, and her huge green eyes were full of pain, as she spoke quietly, and with obvious encouragement from her aunt and Chloe, sitting on either side of her. She begged whoever it was to bring her baby back; she was only one day old, from an eight-month pregnancy, and she needed medication to control her jaundice. It was plain to see how heartbroken Diana was. His heart went out to her, and he wondered how anyone with an ounce of decency could put her through such heartbreak.

Names were then mentioned by Dave of people they needed to interview, asking would they please come forward: Neil Morris, the baby's father, Clare Spencer, Diana's friend, and Rachel Morris, her twin sister. Jake was filled with a desire to know all about this case. Had there been an argument with the baby's father, causing him to take off with the child? So many thoughts flashed through his mind, but his main concern was for Diana. Over the past seven years she had barely changed; with her hair in a ponytail, she could pass for a teenager. He felt those all too familiar pangs of love for her. She was so vulnerable right now, and he so wished he could put his arms around her, comfort her, and tell her it would be OK.

Although his immediate wish was obviously impossible, he could do the next best thing. He felt such anger deep inside that anyone could abduct her baby and leave her in such distress. He could join forces with Dave and help him find the abductor. In the past they had worked well together, but he knew he must not let Dave think that he had ever been close to Diana, or else he would say he couldn't be involved because he was too close to her and might be biased. Well damn right he was biased, who wouldn't be when they saw her breaking her heart on camera!

He watched her rise from her chair; she was sobbing, and supported by her aunt and Chloe. It was painful to watch, and Dave finished off by asking anyone who knew anything, or had seen anyone at the hospital, to come forward. Diana was now off camera, but his instinct was to rush over to the station, let her know he was there for her, and get involved. But he knew he could not act that way; all he could do was speak to Dave tomorrow, and offer to help him with the case. He wanted the bastard who had done this to be found quickly, but all his discipline and training in the past few years had taught him he must wait, and then it might work out.

So he ignored his instincts, but for the rest of the day his mind was in turmoil. Tomorrow he would put in some work checking out all the people mentioned, just to make sure none of them had any previous convictions. Then there was Diana; seeing him after seven years would give her such a shock. She might have bad memories of him and be put off, so he had to gain her trust, because he truly wanted to help her. If all she wanted was a friendship, he would even settle for that; just being part of her life would make him happy. As for the father of her baby, he must want his head examined going off and leaving a beautiful girl like Diana, and the child. But had he left the child? There were so many questions rolling around in his head, together with the shock of seeing the girl of his dreams in such a vulnerable situation, that he did not have a good night's sleep.

He dozed off finally about five o'clock, then woke up at seven when his alarm went off. He staggered out of bed feeling bleary eyed, and jumped in the shower. The hot water invigorated him, and then by the time he had eaten some toast, and drunk some coffee, he was feeling more alert. He couldn't wait to get to work, and so he presented himself in Dave's office, smartly dressed in a grey suit, white shirt and blue tie, just before nine o'clock.

Dave greeted him warmly, since Jake had joined the force, he had impressed everyone. He knew he had come from lowly beginnings, and respected this young man who was making something of his life.

"Well done with your work at Brighton. I thought you were having a couple of days off?"

"I was, until I saw the news appeal yesterday for the abducted newborn baby."

"Yes, such a tragic case. A beautiful young woman, and she is devastated, naturally. It's quite hard to interview her, Chloe found her so emotional."

"Dave, believe it or not, I have actually met her once before, when I worked on the fairground; she came with a friend one afternoon."

Jake was not about to tell him anything else. Not only was he ashamed of the person he had been then, but also that afternoon was sacred to him, it had meant everything, and he would never forget it no matter what happened in the future.

"Are you sure it's the same girl."

"Absolutely. She has barely changed."

How could he forget her beautiful hair and those eyes?

Dave was thoughtful. There were so many questions he needed to ask her. All the suspects were not around, and his men were making enquiries everywhere. He had contacted the British Embassy in Uganda, and all the hospitals and hotels had been made aware of the situation. A white woman with a newborn baby would stick out like a sore thumb in that country. If it was Clare, she would find it hard to stay hidden.

"Well how about you join me in trying to solve this? If you already know her, she might open up a bit more. Surely, with Chloe as well, because we need a woman on board, we can find the abductor."

"I'd be glad to, Dave."

This had worked out well for Jake. He was in, and he went over to the board which had, pinned up, photographs of the three main suspects. He felt a wave of jealousy when he saw Neil Morris; he was very handsome, but he knew he was being ridiculous. He wondered what had gone wrong between Neil and Diana, especially when there was a young baby involved. But then it hit him; her twin was also called Morris, yet he knew Diana would not have gone with her sister's husband.

142

Dave came up behind him and explained.

"Neil Morris married Diana's twin sister Rachel, who was pregnant, but then miscarried." He stubbed his finger at the photo. "They are identical twins. Diana told me Morris raped her and the baby was the result. Her sister disowned her because she didn't believe he had raped her. Now here the tale gets more complicated. Diana agreed for her friend Clare to adopt the baby, but after the baby was born she changed her mind. This is why she is convinced that Clare has taken the baby to Uganda."

"I see."

Jake was struggling to check his emotions when he heard that Diana had been raped. What a bastard this Morris was! He knew what he would like to do to him! There was no doubt in his mind that Diana would have spoken the truth. There was so much loyalty between twins, he was sure she would not have gone after her sister's husband. She was not a brazen marriage wrecker; she had been badly wronged by her twin.

"Yes, I met her sister too, they are identical to look at, but Rachel was quite a serious girl and Diana was more vivacious."

He studied all the photos. Clare was very dark haired, and the twins looked identical. These pictures would have been circulated everywhere, and they had been asked to come forward, but so far none of them had, and all the telephone calls from the public claiming to have seen any one of them had led to nothing.

Dave voiced Jake's thoughts.

"They all seemed to have vanished into thin air. One of these women could have put on a wig and big glasses and posed as the agency nurse, or maybe we have a frustrated middle-aged woman who is childless and has taken the baby. Maybe this nurse does exist!"

"It certainly is a puzzle," agreed Jake. He knew exactly what he was going to do. He was going to check out Neil Morris to see if he had a criminal record; maybe he had raped other women. It would give him the greatest pleasure to be able to get that evil vile man convicted of something. His face concealed his anger as he discussed the case with Dave. It certainly was a puzzling one.

Susan and Clive were glad to have Diana back with them at their home, as it was unthinkable that she should go back to her flat right now. They hardly recognised the silent withdrawn person she had become since her baby had been stolen, from the Diana of old, vivacious, dramatic, and attention seeking. She may have been hard work then, but to see her withdraw like this, and to hear her pacing about in her bedroom, unable to have peace of mind, was soul-destroying.

The doctor had put her on some pills to help her, but today she was seeing life through a haze, and not moving from her bed. Susan had tried to encourage her to get up, but it seemed that Diana had cut herself off from everything; it was almost like she didn't want to live any more. Susan had hoped that with the love and support of her family, Diana would try and fight this depression, but it seemed almost as though she had already given up on seeing her baby again.

When she heard the doorbell, she knew it would be the police again. Obviously they needed to make sure they had not missed anything, but so far interviewing Diana had not been successful. She was sure, with Diana refusing to get out of bed, today would not go any better than before.

She came downstairs just as Sandra was letting them in. She knew that if it was the police, they must be allowed to do their job. Susan noted there was another man with them, younger than DCI Wilson, he looked about mid twenties and he was very smartly dressed. He had black curly hair, and her first impression was that she liked him. He had an earnest look in his eyes, and when he was introduced as Jake Maloney, his firm handshake and respectful manner was enough to make her warm to him.

"Do come in gentlemen, and Chloe," she smiled at the female PC, who smiled back. "I am afraid Diana won't get out of bed today. The doctor has put her on something that has knocked her out."

Jake was not pleased to hear that, because doping Diana up was not the answer, she had to be helped to face up to all that had happened to her, and he had vowed to himself that he would help her. The only intention in his mind was to be her friend and do his utmost to find baby Ella.

Dave smiled at Susan, apologising for once more intruding on them.

"Just as a matter of interest Mrs Scott, have you heard anything from your niece Rachel since she left, and do you know exactly where she went?"

"I wish I could say yes, the agreement was that she would keep in touch via her mobile phone. She only said her company were sending her world-wide and she would be living in hotel rooms. She is a scientist, and in great demand in helping to solve the cause and treatment of cancer."

Dave was impressed, so he took note of the mobile phone number that Susan said belonged to Rachel, and also the name of the company she worked for. This could all be checked out at the office later.

"I am worried that I haven't heard from Rachel," said Susan. "She normally always keeps her word, and I know how depressed she was. She thought going away from all this would help her to move on."

"Well let us know if you do hear," said Dave, trying to inject some sort of positivity into his voice. It seemed like this poor lady had two depressed nieces to cope with, which then reminded him to ask another question.

"Are their parents alive?"

"Oh no, they were killed in a car crash when the girls were eight, so we brought them to live with us. This is what makes this so tragic, because the girls were so close, almost inseparable, until Neil Morris came along."

How Jake hated that name; it seemed like that bloke was nothing but trouble! But first things first, they had to speak to Diana, and he wondered with great trepidation, would she recognise him as a friend after all this time, or would he mean absolutely nothing to her? Whatever it was, he was soon to find out.

Susan showed them into the study. "I will try and rouse Diana, but if not, you may have to speak to her in her bedroom."

Whilst they were waiting, Jake glanced at the photos on the mantelpiece; the twins smiling, always with their arms around each other, two little girls at school with their hair in plaits, and then teenagers, with their hair loose, smiling happily. There was another photo of Rachel's graduation, and then Diana up on stage, obviously performing. It brought a lump to his throat to realise how much the situation had changed.

Susan mounted the stairs and went into Diana's room. Her niece had pulled the duvet right over herself, even her head was beneath it, and Susan steeled herself. Today she had to be tough with her for her own good.

g

"Diana, you can't hide away up here you know, the police are here to interview you."

"I don't want to see them unless they bring Ella back. I need my baby!"

Now her body was racked with sobs, and her tear-stained face emerged from under the duvet. Susan tried to harden her heart to it; being like this would never get her baby back.

"They can't do that without your help. Today we have an inspector as well, I think his name is Jake Maloney, he has been called in to help."

Through the mist of confusion in her mind, the name Jake Maloney assaulted the emptiness that surrounded Diana. Was there more than one man with that name? Her Jake had been a Romany gypsy, but her curiosity was roused, and she sat up abruptly.

"What does he look like?"

Susan wondered why she cared what he looked like, but at least it had caused her to sit up and take notice.

"Well, he's dressed in a very smart suit, about mid-twenties I should think, with black curly hair."

Diana was amazed, the man she had wanted to see again for so many years was downstairs at her aunt's house, but the timing was all wrong, because she needed her baby back, and that was all she could think about. But she couldn't help wondering why he had gone from a fairground into the police force.

"I met him once, when we were at boarding school. He's Irish, isn't he? It's a name you can't forget."

She refrained from telling Susan where she met him, as he had obviously changed his lifestyle, and she wondered why. This was enough to encourage her to get dressed and go down to the library, much to Susan's relief. She was glad that this Jake had accompanied the other two today, otherwise Diana might not have got up.

Jake held his breath when Susan entered the study with Diana just behind her. She wasn't looking her best, she had obviously quickly pulled on some jogging trousers and a sweat shirt, her hair was untidy, her face was marked with recent tears, and her eyes were swollen. But to him she was beautiful, she had always been beautiful. Right now she was so vulnerable, and he felt a powerful surge of emotion towards her that he knew he had to keep inside himself.

146

Diana entered the study. She knew she looked a mess, but her appearance was the last thing on her mind. When she saw Jake standing there in his suit, she felt a glow of pride in him. He had not altered much; his skin still had a bronzed look, his blue eyes had warmth and compassion in them as he met her gaze, and his black curls had defied his efforts to brush them flatter. So the gypsy boy had joined the police, if she hadn't been so heartbroken, it would have made her laugh.

She would have thought that after seven years, she would feel shyness towards him, but it seemed the most natural thing in the world to put her hand out and shake his warmly.

"It's nice to see you again Jake, but I wish it had been in happier circumstances."

Jake was silently enjoying the touch of her hand. He had often wondered if he ever met Diana again, would that first encounter with her fade when they found that the years had made them grow apart. But now his feelings were even stronger, and he knew without a doubt that the love he had for her would last forever, and he also knew that he would work for however long it took to bring baby Ella back to her, and make sure the culprit was punished. If all she wanted was friendship, he would settle for that, no one had ever made him feel the way Diana did.

He reluctantly released her soft warm hand, assuring her of their intention to find her daughter. Then he sat observing whilst Dave asked her some more questions, and Susan's housekeeper came in with a tray of tea and biscuits for all of them.

Susan was relieved to see Diana making an effort. It seemed seeing this man Jake had been enough to make her pull herself together. Until he had turned up she was wondering how she could help her, and had been seriously thinking of getting a private nurse in. She had thought that maybe a psychiatrist might be able to help her troubled mind, but maybe, with the support of her family, Diana would learn to cope.

There was something else that Susan was worried about which she dare not voice. Was the reason that Rachel had not kept in touch because she had abducted Ella? The only person she could discuss this with was Clive, and she would later. But in the meantime, they had provided the police with everything they could remember, and Diana had actually left her bed. After the police had gone, Diana took a shower and washed her hair, and when Susan suggested calling a mobile hairdresser in the next day to give her a trim and blow dry, to her delighted astonishment, Diana agreed, at last she was going to make an effort.

Chapter Twenty-one

Dave and Jake, together with their team, worked hard for the next few days trying to gather information. Rachel's company had been contacted, and it was confirmed that she had worked for them for over a year, and then a few months ago had told them that she would be leaving because she had been offered a contract travelling around and working at laboratories in America. Her departure seemed to coincide with all her marital problems, and although it wasn't quite the same as the story she had told Susan, it was close enough to be considered the truth. The company representative confirmed they had given her a glowing reference, as her work had been outstanding.

Dave was not surprised to find that Rachel's mobile phone was now out of service. For some reason best known to herself, she had wanted to break all contact with her aunt. This made him very suspicious about her, especially when he got a call from Heathrow Airport confirming that the grey-haired lady had been picked up on CCTV sitting in a lounge near to the departure area for New York, giving the baby a bottle. One or two people remembered seeing her there, and assumed it was her grandchild, but nobody could actually remember seeing her board a plane.

It was the same at JFK airport; no one remembered her, it was so frustrating, she seemed to have vanished into thin air. Dave now viewed Rachel as the most likely person to have taken her sister's baby. He confided this to Jake, but they decided, without any proof, to keep their observations to themselves. Susan had already voiced her worries to them about not hearing from Rachel, but Diana still thought that Clare had taken baby Ella.

Diana was a little calmer since Jake had arrived, so Dave was pleased about that. She was more co-operative, and in return, Jake had worked hard to gain her trust, always treating her with respect and listening to what she had to say. There was something soothing about Jake that made Diana feel safe. She had lost so much; her sister's love and trust, her new born baby, but now her aunt and uncle believed her and so did Jake. He had promised her he would track down Neil Morris and he would be punished for his vile deeds, and she found it comforting to know he would not get away with it. Aunt Susan had said he had extorted money from Rachel's bank account, so that, at least, was one crime they could have him for. Even if they could not prove the rape, at least her aunt and uncle now believed her, and so did Jake. Jake's opinion meant a lot to her, he felt like her saviour right now, and his presence in her life was a reason to keep going.

Jake was realising just what a strong young woman Diana was, even though she didn't know it. The past year must have been a nightmare for her. Firstly she was pursued and terrorised by her sister's husband, and then raped by him. Then she tried to tell her family, and they didn't believe her. She lost the love and trust of her twin sister, who was her whole world. Finally, she gave birth to her baby and unexpectedly bonded with her. At that moment she must have felt she had something to focus her life on, but then that baby was taken from her before it was even a day old. Most women would have lost their mind by now, but Diana was so brave, and he loved her for it, and felt so proud of her. He kept his manner towards Diana very professional, because he could not afford for Dave to think he had feelings for her. Staying close to Diana at this difficult time was what he needed as well as her.

There had also been enquiries in Uganda. All hospitals and Community Centres had been checked out, but nobody had seen a white lady with a newborn baby, so they had to assume that Clare had just told Diana she was going to Uganda, deliberately creating a false trail. She might have been in the lounge at Heathrow, but where had she gone after that? Diana had confirmed how desperate she was for her own baby after suffering a miscarriage, but they couldn't trace the husband she had said she was divorcing, so that was another puzzle too.

Neil Morris had also vanished from the scene, but was it any wonder after raping his sister-in-law, and stealing money from his estranged wife? His photograph had been circulated everywhere, so he must be lying low somewhere, or else he had changed his appearance. Had he paid someone to pose as a nurse and steal his daughter?

But then a breakthrough came when Jake came across a photograph on the police files. It looked very much like Neil, but the name was Adam Spencer. His police record showed he had served time for fraud, and grievous bodily harm, but the most interesting part of it was a mention on the file that he had also been tried for rape after a complaint by Naomi Harris some three years earlier, but was acquitted.

Buoyed up by this new evidence, Jake took it into Dave's office to discuss it. It had happened before Dave had come to that branch, but it did not take them long to find contact details for Naomi Harris. Her last known address had been in Mitcham.

"Well done, Jake, for finding all this! We need to go and check her out."

"Yes," said Jake, "I can't wait to hear what she's got to tell us about Adam Spencer."

But when they arrived at the house, which was situated close to Mitcham Common, the man living there said that Naomi no longer lived there, he had bought the house from her three years ago. He was a bit loath to say much, but when they showed their identity cards, and said they were investigating the abduction of a baby, he gave them a forwarding address to which he had sent her mail in the first three months.

"She was trying to get away from an ex-boyfriend she told me, but please, when you find her, don't say that I gave you her address."

They thanked him for his co-operation, and agreed to keep his involvement confidential. After getting back into the car, Dave studied the new address.

"Well Jake, my lad, fancy a day at the seaside in December? I think not, but we are off to Worthing right now."

When they got out of the car, the wind was blowing strongly, and there was hardly anyone around. Most of the shops and cafes were closed for the winter. The sea looked cold and grey, with big white horses as the waves rolled in. The bungalow looked very

151

small, and it took only a couple of steps to reach the front door from the little wooden gate that was propped open. Dave knocked on the door, and they heard a movement from inside, so they knew someone was there.

Eventually the door was opened by a man, aged about thirty, wearing jeans and a thick cream jumper. He had dark hair, and did not look happy to see them.

"Good morning sir, does Naomi Harris live here?" asked Dave politely.

"Who wants to know?" asked the man curtly, but when he saw their identity cards, he let them in, explaining: "Naomi is my wife, her surname is Johnson now, and she is at work. She came here to live after her name was plastered all over the papers. She didn't feel she could stay on in Mitcham."

"We know about the rape trial, and we are sorry for what an ordeal she must have been put through. We believe the same man changed his name and raped someone else."

"She knew him as Adam Spencer. She went out for a drink with him, this is before she met me, it was only the once, but it didn't stop him from raping her in her own home. She went straight to the police that same night, but it made no difference. The jury decided that as she invited him in for a coffee, she must have liked him, and it was his word against hers. It destroyed her mentally for quite a while, being made to feel like she was on trial, instead of being the victim."

Jake felt angry to think how many lives this evil man had ruined. He went around doing just what he wanted, without a care for anyone else. Thank goodness Naomi had her husband. Curiosity made him ask:

"Have you known Naomi long?"

"Two years, but we have been married for one. I already lived here, in a flat round at the seafront, I work nights up at the factory. Naomi took a job there to try and get her life back on track, but it was ages before she would trust me. Luckily that is all in the past now, but men like him destroy lives; British justice is a joke. I am sure if she had the time again, she would not have reported him!"

Dave agreed with him, as he was only too aware of the fact that so few rape cases could ever be proved for sure. It was unlikely that Diana would have a case against Adam either, and it would do her no good to go through the trauma of court appearances.

Then there was baby Ella to think about. So if they could track down Adam, alias Neil, and charge him for fraud at the very least, that would be a result.

Whilst they were talking, there was the sound of a key being inserted in the lock, and the man turned quickly.

"That is Naomi now. By the way, my name is Ben Johnson; I will just tell her you are here."

He went out into the little hall to greet her, explaining that the police were here to speak to her. Naomi came into the room; she was dressed in a mid-length black skirt and a white blouse. She had an ordinary face, with brown hair and dark eyes; not particularly beautiful, maybe attractive, but right now, her eyes were full of apprehension, as she glanced from her husband towards the two men. Dave and Jake both felt sorry for intruding into the new life she had created for herself and dredging up things she wanted to forget.

"Good afternoon, Mrs Johnson, I am so sorry to bring up a time you would rather forget, but this man, Adam, as you knew him, is destroying so many lives, we wondered if you have anything new you can tell us about him?"

"Well I moved to Worthing to get away from him. I was terrified, because he was very violent, and threatened to strangle me if I resisted. The jury didn't believe that because it was a threat and he didn't actually harm me."

Dave and Jake exchanged glances; her description matched exactly what Diana had said about her attack. Naomi continued:

"I only spent one evening with him, but he was totally convincing, charming, sincere, and he appeared to be lonely, so I invited him in for a coffee."

"Did he speak about having any family?"

Naomi wrinkled her brow thoughtfully.

"Yes, he had two sisters he said, one was an actress, the other a nurse. He also had a brother, but he said they were all in California, and he claimed he had lived in San Diego and really missed the warm weather."

Dave and Jake thanked her for being so helpful, and then left the bungalow to drive back to Wimbledon. Jake remembered that Diana had mentioned something about Neil living in California, and his American accent, so maybe they should take a trip to San Diego. As for the two sisters, would Diana know the one who was

153

an actress, and wasn't Clare's surname Spencer too? What surname was the brother using? So many questions without answers, and were they actually getting any nearer to finding Ella? It didn't feel like it.

The next day Jake and Dave, together with Chloe, arrived at the house to speak to Diana again. She was still fragile after the shock of having her baby abducted, but trying to show some sort of strength. Somehow knowing that Jake was taking such an interest in the case filled her with hope. His support was keeping her going more than any pills that the doctor had prescribed. She had thrown away the anxiety pills she had been prescribed because she was fed up with feeling woolly headed, and like a zombie.

Susan showed them into the library, and Diana joined them, as she had seen the car draw up outside. They were both praying there was some more news. Diana stood next to her aunt waiting to hear what they had to say. Jake spoke first.

"Diana, when you were at acting school, did you know that Clare's sister was also there too?"

"Of course, Ruth Harper, she told me about Clare trying to find somewhere to live away from her violent husband. I felt sorry for her and gave her a room at my flat."

Dave and Jake both reacted at those words. So another piece of the jigsaw was beginning to fit. Jake burst out excitedly.

"Neil Morris has the real name of Adam Spencer and he has a criminal record. Both of those girls are his sisters, and you can bet your life there was no abusive husband. Clare used that sob story to get into your flat and gain your trust. Then your sister moves in, and Neil, alias Adam, who makes a living by defrauding people, sees a chance to do it again."

Diana was incredulous when she heard this theory. Had they really been so easily hoodwinked?

"But Neil and the other two were scientists, they worked in a laboratory near to my sister."

"Did you ever go there, and what was it called?" persisted Jake gently, realising this was a shock to Diana and Susan, who had a look of total disbelief on their faces.

"Well no, they said it was top secret. . ." Diana's voice faltered. So her suspicions about the man she still thought of as Neil had

154

been right, he had been after Rachel's money, and he even had a criminal record. And to make it worse, Clare was the sister of this criminal. They were clearly a family who lived above the law, so there was even more reason to think Clare had Ella. She would not suffer any pangs of conscience.

"What a fool I was to think Clare was my friend," she said miserably, and Susan put her arm around her to try and comfort her. Jake wished he could; he ached to take her in his arms and tell her everything would be all right.

"It's not your fault Diana, we were all fooled by them. I myself was taken in by Clare, she seemed to be such a supportive friend to you."

"Only because she wanted Ella!" said Diana bitterly.

Jake longed to tell her that someone else had been raped by Neil, but he was not sure whether Dave would approve of him discussing the case. Certainly Naomi could not be named; but it seemed that Dave was thinking the same as him, as his next words proved.

"Diana, we can't tell you everything, but you aren't the only person he has raped. Although the other person was brave enough to go to the police, it was never proved."

"I was going to go to the police, but Clare talked me out of it," said Diana thoughtfully.

"Well, of course, she had to keep the police away from her brother, but don't worry, we are getting nearer to the truth," said Jake.

"I think we should go back to the station and check out Neil's two friends Barry and Colin, they might be using assumed names as well," said Dave. "We are going to leave you ladies in peace now, but we will be back in touch when we have more news."

Chloe put her notebook away. She had been busy writing down information, she knew her role was to listen rather than to speak. It amazed her the way that Diana was holding up, especially as they had no way of knowing whether she would ever see her baby again, or whether the poor little mite was even alive. It was an unspoken thought in all their minds.

Jake somehow felt that finding out more about the members of Neil's family would bring him closer to finding baby Ella. He worked diligently, along with other members of the team, checking files and previous cases, and then he came upon something he had not been expecting. It was a file dating back some twenty years; a mother had strangled her own newborn baby and then killed herself with an overdose of pills. That woman's name was Harriet Spencer. Of course, Spencer was not an unusual name, but it was possible this woman had been Neil's mother, and as his sister Ruth seemed to be the only person who had not disappeared into the mist, she must be brought in for an interview. Diana had explained that she lived in hotels due to touring a lot with her job, but there must be a way of contacting her, so he put his team onto finding our exactly where she was staying. He knew time was of the essence here, and he so wanted to give Diana peace of mind and reunite her with Ella.

Chapter Twenty-two

Ruth Harper surveyed her reflexion in the mirror. As an actress she had to make sure she looked her best at all times, because her looks dictated her ability to get work. Her hazel eyes were probably her best feature, big and expressive, and her brown hair had golden lights in it. She wore it long, it tumbled around her shoulders, and curls sprang defiantly framing her oval face. She slightly resembled her brother Adam, he was a year older, but there the similarity ended, in character they could not have been more different.

Ruth could just about remember her mother, who was very beautiful but not at all motherly. She had no idea about her father, who or where he was. Her mother had no idea how to run a home or be a mother. She could not remember ever being cuddled. Her mother had been obsessed with looking good, wearing heavy make-up, and sleeping with as many men as possible. She had no idea whether she shared the same father with Adam, Barry and Clare, but it didn't much matter, and she doubted whether her mother knew either. They all grew up in squalid surroundings and had to fend for themselves, until the day Harriet strangled her newborn baby because its crying was driving her mad, then took an overdose of pills and ended her own life.

The frightened and bewildered siblings had all been taken into care, and then came a series of foster homes until they were old enough to fend for themselves. Ruth knew she had been the luckiest; her family had adopted her and brought her up as their own daughter, and she would always be grateful to daddy for the money he had spent getting her into drama school and then supporting her whenever the work dried up. Although shocking, her mother's actions had toughened her; she was a survivor, and it gave her even more impetus to make a success of her own life.

But her two brothers misbehaved so much they just went from one foster home to another, then had a spell in Borstal after stealing cars. That seemed to set a pattern for their future lives, because later Adam did his first time in prison, for extorting money by defrauding a woman and beating up her father who tried to confront him about his bad treatment of her.

Ruth realised at that time that her brother was bad. He had grown up that way. Maybe their mother had shaped his character by her behaviour, or maybe he had those insane genes that their mother had, but in an effort to distance herself from him and his violent nature, she had changed her surname to Harper, and cut all ties with Adam.

But because her siblings were the only family she had, she still kept contact with Clare and Barry. She didn't want to think they were no-hopers like Adam, who just used his looks to lure vulnerable women to part with their money. His temper was frightening, just like their mother's had been, but she had not seen any sign of it in her other two siblings.

When Clare had suffered her miscarriage, Ruth felt so sorry for her, she knew her man had left her to cope alone and then moved on to someone else, and Clare had been pretty devastated. So she had mentioned it to Diana, who had been so generous and offered her a home. But now she was wishing Clare had never been introduced to that family, because through her Adam had also wormed his way in and left the usual emotional devastation behind him.

She had followed every bit of news about the abduction of baby Ella, and her mind kept flashing to what her mother had done. She now believed that Clare had abducted baby Ella. She thought she knew her sister, but she did hope that her obsession about being a mother would not cause her to harm Ella in any way.

When the telephone in her hotel room rang, and the receptionist informed her that there were a couple from the police who wanted to speak to her, she was filled with dread. She had changed her name to distance herself from Adam, and she knew if any connection between her and him could be proved, it could ruin her career. This was just the sort of publicity that was harmful to her. With trepidation in her heart, she gave permission for them to come to her room and speak to her, then put the kettle on. She knew she had to win them over; she was well versed in acting, so she would put it to good use.

When Dave and Jake entered, she gave them a dazzling smile to hide her thudding heart.

"Good morning. I have the kettle on, can I offer you both a cup of tea or coffee?"

Jake's impression of the smiling young woman was a favourable one. She was smart and well dressed with black trousers and a red top, which gave her a warm glow, she spoke nicely, and obviously came from an affluent background. Her clothes looked expensive, and she certainly did not look like the sister of a criminal. Her accent was not American, it was very polished, as though she had been to a really good school, or had elocution lessons.

"Good morning, Miss Harper, tea sounds nice," said Dave warmly, and Jake nodded to him in response. "We both take milk and one sugar."

They both sat down on the couch. It was a spacious hotel room, and it looked like she ate her meals here too, but then after performing to the public, she probably valued her privacy. Ruth brought the tea over and set it down on the coffee table next to them, also putting down a plate of biscuits.

"Many thanks," said Jake, who in his excitement to get here had skipped breakfast, so a digestive with his tea would go down well. Ruth sat opposite them, she appeared very calm, when she asked:

"What can I do for you today?"

Dave explained they had come to question her about the abduction of her friend Diana Wilcox's baby, and Ruth's face immediately took on a really concerned expression.

"Yes, admittedly I have lost touch with Diana since drama school, but like everyone else, I have been following the case and I do so hope she will soon be reunited with her baby."

She looked sincere, but hadn't Diana remarked that Neil had always looked and sounded sincere? Jake was prepared to give her the benefit of the doubt; it looked like she did care.

"Is it correct that Neil Wilcox, alias Adam Spencer, is your brother?"

Ruth looked them straight in the face. She had nothing to hide, nor had she done anything wrong, so she refused to act in a guilty way.

"His real name is Adam, and yes he is my brother, but we have not lived together since we were very small children."

"But you keep contact with Clare, so you obviously knew he was the father of Diana's baby, and that Clare was planning to adopt baby Ella until Diana changed her mind."

"To be honest, I didn't really know any details, I understood Clare was going to live in Uganda because there were lots of motherless babies out there."

"Do you think your sister is capable of stealing a baby?"

Ruth did not like that question. It was too close to what she was worrying about, and out of loyalty to Clare, how could she answer it? So her reply was a little bit away from what she had been asked.

"I think she might have been disappointed that Diana changed her mind, but if I was in her place, I would not risk stealing a baby if I was going somewhere to work amongst them."

"Clare has never arrived in Uganda," persisted Dave. "We have had all points of communication checked."

Jake then went on to explain that there were three main people they wanted to speak to, and each one of them had disappeared, so they could not be questioned. They were hoping that she could shed some light on it. Ruth assured them that she had not heard from any of them, and in the case of Rachel, the baby's aunt, she had never even met her. Jake had one more question for her.

"If you do hear from anyone in your family, can you let us know straight away?"

"Of course I will, and I will say you want to speak to them." She then asked them: "Can you keep from the press the fact that Adam is my brother?"

They both realised what she was getting at. She had made herself an honest life away from her brother, and if the press got hold of it, they would have a field day at her expense. As she had done nothing wrong, that really wasn't fair, and she had co-operated with them today.

"Don't worry, the press certainly won't hear it from us," Dave reassured her.

They both then thanked her for her time and left. It was interesting to find out that Barry was also part of the family, but why had Neil kept it a secret? If those three were linked together, then maybe they were all hiding out somewhere together, and maybe baby Ella was with them?

When they arrived back at the station, it was to find out a lady called Mary Lou Spencer had telephoned in; she had heard all about the abduction, as the news had travelled worldwide. She lived in San Diego, California, and she had important information to give them about Adam Spencer. Rather than try and take information over the telephone, Dave decided on a trip to California. So after booking tickets, that evening found them on an overnight flight to San Diego.

Diana was distressed that Jake was going off to California. She realised they had to check whether Neil was there or not, as they had all believed he was American, and he could have returned there. But after he had raped her, she had been left with this fear that she might see him again. The days were passing by now, and she had hoped she might be able to pluck up the courage to go home and get on with her life. She didn't want what Neil had done to affect her, and take away her independence, but whilst Jake was away, she felt she was on the back foot.

Sitting around moping at her aunt's house was no good. She needed to go back to work; anything to keep her mind focused. It was now over a month since that fateful day, and during that month, Jake had been a frequent visitor, always making sure that she was all right. Sometimes he came with Dave if they had anything to discuss with her, but more often than not he came alone, and the concern and softening of his eyes when he looked at her had been so comforting. She was beginning to realise how much she needed him in her life, how much she truly loved this kind and supportive man. Even though the loss of Ella filled her mind, Jake felt like the rock she so badly needed. But it was a hopeless situation. Here she was, so in love with him, she had been right from the first time she met him, but he was a police inspector just doing his job. The last thing he was thinking about was a relationship with her, but she wished so fervently that she could cuddle up to him at night and feel safe. Her arms felt so empty without Ella to fill them. She brushed the tears away fiercely; this was not helping her, all this self pity. She wanted to prove to Jake, and herself, that she could and would pick up her life again and survive. She had to, because one day she would get her daughter back, and she must stay strong.

She took a bath and washed her hair, then dressed herself in a smart long black skirt with boots, as the January weather was very cold. She had a grey coat, which she pulled on, then she ran downstairs. Putting on a bright smile, Diana opened the lounge door where her aunt was sitting doing some crochet, and she spoke quickly, before Susan could intervene.

"Bye, Aunt Susan, I am popping into London to the agency, to see what work there is for me."

Susan was completely taken by surprise by this, because with Jake in America for a while, she had expected to see Diana being very melancholy, as she had noticed how much seeing him seemed to help keep her together. If only they could become a couple. Susan had spotted true concern in Jake's eyes when he was with Diana, but of course he was just doing his job, and it wasn't the time to think about a relationship with her baby missing. What a sad little Christmas they had just spent; she had been glad when it was over. But maybe getting back to work was just what Diana needed. If she could cope, it would keep her mind occupied. Diana was proving to be stronger than Susan had ever thought she would be, and at that moment, she felt proud of her.

"You look very nice. I am sure there will be some work for you!" she said warmly, as she squashed down any feelings of misgivings, and smiled back at her.

Neil was fed up with lying low in Bodmin. It had been almost a month now since he had fled back to the studio flat. His face was being circulated, so in the past month, he had grown a thick beard and was now wearing glasses. Going to the police to help them with their enquiries was not an option, because he knew with his criminal record, if they could put him away again they would.

What was making him so angry was not knowing what had happened to his kid. Anna had left the flat that day in a taxi, and he had never seen her since. She had obviously done what he wanted, but he had no idea where she had taken his kid, and why she had not brought her back to him. She had been reluctant in the first place to snatch that baby, but wearing a grey wig had been a master stroke; he hadn't thought of that, but she must have.

Anna would do anything for him because she was besotted with him, so disappearing with his kid made no sense. A letter had come this last week to say that the studio flat was being let to someone else as from the beginning of February, so he had no choice but to go. He had no more rent money anyway. There were so many questions he would have liked to ask Anna, but now he had to get out of Cornwall, hit the road again and find somewhere new. He was so angry with her. He wasn't sure that he would control that anger if he met up with her, but then she only had herself to blame, she had roused his anger with her actions, and as for his kid, unless he was able to track Anna down, it would grow up without ever knowing him.

How he wished he had got to know Anna's father, as she might have fled back home. But he had only met him once, not long enough to strike up an acquaintance, and he had no idea of his address; somewhere in London, that is all he knew. So he was leaving Cornwall, but Barry would have to stay here and keep his mouth shut if they tracked him down. In this case blood was almost certainly thicker than water.

Clare smiled tenderly at the baby that nestled in her arms. Her journey to Australia had been a long one with a change of plane at Bangkok. She had kept a low profile on the plane; after all, she had told them she was going to Uganda. As soon as Ella had been abducted, the news was everywhere; in newspapers, on TV screens, and what was even worse, there was a photograph of Clare circulated, as they wanted her to help with their enquiries. All Clare wanted was a new life away from her troublesome brothers, although she would miss Ruth, but she knew if she had any chance of achieving a happy future, then cutting all ties was the only way. Australia was as far away as she could get from all of them, and she would not have had to take such measures if only Diana had stuck to her word and let her adopt Ella. Her journey that day to the hospital had not worked out. The taxi she had travelled in had been hit in the back, and then a huge traffic pile-up had resulted whilst angry words were said, and details exchanged between the driver and the lady who had hit him in the back.

With her experience as a midwife, it had been so easy to get a hospital job. The local hospital was desperate for staff, so with her newly dyed blonde hair, now cut short in an elfin style, and her assumed name of Mary Hamilton, she was able to start a new life in another place. It was amazing how a change of hair colour and style could alter a face, and being so far away, it was like another world.

She had been there for a month, and was enjoying the casual life and warm sunshine. January in England would be very cold and grey, but here it was summer. Australians seemed very friendly, and they didn't probe too much into her life; they were out for a good time, with barbecues and outdoor activities going on constantly. The rolling waves and beautiful sandy beaches, with lots of men with golden tanned torsos playing beach tennis and surfing; it was just perfect. There was already someone she really hoped to have a future with. His tall blond good looks had attracted her straight away. Clare, alias Mary, felt sure her dream of marriage and motherhood would be realised here.

Chapter Twenty-three

Dave and Jake got out of the car that had been provided for them by the FBI. The driver had said he would wait outside whilst they spoke to Mary Lou Spencer. Jake was wondering if this was yet another sister, and whether this had been Neil's home before he travelled to England.

The house was similar to many American properties; the outside walls were timber framed, there was a veranda, and large wooded gardens surrounded it. It was a fairly large property, but with paint peeling, and overgrown grass, it looked neglected. Mary Lou had noted their arrival, and was standing at the door waiting to receive them.

"Ain't ya coming in too!" she demanded of the FBI man loudly, and he shook his head; it seemed they already knew each other.

"Well that son of a bitch don't wanna know, he never did!" she exclaimed as she let them in.

"Married to a psychopath I was, and they were useless, said now he had gone to England that was the end of it!"

Jake and Dave exchanged surprised glances at the word "married", the plot was definitely getting thicker. Jake studied her as they stood in the hallway. Although Mary Lou had a loud voice and an intimidating manner, her size did not fit with her personality. She was tiny, probably less than five feet in height, slim with a mass of very dark curly hair which tumbled around her shoulders. Her eyes were very dark, and she was of mixed race, with tanned skin. Her eyes were arresting, dark pools of mystery, but right now they flashed with unsuppressed anger.

Dave introduced them both, but Mary Lou was in no mood to shake hands as they stood in the hallway, although she did at last lead the way into a room she referred to as the parlour. It had a couple of two seater sofas and a dining table with four wooden chairs. The wallpaper had not been changed for a number of years, and the rugs looked old, but it was clean and tidy.

Mary Lou suddenly stopped talking, almost as if she had unexpectedly remembered that she had visitors. "Oh dang, it's hot out there, would you like some water?"

"That would be nice," agreed Jake. It had been a shock to leave the icy blasts of the winds of January in England, and then to land in San Diego to find everyone was in t-shirts, on the beach, and enjoying the Californian sun. It was a hot and sultry day, and neither himself nor Dave were dressed for it; trousers and jackets were just too much.

Mary Lou disappeared outside into a kitchen, and then returned with a jug of water with ice cubes, and glasses on a tray. She invited them to have one of her home made cookies, which they both accepted, and whilst they were munching, she explained why she had contacted the English CIA.

"That story about the infant being snatched was on CNN news; in fact, it's worldwide, but as soon as I saw his picture, I knew it was him. Neil Morris is not his name, he's my husband, and his name is Adam Spencer."

"How long have you been married to him?"

"We've been married two years. I met him in 2001, he was on vacation and we were married after a month, I didn't know he only married me to stay in the USA cos his visa would run out. No one ain't s'posed to enter this country with a criminal record, but that son of a bitch used so many different names, even our FBI couldn't keep up with him."

"Why do you refer to him as a psychopath?"

"His temper; he changes, and damn near put me in hospital one day. He was always wanting money. He had no job, and neither did I. Spent years looking after my mammy; she had a heart condition, then just before he came over, she passed. After we married he wanted me to sell the house so we could have a good time, but I said: 'No, it's all I have, my mama left it to me.'"

Jake really felt pity for her, it was so obvious that after her mother died, Mary Lou must have been so lonely, and an easy

166

target for Neil alias Adam. He was an evil predator. If only they could find him, and put him away for a very long time.

"So how did you come to part? Did he leave you?"

"I threw him out when I found him in our bed with my best friend. She ain't my best friend any more, and although we been hitched for two years, that man only spent three months of it with me. There's been no divorce, so if he's married someone else, then he's a bigamist, and boy does he deserve locking up!"

Although he concealed it very carefully, Jake was beginning to feel the same anger as Mary Lou towards this man. Ever since he was sixteen years old, Neil had been in and out of trouble, he had abused so many women both mentally and physically, and he had got away with it. If they ever managed to track him down, the only thing they could charge him with was bigamy, and he would be out of prison within the year to cause more misery. He may have been endowed with good looks and charm, which fooled so many women, but his heart was hard and cold, and his temper was frightening. He was a very dangerous man, but Jake felt no fear of him, he was sure if Neil was standing in front of him now, he would forget he was a policeman, and would not be responsible for his actions!

Dave thanked Mary Lou for all her help, and expressed how sorry they were for her predicament. He assured her that they would do their utmost to get her justice, and catch her husband. She in turn agreed to give any evidence against him that they wanted. Jake then remembered to ask one more question.

"Have you any idea why Adam, as you knew him, came to America? He actually spent most of his life in England, and he has a brother and two sisters there. I have been told he has a convincing American accent though, and tries to pass himself off as being American."

Mary Lou laughed scornfully.

"In his dreams. He would like to be, but the accent is as phony as he is. I think he came to the States to get away from some girl in Mitcham; she said he had raped her. He laughed when he told me, saying she was a poor desperate bitch and he didn't fancy her, but she wanted him, and when he rejected her, she turned angry. He was not jailed for it, her word against his, and like a fool, I believed that man. He seemed like my future, coming so soon after mammy died, but there were times when he lost it big time

167

and I felt scared of him. It was just like a balloon bursting, but within a minute or two, he was as charming as ever. It was so confusing. Sometimes I thought I was imagining it, and felt I was going mad, but after I threw him out my life became calmer, and I realised it was not me, it was him. Trouble is, he has left me with a lot of anger, and if he is mixed up in a custody battle, I certainly would not trust him with a tiny infant."

Dave and Jake knew only too well just how true her words were, and when they took their leave of her, they were both wondering why the FBI had not done more to help her. Dave asked their driver whilst they were travelling back to the hotel, if he could explain more about it, as he obviously knew Mary Lou.

"Well, we used to walk out together. It wasn't very often 'cos after her daddy died, Mary Lou's marmee was never quite the same. She took to her bed, and the doc said her heart weren't great, so Mary Lou gave up her job at the factory to care for her. I was gonna wait for her, but suddenly her marmee has gone, and before she's even cold in her grave, the charmer arrives, and he damn well charmed the knickers off her; and before I knew it, he had married her."

"Did Mary Lou complain about his temper?"

"Not a word said until after she slung him out, then she said he was spending her money; but until she found him in bed with her friend, she was going out with him and spending the money too. It just seemed like she was hitting back 'cos she was a woman scorned; and then he takes off to England, so we thought it was the best thing for everyone."

Dave turned to the young FBI man with a smile as they got out of the car.

"Well now is your chance. It seems like he stole your sweetheart. Tell Mary Lou what you just told us, and say sorry, in time she will come round, I am sure."

The young man sat deep in thought after they had gone. It was staring him in the face and he hadn't realised; he loved Mary Lou, and he was going to make his peace with her, then maybe they could go back to walking out again. Her criminal husband was gone, and in time she would get a divorce from him. Now the future was looking rosy again.

* * * *

168

Later, in their hotel, Dave and Jake discussed their findings. Dave was glad they had visited Mary Lou; she had shown them her marriage certificate, so they knew she was speaking the truth.

"Well, if we could only track down Rachel, I am sure she would be relieved to find that she is not married to him," said Dave thoughtfully.

"She doesn't want to be found. But it's so unfair on Diana, she has misjudged her badly!" said Jake with feeling.

Dave said nothing, but he looked at Jake closely. He was not fooled; Jake was getting emotionally involved with Diana, and as much as he enjoyed working with him, it would have to cease. He decided he would tell him when they got back to England. In his opinion, Diana may have been just an acquaintance at the beginning, but Jake was clearly smitten and in protective mode of her. He could not risk him compromising the situation.

The more Jake learned about Neil Morris, the more he wanted to make sure he got his punishment. When he thought about what that man had done to Diana, and how he had split the twins, the more anger he felt towards him. Then she had to cope with losing her baby too, after unexpectedly bonding with her. He would have happily taken care of Diana and Ella for the rest of his life, and Neil Morris would not have been allowed anywhere near either of them. Diana had confessed to him that she still had nightmares about bumping into that man again one day, and Jake would always protect her from him.

Now that they had interviewed Mary Lou, and got her statement, all he could think about was returning to England and Diana. He sent her a text to find out if she was OK; with the eight hour time difference, it would be about seven o'clock in the evening over there. He was surprised when she replied to say she had visited the agency that day to see if there was any work. He had assumed with her baby missing, Diana would find it hard to concentrate on anything else. He had huge admiration for her courage. Finding himself on his own because Dave had gone down to order them some sandwiches, he rang her, and his heart flipped when he heard her voice.

"Diana, it's Jake, we have interviewed Mary Lou. You mustn't let Dave know I told you, but Neil Morris is already married to her, so if we could only get hold of Rachel, we could tell her that. I am sure she would be relieved."

169

h

"You don't know how glad I am to know that he is not part of our family, but I have no way of contacting Rachel, and neither do my aunt and uncle. I think she wanted to move right on and forget us all."

He heard the catch in her voice. It was still raw, that pain of losing all contact with Rachel. Her love for her sister would remain in her heart. He so wished he could make it better for her!

"How did you get on at the agency?"

"Well they have plenty of work for me. After being headlined in the newspapers, everyone wants me, but it's for curiosity, not for the right reasons. I think I am going to wait a bit. It's a month since Ella was snatched, it's too soon!"

"You're right," he said warmly. "There is no rush, get yourself fit and well, and have a few good night's sleep."

"Aunt Susan is still trying to keep the press away. They never give up!"

"I know," he sighed. "Dave has just brought us some food and I have to go, but keep your chin up, we'll be home in a few days."

He switched off his mobile quickly, but Dave guessed who he was speaking to, and he wasn't surprised. It seemed Jake couldn't go long without contact with her; he had got it bad. He thought an awful lot of Jake, he was a good worker, and he really hoped Jake and Diana did get together once he had freed Jake of this case. He knew Jake would take good care of her so she could put her ordeal with Morris behind her.

"I was just checking Diana is OK. She's trying to go back to work, but it's too soon; everyone wants her, but for all the wrong reasons," he explained.

"Well that won't last forever, people do forget, and once we get some major drama like a murder, then this case will be old news. But we have to make sure we keep it fresh in people's minds, because one day the person that stole baby Ella will have nowhere to hide!" said Dave firmly. He continued on, "Here are some roast beef sandwiches; twice the thickness of what we call a sandwich in England, no wonder everyone is so big out here!"

Dave produced the evidence of his statement, and the two men sat down with their cans of Coke and Subway sandwiches. They both had the same thought in their minds; to get back to England and see what else they could find out about this case.

After lunch, they were picked up again by the FBI and taken to the local headquarters. It was a big white building, with one floor housing the offices. The floors were marble, and the air conditioning made it a pleasant place to be. They sat down with the agents to discuss their findings, and once again they heard that when Neil, alias Adam, had departed, they had no reason to chase after him. Mary Lou had no marks to prove he had ever assaulted her, and she was very angry when she found him in bed with her best friend.

Dave filled them in about Neil's other crimes in England, also explaining about their unbalanced mother Harriet, who had killed her own baby and then took her own life. Although they had no way of knowing if Neil did have baby Ella, if he did they would be concerned, as indeed they would be if Clare had her too. With the family history of instability, they considered Ella would be in grave danger. Meanwhile her mother was breaking her heart at the loss of her baby. He finished off by saying the only positive to come out of their interview with Mary Lou was knowing that she was still married to him, which meant that Rachel was not.

Because of his bigamy, there would be a reason to arrest him if anyone could catch up with him, but there were far more serious crimes to charge him with if they could be proved. The FBI agents were now beginning to realise what an evil man he was, and how lucky Mary Lou was that he was no longer around. If he did dare to come back, which was now very unlikely, as even more vigilance would be used when anyone entered the country, they would capture and hold him.

Eventually Dave and Jake were driven back to their hotel, and they packed ready to leave for England the next day. Although Jake had only been away from Diana for three days, it felt like a lifetime to him. Dave was complaining on the plane about the jet lag they would suffer after fitting so much into three days, but then added he was going to enjoy a nice relaxing weekend to get over it, that is if his wife didn't find him any jobs to do at home.

Jake smiled, but all the while he was wondering what excuse he would have to go and visit Diana at the weekend. Chloe was her family liaison officer, ensuring that Diana was coping, and he had no reason to go there without Dave, but all he knew was he had to see her. Diana was becoming a huge part of his life, and he had no idea if she had any feelings for him other than gratitude for the help and support he was giving her. But that in no way diminished the strength of his love for her.

They arrived in England on Friday morning. Jake had not slept on the flight, as his mind had been too full of Diana, and he suggested to Dave that they could report to headquarters before going home, just in case there were any new developments. Dave wanted to get home, but said he was happy for Jake to do it. Now that he had decided to take Jake off the case next week, and find him something else, it seemed only right he should let him check in today for the last time. He wasn't looking forward to telling Jake, so after the weekend would do.

When Jake arrived at headquarters, he was stopped by the duty sergeant as he came in.

"So glad you are back Inspector Maloney, is DCI Wilson with you?"

"No, he's gone home. We only just landed, and I was just checking in."

"Well we have Morris here for questioning. Thought you might like to interview him!"

Jake couldn't believe his luck; he was going to interview the bastard. He felt his adrenalin rise.

"I certainly would like to do that!" he said with feeling.

Chapter Twenty-four

Danny Lee was sitting in his apartment overlooking the river Thames. On this grey January day, no matter how splendid the view, nor how opulent his home was, he needed something to inspire him. He was a very successful producer, and his lifestyle reflected this. He only dined in the finest restaurants and stayed in the best hotels.

He had worked his way up from training as an actor, but then found moving onto being a producer was what he found most satisfying. He was still only thirty, but his film star good looks with very dark hair and expressive brown eyes, had been his fortune. He could have dated any woman, and occasionally he did, but to him work came first, and the satisfaction he got from seeing his productions succeed and make money took precedence over everything.

Right now he needed to fill the part in his new production. The leading man was sorted, but he knew without a shadow of a doubt, after their paths had crossed yesterday at the agency, just how perfect Diana would be, with her red gold hair, and amazing green eyes, for the leading lady; the tragic heroine.

He had seen her act before, and he knew she had great stage presence. Her sense of drama was inborn into her personality, and she could also be vivacious, but this part required a tragic hard done by heroine, and right now Diana was in exactly that frame of mind. Like everyone else in England, Danny was well aware of her situation; a new mother whose baby had been snatched. There didn't seem to be a man to support her, which made it even more tragic, and her name must be on the lips of the whole world. So anything she appeared in would get maximum coverage, and people would flock to see the woman who had dominated the news now for a month.

If Danny was being ruthless, and not thinking about how Diana might feel, it was because he had got where he was by being that way, and after chatting with her and sharing a coffee yesterday at the local Costa, she had left such an impression on him, he knew he would not rest until he had tried to get her in his play. He knew she lived at Wimbledon, so she would be close to the theatre, and not much travelling would be needed, but now he needed to get on the right side of her and convince her that a stint in his play would be the very best thing for her. She had given him her mobile number yesterday, saying she might be available later in the year after her life was more sorted, but he wanted her now.

He texted her to say he had something to tell her, feeling it was best to be a bit obtuse to rouse her interest. So all he had to do now was pick up a bouquet of flowers on the way, and get a taxi to the address she had just sent to him.

When he arrived with the flowers, Susan opened the door to him, and seeing the flowers, assumed Danny was an admirer. She wondered where Diana had met him, as he had never been mentioned. She was impressed by his dark clean cut looks and polite manner. He was smartly dressed in navy trousers, a grey jacket and a pale blue jumper. She hovered by the door of the study when Diana greeted him, and was pleased to see Diana's face light up when she saw him. Sitting around waiting for news of Ella was stressful, so here was someone to take her mind off it. She went out into the kitchen to organise some tea and biscuits, but when she came back, Diana explained.

"Danny is taking me out for lunch, aunt Susan. Look at these lovely flowers he has brought for me!"

"Yes, they are beautiful," murmured Susan. "I will get Sandra to put them in a vase for you."

Danny smiled at them both, totally disarming them. He had decided that taking her on a date, and getting her talking, was a good way of gaining Diana's trust before putting his proposition to her. So when the taxi arrived, they would go to a steak house. Hopefully after a nice meal and some red wine, he may have wooed Diana into taking that part.

174

Before Jake entered the interview room with Chloe, he was filled in about how Neil Morris had been captured. Somebody had telephoned in from a remote part of Northumbria to say that a man living in a terraced rented cottage next to him looked very much like Morris, except he had a beard.

He had only spoken to him once, but had noticed his American accent, which stood out against the locals as being so different. He drove a battered old Ford Fiesta, which he had taken off in when the police arrived. During the chase that ensued, he had crashed the car, writing it off, and it was subsequently found to be stolen. He had not been hurt by the crash, nor luckily had the officers chasing him, but he had been arrested for stealing the car and other driving offences, and then brought back to Wimbledon for further questioning.

"Well done to everyone involved!" said Jake, adding, "Now he's finally captured, there are a lot of questions he needs to answer, and hopefully a lot more crimes we can charge him with. This man is a danger to society!"

Chloe noticed the anger in Jake's voice as he spoke about him, and wondered whether she should call Dave in as well, even though he was off-duty. She, too, had seen it in Jake's face when he was with Diana; he was smitten, so he might not be the right person to interview a man he clearly hated for what he had done to Diana.

"Shall I get the duty sergeant to give Dave a ring? He might not want to miss out on this," she asked casually. But Jake was not to be swayed. He had longed for this man to be captured for so long, and he couldn't wait to interview him.

"Let's not trouble him; he wanted the weekend off. I can fill him in on Monday," he said confidently.

They entered the interview room, and Chloe had the tape ready to record the interview. As soon as Jake saw Neil, he felt such hatred go through him. Neil was lounging in the chair without a care in the world, and there was not the slightest sign of remorse on his face. Jake reminded himself he must be professional.

"Good afternoon, sir, I am Inspector Jake Maloney, and this is my colleague WPC Chloe Martin, and we are here to interview you. The time of this interview is eleven o'clock. For the benefit of the tape, can you please give us your name and address?"

175

"No comment."

Jake hated this bastard so much. He had a sneering manner about him, his beard was unkempt, and he was dressed in jeans and a black sweater which were both creased. He looked as if he had got dressed in a hurry and not had time to wash and shave. Jake didn't like his eyes, they were cold, grey and staring. He tried again.

"OK, we know you are at the moment using the assumed name of Neil Morris, and that you committed bigamy when you married Rachel Wilcox some nine months ago. You have a wife in California who tells us your real name is Adam Spencer. You have a brother Barry, and two sisters, one is called Clare, and the other is called Ruth."

If Morris was surprised that they knew so much he never showed it. The sneer on his face spread even more, and he stood up to clap his hands together mockingly. Jake would have liked to smash him to the ground, but common sense had to prevail.

"Several women have made complaints against you, claiming you abused them."

"No comment."

Jake was getting exasperated; this apology for a man looked so pleased with himself, and was deliberately wasting time. He decided to try and mention something that might prompt a response.

"We have enough evidence to put you away for a while whether you speak up or not."

He knew that was a slight exaggeration, as bigamy and car stealing would hardly put him away for long, but Morris could not resist jeering back.

"Oh yes, women love me you know, they can't get enough of me, and that is no crime."

That was the one remark that fired Jake up. He knew that evil creature was suggesting that Diana had welcomed his advances, and suddenly he felt his rage inside him burning like a white hot flame which was about to erupt. He leapt from his chair. He felt like throttling the bastard, so he could not spew out any more lies. Jake, the easy going and gentle man, had been goaded until he lost control, but just as he reached the chair that Morris was slouched in, there was a knock on the door, and all eyes turned towards Dave, who stood there with the duty sergeant.

176

"Stop the tape, I have come to sit in on this interview!" he said commandingly, and Chloe did as he asked.

Jake could tell that Dave was not happy with him; he was glowering at him, and next to him stood another man, who was introduced as Morris's solicitor. He looked about as shifty as his client, and Jake watched him cross the room towards the empty chair next to Morris, who was now looking so pleased with himself.

Dave told them they could have a cup of tea, and then asked Jake to leave the room with him. Jake was feeling a little crestfallen. He had really hoped he could handle that interview, but he had lost it and had let himself and Dave down. Dave led him into a side room.

"Jake, what were you thinking of? Did you want him to make a complaint against you for assault? That won't help the case!"

"I know. It was his smug face; I just lost it."

"Look I understand why, but for that reason I have to take you off this case. Anyone can see a mile away how much you care about Diana. You are too emotionally involved to make clear decisions. I am just glad the duty sergeant rang me, because it looked like you were about to attack him."

Jake's head whirled. He could not come off the case; he would have no reason to visit Diana, and he so needed her in his life. Not only that, but he wanted to give her the support she needed. He spoke desperately.

"I know I should not have let him get to me, but just think of all those poor women he has abused, at least three that we know of. It won't happen again. Please let me stay on the case."

But Dave was adamant, and he tried to soften the blow.

"Jake I can't, but I know what you should be doing, and you don't need an excuse to do it. I have seen Diana's eyes when she looks at you, and the respect she shows you, and I believe she feels the same as you do. Go and see her, and tell her how you feel; it may help her considerably at this time. Even if she is not ready for a relationship at the moment, just to know you are there, and you care, would lift her spirits considerably, especially if she knows it's not just because of the case, but because you love her."

Jake considered his words; they did make a lot of sense. He really did find it hard masking his feelings to Diana. He so wanted to put his arms around her, show how much he cared, and protect her. If Dave had noticed that she seemed to care for him, and he had been too blind to see it, that was so heartening. He had a good reason to visit today, because the newspapers would soon be full of the car chase and capture of Morris. Somehow, no matter how careful they were, this stuff always leaked out. He could go and reassure her that everything was all right.

Buoyed on by this encouragement, he forgot any tiredness he might have felt from not sleeping on the flight. Dave reassured him that although he was off the case, he would still let him know how his interview with Morris went. So Jake jumped in a taxi and went home to take a shower, and generally smarten himself up before he went to see Diana. He put on some thick jeans and a navy blue jumper, as the wind was very cold. Usually he visited Diana in plain but smart clothes, and jeans were for relaxing, but he would have to explain he was off the case.

There had been a murder of a black teenager, and Dave was going to recommend him to head the investigation, as this case was so far removed from the current one and he didn't know any of the people involved. Dave had told him he knew he would do a good job, and Jake was relieved that his outburst had not made him go down in Dave's estimation, because he so wanted to keep the respect of his boss and he felt ashamed that he had let his emotions get the better of him.

The new case was taking precedence over the abduction of baby Ella. It had been a racial attack, and the police force were well aware that racial hatred always needed to be stamped down on. The devastated parents were on TV pleading for any information about the attack and, as always, there would be plenty of feedback from the public afterwards. Jake made a vow to himself that he would work hard to find the culprit. He would put his heart and soul into this new case, to prove to Dave that he deserved the title of inspector. The abduction of baby Ella would continue on the back burner, but that certainly did not mean the case was closed, it never would be, and hopefully before the not too distant future, she would be found safe and well.

It was midday when the taxi arrived at the house, and he was just in time to see Diana in another taxi, with a man he did not recognise, coming out of the gates and heading towards London. He tried but failed to catch her attention, and he felt disappointment sweep through him that he had missed her, as well as wondering who the man was.

He asked his driver to wait whilst he popped in to see Susan. Without Diana there, he had no reason to stay. When Sandra opened the door to him, Susan was standing next to a huge bouquet of flowers, arranged on the hall table in all their glory.

"Welcome back Jake, I was just arranging these beautiful flowers that Danny brought?"

"Danny?" enquired Jake, and his heart was thudding with apprehension and fear at what she might tell him.

Susan had thought for a while that something might happen between Jake and Diana, because they always seemed at one with each other. But when she thought about it, that was his job, and if Diana was clinging to him with aspirations that he might care for her, then Susan didn't want her to be hurt any more. She had been hurt enough in the last year to last a lifetime.

But today Danny had walked into her life with a big bouquet of flowers and taken her on a date, and although she didn't know anything about him, Diana clearly liked him or else she wouldn't have gone. So she gave what she considered was a true answer.

"Yes, I don't know him as yet, but Diana has gone out for lunch with him, and he certainly seems to be very keen on her. It's about time she had some happiness!"

Jake was very careful to mask his disappointment when he heard those words. Susan was absolutely right, Diana did deserve some happiness, but his heart ached to know he had been too late. Someone else had come along to help her mend her broken heart, he had been too slow. After loving her for all these years, and then meeting her again, he had been filled with hope. He just murmured politely:

"She certainly does deserve some happiness!"

"Did you have a good trip to America?" said Susan, changing the subject quickly; although Jake had shown no signs of jealousy when Danny had been mentioned.

"A short one. I expect Diana has told you that Morris is a bigamist."

"Yes, amongst all his other crimes."

Jake remembered why he had come, but aware of the taxi man patiently waiting, he knew he must tell Susan this before they read the newspapers tomorrow.

179

"Can you tell Diana that Morris has been captured, and he is at the police station as we speak."

Susan was impressed, as she knew it wouldn't have been easy tracking him down.

"Oh, well done. Let's hope he will soon go to prison and be unable to wreck any more lives."

"I hope so too, but just to let you know, I am no longer on the case. I have been given another one as from Monday. I have to say goodbye now, my taxi is waiting."

Susan was taken aback by this news. It was true that it was a complex case with so many witnesses disappearing, but she hoped that they were not giving up on it. If Jake was no longer investigating it, that meant he would not come round to see them. They had got used to seeing him in the past month, and she felt a sense of loss. She was sure Diana would too. He was such a sincere and caring young man. Thank goodness Diana had got herself back out there and wasn't moping at home any more, because it felt like they were on their own again. Thank goodness she had met Danny.

Chapter Twenty-five

"So you'll do it then, Diana?"

Danny lifted up his glass of red wine and took a sip. He was enjoying Diana's company very much. Women had always been secondary to his work, but Diana was different. She wasn't only beautiful and talented, she was also extremely brave. She had explained how she could no longer sit at home waiting for her baby to be returned to her; she had to keep busy. The part in the play was a challenge, but she would do it.

Diana lifted her glass and clinked it against his.

"Yes I will, as long as you keep the press away from me."

"Indeed, you won't go home via the stage door, instead we have a special exit for you."

The heroine in the script was fighting against everyone to get justice, and Diana knew that acting in this play was going to be so cathartic for her. She could indulge all the tears and anger she was feeling inside. She had made up her mind she wanted to be earning again, and able to return to her flat. Her uncle and aunt had been brilliant, but she wanted her life and her freedom back.

It was over a month now since that fateful day, and she almost felt like it had never happened and it was all a dream. She had bonded with her baby right after her birth, then held and fed her for less than a day, and then she was gone. She had made herself believe that Ella was alive and well somewhere, but she was slowly accepting that she might never see her again. No matter how much it hurt, she recognised that to keep her sanity, life had to go on.

Sitting here with Danny enjoying a nice meal and a glass of wine felt normal, instead of pacing around at home waiting for the phone to ring, or for someone to arrive with some news. She did care very much, but she felt she could no longer put her life on hold any more. She was happy to be seen with him, and he was a known figure, so it would not be long before they would be mentioned in celebrity magazines. He had warned her she might be criticised for going back to work, but Diana did not care, she knew working was going to help her cope. She was prepared for the amount of public interest levelled at her; some would be kind, and some would not, but there was a saying that there is no such thing as negative publicity, and for a jobbing actor, all publicity is good, so she made up her mind to weather it. After what she had been through this last year, a few critical remarks would simply bounce off her.

By the time they had finished their meal it was three o'clock, and she suddenly remembered that Jake was returning from America today. Her heart gave the usual flip when she thought about him. She cared so much about him, but she had no idea if he felt the same. She wondered if he had any more news. He had already told her that Morris was a bigamist, and even though Rachel was now lost to her, she felt relieved that he was not her husband. It was strange that her aunt had never heard any more from her. She had accepted that she was never going to feel complete without her twin in her life, and she would so have loved to tell her about Morris, but wherever Rachel was, she just hoped she was happy.

Danny helped her on with her coat, and they left the restaurant and got in the taxi. He gave the driver directions to drop Diana off first. He was hoping he might be invited in, because he had enjoyed his time with her so much, he didn't want it to end. He could easily pay off the driver and send him away. They had discussed the play at great length, and Diana had agreed to report for rehearsals tomorrow.

By the time they arrived at her aunt's house, Diana's thoughts had turned to Jake. When she entered the house it was clear that Susan had something to tell her, so she said goodbye to Danny, promising to see him at rehearsals the next day. She guessed the news would be something to do with the investigation, no matter what she did or where she went, it was always there in her mind.

She was so preoccupied she failed to see the look of disappointment on Danny's face when he went.

"Jake came round whilst you were out. They caught Morris!" Susan announced triumphantly. "He's being questioned at the police station now."

Diana felt a shiver of fear go through her. He still had the power to scare her, but she didn't want to be a victim, nor did she want to dwell on the rape. She had explained to Dave and Jake that she didn't want to ever go to court and testify against him, and the reason was that Ella was the one good thing that had come out of it, and she loved her, and did not want her daughter to grow up knowing how she had been conceived. They had agreed with her, because it was highly unlikely that she could even win the case and, after the way she had suffered, there was no reason to put her through that sort of stress.

"Are they going to charge him?" she asked.

"Well, with bigamy yes, and he was driving a stolen car, but Jake spoke as though they were hoping for more charges so he goes away for a long time."

"I hope so, he's managed to split up our family!" said Diana feeling that all too familiar pain in her heart.

"Yes," sighed Susan. "I wish we could hear from Rachel so I could know she is all right."

"Is Jake coming round tomorrow?" asked Diana. She always found his presence comforting.

"Oh no, I nearly forgot to tell you, he's been taken off the case."

Diana looked at her in horror; this couldn't be true surely? But she knew by her aunt's expression, that it was. Suddenly she was filled with fear. Jake was the reason she was coping. He had been her rock, and now her rock was gone, and she felt so incomplete. Now it felt like her life was falling apart again. She burst into tears, and Susan wrapped her arms around her, promising everything would be all right. But even as she said it, Susan wondered if it would be true. Losing Jake was like losing her right arm, but somehow they would have to get through it.

By the time Diana had reported for rehearsals the next day, she had got herself together, and was determined to cope. Today she was wearing jeans and a cable knit sweater, as sometimes at rehearsals the old theatres could be quite cold, although the heating was always put on when the public came. It was only just over four weeks since Ella's birth, but her figure had gone back to normal; maybe it was because she had not eaten much, although she had enjoyed the steak yesterday. It was nice to be able to fit into the same size jeans again, and she had washed her hair and showered, but refrained from putting on too much make-up. She would be made up on the night, make-up girls always commented how easy it was to enhance her beauty because she had such big eyes and they were such an arresting shade of green. Remembering this restored her confidence a little as, apart from yesterday when she had gone out with Danny, she had not been wearing any make-up. It was time to get back out there and be noticed again.

Danny was delighted to see her and took her over to meet the rest of the cast. She had not worked with any of them before, so it was all very new. Her leading man was tall and well built but as he was playing an abusive husband, and she was the feisty wife who would not let him ruin her life, he seemed well cast. He grinned when introduced to her. His face totally changed when he smiled, and she thought he looked kindly in spite of his strong build, and felt they would get on.

Diana spent most of the day rehearsing with her script, although she promised herself that tonight she would learn it so she wouldn't need the script anyway. Some of her scenes were very dramatic, she had to rage and cry in equal measure, so her acting came straight from her heart in such a way it really made them all sit up and take notice of her. Danny stood there with a proud look on his face, as he knew he had struck gold with Diana.

He was really fascinated by Diana, she was unlike some of his other leading ladies. She had a natural beauty, an aura seemed to shine from her, and those scenes she had just performed were so moving and believable, he knew she would have the audience right there with her, willing her on, and that is what acting was all about. Diana had the makings of a star, and Danny felt so proud to think that he had found her. What a talent!

Danny had not expected her to have such an impact on him. It wasn't just that she was beautiful and talented, but kindness and love seemed to flow out of her. She cared about people. She had spoken about her twin sister with such warmth, and although she had chosen only to tell him what she wanted to, he knew that her sister was now working abroad, and how much she missed her. She also spoke very warmly about her aunt and uncle, the way they had given them both a home when their parents had died, and also the support they had offered since Ella had been abducted.

She had character too, as she had said quite firmly that now she was back on her feet and earning again, she was going back to her flat, as she didn't want to return to the days when her uncle had helped to subsidise her. Danny found this quite refreshing after some of the women he had known in the past, all up for a good time, and if family chipped in to help, so much the better. He could feel himself being taken over by a strange new emotion that he had never experienced before, and it was all because of Diana.

Neil Morris was held for questioning over the weekend. He was very uncooperative, and Dave, who had lost his weekend off because of it, although in control of himself, could see exactly why Jake had almost clocked him one. The bloke was a pathetic excuse for a man, a small time crook with a violent bullying nature where poor unfortunate women were concerned. Of course, they had never been able to prove any of the rapes, and there had been at least three counting his wife, but they had proof of his bigamy, and various charges of stealing the car, no tax and no insurance. Normally these charges would not involve a prison sentence, but due to his past record of extorting money, they could hopefully get him off the streets for a few years, and there were certain men inside who didn't take kindly to blokes who abused women, so he might just get his comeuppance whilst the prison warder looked the other way. In the meantime, his dodgy lawyer had been unable to help him much, so he would be held until his court hearing, as no judge would allow bail to a man like him who had no security to offer in case he absconded.

It was the sneering that got to Dave, as Neil swaggered about as though he was Ronnie Kray; he was just a jumped up petty thief who had adopted an American accent to cover up his East End one. Neil was no different to his brother Barry, born and bred in the East End of London. No wonder his sister Ruth had disowned him and changed her name. If she wanted her career to succeed, then she needed to make sure there was no link between them. On Monday Morris was charged and taken to a cell. It was amazing that he still had that sneer on his face, because he would go back to prison, but people like him never showed any remorse for their crimes. Dave felt relieved that he had finally got him locked up and out of the way of any other poor unsuspecting females. Now he could take a couple of days off and relax. He felt he had earned it.

Today was the first day of Jake investigating the murder of the black teenager, and Dave knew he would leave no stone unturned to get justice for the bereaved parents. He hoped that Jake had understood that he had no choice but to take him off the case of the abduction of baby Ella. It was too close to home, and he also hoped that Jake would take his advice, and tell Diana how he felt, because she was a beautiful young woman, and unless he did, he might lose her. Maybe if Diana had not been so distracted by all the other emotional turmoil in her life, she would have realised by now just how in love with her Jake was. He wore his heart on his sleeve, and his eyes lit up every time he mentioned her. If she felt the same, then some good would come out of this sorry mess, because Jake would take care of her for the rest of their lives, he was a good decent bloke, and they both deserved some happiness.

Dave knew how much his own wife and two daughters meant to him and, although he worked long hours, they were everything to him. When life throws up challenges the love of the family really does help, and he was sure that although he would not be working on the case, if Jake was with Diana, together they would cope with the loss of Ella. He would never give up hope of finding her, and the case would always remain open, but in the meantime, Jake would help her to remain strong.

Chapter Twenty-six

During the next six months, Diana's career went from strength to strength. The play was a huge box office success, and the offers came flooding in. But she was choosy, because still at the back of her mind was the desire not to go too far in case the police found Ella. The ache inside her never went away, but she just plunged herself even more into her work.

Danny had made sure she got a good agent, and Diana told her to ignore any offers from abroad, especially America, as it was so far away; she would only work in England. Although the world could have been her oyster, because an American film director wanted to put her in a block buster movie, which would have made her a millionaire overnight, nobody could influence her, Diana knew her own mind.

Danny wanted more for her; he knew she would become a superstar if she took up the offer from the USA, but selfishly he didn't want her too far away from him, so when she accepted a lead character role in a British soap, he felt relieved, and happy for her too. She then went on to win an award for her acting in it. Tragic and feisty roles suited Diana so well. She moved her audiences to tears, and inspired many women to stand up and fight for themselves when the going became tough.

Most people knew the story of her baby being abducted so soon after birth, and how she had picked herself up and got her life back on track. Nobody except the police and her aunt and uncle knew about her rape, and they never would from her. Diana never wanted to be a victim, she wanted to be a survivor, and get on with her life.

She was frequently seen at celebrity dinners and functions with Danny, and rumours abounded everywhere that she had bagged herself one of the most eligible bachelors, and the richest, in England. She laughed when she saw the headlines, because she only thought of Danny as a good friend, and she was grateful for the help he had given her by putting her in the play.

Danny was completely in love with her. He admired this feisty and plucky woman, and was truly happy that people thought they were already a couple. He had not even kissed her yet, as he didn't want to rush it and lose her, but if he had it his way, they would be married in September of this year; it was now June, and he so wanted to get engaged, then he would know she would be his forever.

Jake spent those months solving his case, and bringing to justice two teenage brothers who had killed the black teenager. It had been a racially motivated crime. They had picked on him because of his colour, he had tried to defend himself, but one brother had stabbed him through the heart, and he had never recovered.

Initially Jake had been met with a wall of silence after the initial appeal by the parents. All the teenagers lived on the same estate, and the two brothers were feared by many. They came from a family where their father had done time and had links with other thugs, so most people said they had seen nothing, as they all valued their own lives.

The breakthrough had come when one of the brothers had dumped his girlfriend in favour of her friend. The irate female had secretly come to the station and explained she had been there and seen it all. The police promised her anonymity, and had agreed she could give her evidence by video link, so with her help they had got their conviction, and the brothers were imprisoned for life.

Jake was commended for the way he had handled the case, but although he had strived to prove himself to Dave, somehow that praise didn't mean as much as it should have. It would have meant more to him to solve the disappearance of Ella, and bring the culprit to justice, for Diana's sake.

It was impossible to miss all the photographs of Diana on the arm of Danny at various events, and newspaper reports about this "beautiful couple." Jake was usurped, as he didn't know how to compete with this rich and distinguished man, and although his heart ached so much, his love for Diana was so strong that, if Danny Lee made her happy, then he must accept it, because she certainly deserved some happiness. Dave had told him he must fight for her, but after that afternoon when he had arrived at her aunt's house to find her out with Danny, he had bowed out. Since then her career had taken off, and she was now living in a very grand apartment in Chelsea. Jake had a good job with a decent wage, but this Danny Lee was loaded, and well out of his league.

He had kept in touch with her by phone. Hearing her voice was like balm to his wounded spirit, and she had even asked him round to show him her new home when she moved in. He was planning to ask her out for a celebration drink when he got there, but Danny Lee had turned up; his smart appearance, and clear annoyance that Jake was there had curtailed all Jake's plans, and he had felt like he was an unwanted guest. Diana had given him a quick hug as he left, and thanked him for coming round, but Danny Lee had given him the look that said "get lost," and because he didn't want to give Diana any extra stress, he had done just that. He really didn't like the bloke, he was too full of himself, but if Diana did, then it was her life.

Dave had some important news to share with Jake when he reported for work that day. He had received information about a handbag that had been recovered from the river Thames. It had been in the water for a long time, and most of the contents were unrecognisable, except for a credit card in a plastic case. That credit card had the name of Rachel Wilcox on it.

After contacting her bank manager and interviewing him, Dave had been allowed access to her account. Clearly she had not altered her surname to Morris, given the outcome of her fateful wedding day. She also had another account, which was the one that Morris had been given access to via a third party credit card, and he had removed five thousand pounds from it by using his card. As she had freely given him the card, they could not do much about that.

The thing that worried Dave was her current account had not been used since the day she disappeared. There had been no movement on it whatsoever, and the bank confirmed they had not been notified about a change of address. She had over twenty thousand pounds in that account, and her handbag had been found in the river Thames. If anyone had murdered her, they would surely have tried to get to her money, especially if it was Morris. Maybe Rachel had taken her own life, and even the life of baby Ella? It was a possibility they could not rule out, as that evil man had messed with the minds of both of these women. Who knows how Rachel might have reacted?

Danny arrived with two bottles of red wine; Diana's favourite he believed. He wanted to celebrate another resounding success, because she had been voted WOMAN OF THE YEAR by a celebrity magazine, and her face graced the cover. Diana's face was everywhere, she was the woman every young woman wanted to look like. They copied her strawberry blonde hair, her dress sense, and everything about her that they could. It was cool to be a fan of Diana Wilcox.

He had decided that now was the time; with a couple of glasses of red wine inside him, he was going to tell her how he felt. It was difficult to start a love affair with someone who had been parted from her baby, this is why he had held back, but it was over seven months now and, quite frankly, Danny didn't believe they would ever trace that baby again. Maybe she had been sold in another country, it happened, but he had never said that to Diana. Maybe his love for her would ease her loss; he hoped so, and they could marry and have their own family.

If anyone had told Danny a year ago that he would have these sort of thoughts, he would have thought they were barking mad. But Diana had changed him, he was incredibly proud of her courage, he loved everything about her. For the first time in his life Danny Lee was in love, at the age of thirty he had fallen hard for her.

He had not been pleased to see that Maloney bloke sniffing round her. He had caught him at her house when he was off duty. If he thought he could win her over with his Irish blarney, then Danny was going to make sure he didn't. Diana had laughed when he mentioned him, saying he was a good friend who had helped her at a very difficult time. But Danny was used to having his own way, and if he was acting possessively, it was because he didn't want to lose her, so he was going to make sure that he would be the one she would turn to in the future, and that Irish bloke could butt out!

When she opened the door to him she was dressed very casually, as it was her day off, and his visit was an unexpected one. To him she looked beautiful, with her hair shining as the June sun reflected from behind her. She wore white shorts with a peach coloured top, and her shapely legs had a light tan. Her face broke into a smile.

"Hi Danny, I wasn't expecting to see you today."

He waved the magazine with the picture in front of her.

"I've come to celebrate with you, WOMAN OF THE YEAR."

"Oh that, it's just a celebrity thing," she said modestly.

Danny flourished the bottles in front of her.

"Where is your corkscrew, we must celebrate."

Diana let him in and went to find some glasses. She knew Danny liked his red wine, he had introduced her to Beaujolais, but she didn't usually drink during the day, it made her sleepy. In her profession, many actresses did drink, some even took drugs, but it was not something that appealed to her, she was just a social drinker, she never drank when she was alone. There was a reason for that, having a drink to try and block out what had happened to her might work for a few hours, but she also realised she might become dependent on it, so rather than risk that, she didn't do it.

She watched Danny pouring out the wine. He was over generous with her glass, so she laughed and told him to stop. They clinked glasses, and she sipped hers whilst he drank his quite quickly. He was chatting about how well she had done, and she smiled and reminded him that if he had not had faith in her, she would not be in the lucky position that she was now. Danny continued to refill his glass, he was on to the second bottle now, and urging her to drink up and have more.

Diana let him refill her glass. Why not let her hair down for once, they were not hurting anyone else. Danny had been her rock since her career took off, but yet no one could replace Jake. Her love for him continued to burn brightly inside her but, sadly, she believed it was unrequited love. She had been so upset when he had come off the case. She felt abandoned, even though Dave Wilson had explained Jake was needed to solve a murder case.

She had been used to confiding her worries and fears to Jake, but at least losing him had made her focus on her career; and look at her now, the sky was her limit. Maybe she should be grateful to him for showing her she could manage, but she knew that given the choice, she would have settled for being with Jake if he wanted her, with or without her career.

Danny was a bit drunk now, and she couldn't stop giggling. Her head felt a bit dizzy, and she exploded with laughter as he lurched towards her. It had been a while since she had let her hair down, and it felt good. Danny collapsed onto the sofa, taking her with him, and then it happened, his arms were round her, and his face was close. She looked deep into his eyes, and saw his love for her, and then his lips met hers, gently at first, but then exploding with passion.

She found herself responding; up until now she had kept all her love tightly locked inside her heart for Jake, but it seemed he didn't want it. In her present state of euphoria, her need to be loved and cherished was so strong her heart had stopped arguing with her. Danny was here with her, and he said those magic words.

"Oh God, Diana, I love you so much, please marry me, we would make such a great team."

Without even hesitating, she replied, "Danny, maybe I will." She was chuckling.

Danny was ready at that moment to make love to her on the sofa. All his inhibitions were gone, and after that she would surely say she loved him too, but at that moment the intercom buzzed.

"Leave it," he said impatiently. He didn't want anyone to spoil this moment.

But Diana couldn't leave it, it was always there at the back of her mind, was there any news? She got up from the sofa, pulling her jumper down, and running her fingers through her tousled hair. Danny was not happy to see her pick up the intercom, and even less happy to hear that DCI Wilson and Jake Maloney were downstairs. That dratted bloke was like a limpet, always clinging onto her! Diana immediately sobered up, and went to her door to let them in.

Jake tried not to look at the empty glasses and half finished bottle of wine as they came in. Jealousy coursed through him.

192

They had obviously disturbed an intimate moment, as Danny looked really annoyed. Dave had asked him to come with him because the news was not good, but with her boyfriend there it was going to be harder to talk to her.

Dave spoke politely after shaking hands with Danny, this was the first time he had met him, but he had seen the photos and press coverage of him. There was an arrogance about Danny which he didn't like, or was it because Jake was his friend, he couldn't be sure?

"Good morning to you both. We were wondering if you, Diana, would come to the station to do an identification, and also your aunt might like to come with you."

Diana's heart missed a beat; why were they being so secretive, was it because Danny was here? She realised that until they turned up, she had almost promised to marry Danny. It had felt right at the time, but now, after seeing Jake, could she really marry a man whom she liked but did not love? Would that love grow later, as they did have a lot in common?

"You can tell me in front of Danny; I totally trust him."

"We have found a handbag. It's been in the water for sometime, but there was a bank card belonging to Rachel in it, and we need you and Susan to identify it."

Dave refrained from telling her their worries; that was enough for now, and the boyfriend was clearly not impressed by their visit. Danny responded as politely as he could muster. This investigation was always putting a cloud over their lives. He wanted to take Diana to the States as his wife. She had a big future out there, and once they were married he was sure she would go with him because, after all this time, it was unlikely she would get her baby back.

"You best go and sort it out babe, I can wait here until you return if you like."

He used that word just to let the Irish bloke know they were an item, well almost an item; they would have been if this lot had not turned up right now. He, Danny Lee, was not used to chasing after women, nor used to being in love either. He could tell by this paddy's eyes that he loved her too, so the quicker Danny could marry her and whisk her away from him, the better. At that moment he abandoned the idea of a big celebrity wedding in September, and the photos in OK Magazine, it was going to have

j

to be a trip to Vegas and a special licence, because time was of the essence.

The police car stopped off to pick up Susan too, and in almost silence they drove to the police station, each one thinking their private thoughts. Dave and Jake realised they had to voice their thoughts after the identification. Susan and Diana were wondering why the bag had been dumped in the Thames; was it because Rachel had assumed a new identity, and if so, was it because she had stolen Ella?

The bag had been in the water a long time. It was an expensive leather one, but Diana recognised it as originally white, with a shoulder strap, she had been with Rachel when she bought it. None of the contents were recognisable except the bank card, which had been saved by the polythene window covering it in her purse.

Dave looked at Jake before he spoke gently to them; Chloe was also there in case they needed the support. He didn't want to say it, but he had to, they must be prepared for this.

"Diana, we have worked so hard over the last few months to find Ella. So many people have been interviewed, and as you know, the three main suspects have been Clare, Rachel and Morris. We are satisfied that Morris hasn't got her, and he is safely locked up for a number of years now. But we have never been able to trace Clare, who apart from being Ella's aunt, had her own reasons for wanting to adopt her. Then there was Rachel, who went away when the balance of her mind was disturbed by the events."

He stopped when he saw the look of pain in Diana's eyes, and Jake cut in quickly, realising how much it still hurt her.

". . . It was never your fault Diana, none of it, so don't blame yourself," and without even thinking about it, he put his arm protectively around her shoulder, and she looked at him gratefully, realising he understood her emotions.

Dave took a breath and continued.

"Since we found the bank card, we have investigated, and there has been no movement on Rachel's account since the day she left, and there is a large amount of money still in there. Having found the handbag in the river, we cannot rule out the possibility that she may have taken her own life."

Diana stood there stunned, as the words slowly invaded her mind. She covered her ears; this was ludicrous. Rachel could not be dead, she was her twin, she would know if she was dead!

"Oh no, what about Ella?" asked Susan, fear now coursing through her when she remembered just how depressed Rachel had been. Then she answered her own question. "Surely you don't think Rachel took her life as well?"

After all this time of waiting and wondering, something snapped inside Diana, all she could think about was getting out of there and going home. Her whole life had collapsed, and it felt like all hope was gone. Was it true that she would never see her sister or her baby again because they were dead? She gave a scream of anguish, which came from deep inside her, and she felt nobody could understand how much pain she was suffering. In that moment of madness she felt there was only one thing left to her; she must go home and end her own life, only then could she have peace, and be reunited with her sister and her daughter.

Diana had forgotten that Danny would still be there when she arrived back at her flat. She didn't remember getting in a taxi, or the journey, or even paying the man, all she could think about was the big black pit that surrounded her and was dragging her down.

When Danny saw her face, her eyes wide with fear, and heard her uncontrollable sobs, he knew it must be bad; maybe they had found a body. He moved to put his arms around her, trying to soothe her, and she laid her head against his chest and sobbed out what had happened. But Danny had always had his own theory, so he voiced it.

"You don't know for sure they are dead. Your sister I never knew, so can't comment, but people steal babies you know, especially fair skinned ones to sell in foreign countries."

"Well they are lost to me forever!" said Diana dramatically.

Danny adopted his most soothing manner, stroking her hair and murmuring.

"Babe, let's get married by special licence tomorrow. I can book a flight to Vegas. How about it, we can start our new life?"

Diana broke away from him in horror. He just didn't get it; always inside her would be that hope, it would never die, and all he could talk about was getting married and going to America!

"Danny, you are my friend, but I don't love you. I was only joking earlier, and I thought you were too, and I certainly cannot leave the UK."

Danny had never been a very patient man, and he always managed to get what he wanted as very few people argued with him. But he had reached the end of his tolerance, his jealousy flamed inside him at her change of heart; it must be something to do with that paddy.

"Diana, I was not joking. What has changed your mind, that Irish git! Don't forget I made you, and I can just as easily cause your career to fall from a very big height."

Then Diana saw him for what he was, a man who wanted to marry her and control her. Maybe he did love her in his own way, but she didn't want that kind of love. His words were full of spite, and she had no idea why Jake had got the blame for her change of heart, but she would always defend him.

"He's no git, he's worth ten of you!" she said fiercely, "now get out of my house!"

After he had gone she felt drained of energy, so she sat on the sofa with her head in her hands. Her moment of self-destruction had passed, and she began to doze, but was immediately woken by the sound of her buzzer going frantically.

Chapter Twenty-seven

Jake followed quickly after Diana when she ran from the room, whilst the others stood rooted to the spot with shock. It wasn't the sort of news that could be broken gently, but it had to be said, and he could see it had been the final straw for Diana, and he was really worried about what she might do.

His way along the corridor had been temporarily barred by the bulky frame of the duty constable. He told him that whatever it was it had to wait, or to tell Dave, but by the time he reached the street Diana had gone. He guessed she had either hopped on a bus or taken a taxi, and then he remembered that Danny was waiting for her at the flat, so he hailed himself a cab and set off in pursuit.

When he arrived, he was just in time to see Danny letting himself out of the flat with a face like thunder.

"Is Diana up there?" he asked politely, but Danny was all out of politeness by now.

"Find out for yourself paddy. You just couldn't keep your hands off her, could you! But she's had it, her career is over, she's nothing without me!"

Jake wondered what that was all about, and he felt uneasy. He had to make sure she was not doing anything silly, because right now she must be feeling that the whole world was against her. He pressed the buzzer several times, but there was no answer, and now he was sweating with fear, so he leaned on it until at last she spoke in a sleepy voice.

"Who is it now?" she asked wearily, today had been exhausting, and she was nursing a headache.

197

"It's Jake, please let me in, I want to make sure you are OK."

If it had been anyone else, even her aunt, she would have told them she was OK and asked them to go, but she was sure that Jake was the only person who got it, understanding just how she felt and what a tightrope she had been walking for the past few months, so she let him in.

First of all he tucked her back on the sofa with a duvet round her. Diana's face was pale and her huge eyes looked troubled, so he made a pot of tea then sat drinking it with her. He didn't ask her any questions, he was just content to be with her. She looked such a forlorn figure underneath the duvet, but his presence felt comforting, and for the first time for a long time she felt safe.

Jake could see that this was a defining moment in her life. She would always hope that one day she would see her sister and Ella again. It was human nature never to give up, but her acceptance of the situation was necessary for her to move on. This girl, who was always so feisty and determined, had reached her lowest point, and because he loved her with all his heart, he knew he had to speak out. He sat on the sofa and put his arms around her, stroking her hair back from her tear stained face, and Diana felt at peace at last because he was there.

"Diana, I just met your boyfriend outside, Danny, and he seems very angry, threatening all manner of things like ruining your career."

Diana nestled closer in his arms, it was like heaven to Jake, and he felt he wanted it to go on for ever. He could not give up on her unless she told him to go.

"He's not my boyfriend, he was my producer, but he is so spiteful. He did want to marry me, and I turned him down because I don't love him."

"Oh, I get it." Jake understood now, and his heart had flipped when she had said she didn't love Danny. He had enough love to last them both a lifetime even if she could only love him a little bit back. He could feel a closeness towards her, as though they were finally on the same wave length at last, so he took advantage of the situation, and finally poured out the words he had been longing to say for so long.

"Diana, I am only a humble police inspector, I don't have the wealth and contacts that he has, and I can't help your career, but I do love you with all my heart. I have done since the day I first met you, and I know you are upset and confused at the moment, but that doesn't matter, I am prepared to wait for as long as it takes."

"Wait?" echoed Diana. Were her eyes and ears deceiving her? Could it be that Jake loved her as much as she loved him?"

"To marry you. I want you to be my wife one day. I may not be able to bring Ella and Rachel back to you, but I promise you that I will love and take care of you for all of my life."

His words had lifted Diana right out of that desolate pit. Nothing seemed impossible now because the man of her dreams loved her. She vowed to get back on her feet again, to keep fighting because her life was to be lived; she didn't really want to die. And with Jake by her side, she knew life would take on a new meaning.

Jake's lips met hers, and she felt it, that amazing chemistry flowing between them. His arms tightened around her; she was safe at last, in the arms of the man who understood her inside and out. She stood up and took him by the hand to her bedroom, and when he made love to her she felt the bond of their bodies and souls uniting, and with that came the knowledge that with this man beside her, she could conquer anything.

Aunt Susan was relieved that Diana was all right. She too, had been shaken by the news, but when she heard that finally Jake and Diana were planning their life together, happiness flooded through her. She knew, without a doubt, that Jake would always take great care of Diana.

The next thing was to plan the wedding, and Susan and Clive were both prepared to give her exactly the same day as Rachel, but Diana didn't want that. She just wanted a quiet registry office wedding, with her uncle and aunt as witnesses, and Dave and his wife and children, and Chloe and her fiancé, as the guests.

Jake was happy to go along with whatever she wanted. He understood that a big wedding would attract the attention of the local press, but this way, by the time the newspapers found out, Jake and Diana had left for their honeymoon. With Jake she could travel abroad, because she knew if there was any news at any time about Ella, he would be in direct contact with Dave, so her phobia about never travelling overseas had finally vanished.

Danny had been true to his word, and her career took a downward turn, but Diana had realised exactly what was important in her life, and every day spent with Jake found her loving him even more. Family life meant everything to her, and she became pregnant very soon after her wedding.

She tried not to dwell on the past too much because she knew it was the future that counted, and then one day Dave told them that Neil Morris had been found hanged in his cell. He had suffered various beatings from inmates since he entered prison, because although none of his rapes could be proved, they were known about, and one thing criminals in prison did not like was men who harmed women and children, and then got away with it. Diana did have a grain of sympathy for him because the man had obviously not been right in the head, but she then put it firmly behind her and moved on.

Their son, whom they named Andrew, was born in 2005, just under two years after Ella had been born. It was an emotional moment when he was delivered, as Diana's mind went back to the last time, and she could be forgiven for insisting on a private room, and a nurse in attendance at all times so her son was safe.

They returned home the next day, and she started breast feeding Andrew. The bond she felt with him was very strong, although it would never erase the memory of the short time she had spent with Ella, and hope always remained in her heart that one day she might meet her again.

Andrew and Jake were her whole life. With his black curls inherited from Jake, and her big green eyes, Andrew was a striking boy. He grew very sturdy, and when he was nearly two, they decided to try again for a brother or sister for him. But sadly Diana could not get pregnant again, so she showered all her love on the two men she did have in her life, and tried not to think about the sister that Andrew should have grown up with.

When Andrew started school, Diana went back to work. She never saw Danny again. He had gone to live in America, and according to all the celebrity magazines, he had more money than he knew what to do with. He had married an American girl, and it was now reported he had twin sons, and because she didn't bear him any malice, Diana hoped he had at last found happiness. She worked hard to revive her career, as by now Jake had become a detective chief inspector, and Dave and his wife and family had transferred elsewhere.

Diana was put in TV dramas, as with her striking looks, and big expressive eyes, she was still the perfect tragic heroine. But she wanted to try everything and found she had a flair for comedy. Her timing was perfect, and she was put in a situation comedy, where she found a new sort of enjoyment with acting; laughing at herself and others.

As the years passed, and she reached her thirties, she continued to enjoy balancing her work and her home life. Being a survivor she did not allow herself time to think about the disappointment of never conceiving again. Susan and Clive, now in their sixties, but still very fit, enjoyed being a part of Andrew's life, and when he got to secondary school, just like Jake, he proved to be very good at sport, especially football. He was also interested in computers, and they were now a feature in most people's homes, rather than just in the work place, so as he entered his teens, he had aspirations to work with computers one day.

By the time 2018 came, Andrew was thirteen, he knew all about social media, and actively encouraged Diana to set up a Facebook and Twitter account. This really helped her with her career, and she now had a part time PA who agreed with Andrew that this was the way to go. Many of the fans no longer remembered that fifteen years previously Diana had lost Ella, but there was just the odd troll on Twitter that made reference to it, so she explained about Ella to Andrew. She felt at thirteen he was old enough to know about his sister Ella.

Andrew was impressed, and said the story sounded like a block buster movie, especially as nobody knew for sure who had abducted Ella. She didn't tell him she had been raped, she didn't even say who the father had been, nor that he had taken his own life. One day he might ask that, but for now she felt he knew enough. Then one day their lives were changed for ever when the letter arrived on the mat.

Chapter Twenty-eight
2018

Clare was looking out of the window as the plane was landing at Heathrow Airport. This was her first visit to England for fifteen years. She had gone to Australia as Mary Hamilton because her photograph and real name were everywhere at that time. Now she was returning as Mary Lucas, wife of tall handsome Max Lucas, and mother of three; her adopted fifteen year old daughter Esme, and her two sons by Max, Owen and Scott.

She had adopted Esme because her mother couldn't cope with her, and having a baby to care for had fulfilled all of Clare's longings. Even though she was in a strange country with a young baby, she found her neighbours very helpful and accommodating. She had to work because she was a single parent, so she had taken a job at the local nursery and left her job as a midwife at the hospital. She was able to take Esme to work with her at the nursery, which was just what she wanted.

She truly believed that it was fate that brought Max into her life. No one could fail to notice the man who did all the jobs around the nursery. His lithe body in denim shorts, and his brown torso, greeted her almost every day. His blond hair and piercing blue eyes in a rugged face were impossible to forget, and his cheeky grin. It was not very long before he asked her to come to a barbecue on the beach. So she went, and whilst he was drinking lager, she was enjoying Sangria with the other women and having a laugh, because nobody in Australia took life that seriously. They were so laid back, which was very different to the life she had left behind her.

They were married within six months, and Max had always thought of Esme as his own daughter, and treated her so. Clare felt like she had given birth to her, because she had been so young when she adopted her and her mother had never been seen since. Owen was born in 2005, and two years later along came Scott. The two boys had their father's blond hair, and now Clare had also turned blonde and kept her hair short. Sunglasses were a compulsory fashion extra in Australia, so there was little chance of anyone linking her to the photograph in England.

She had enjoyed a great life in Australia and her marriage was strong. Initially Max had not questioned her past, but as they became closer as a couple, the feeling of wanting to share her past with him became overwhelming, so she told him about her life as a child, her two brothers, and her glamorous sister Ruth. She explained how she had to cut her ties with her brother Neil, also known as Adam, about the life he led, and everything about him. He had ruined so many lives in England, and she needed a fresh start.

She also told him about Diana, the rape, and consequent birth of Ella. Because Diana had done so well for herself as an actress and entertainer she still graced many magazines, and through this Clare had kept up with Diana's life, and marvelled how she had carried on without her baby.

She regretted that she had to cut her ties with Barry and Ruth, but she never wanted to put them in a position where they knew her whereabouts and then had to lie to the police. When Neil had committed suicide, papers all over the world had carried the story, and as evil as he had been, she had still shed tears for her brother. He had inherited their mother's madness, she was sure, and had never been given any treatment or help for it. The whole family had been dysfunctional because of early neglect, but knowing this made her feel thankful for her husband and family, and the stability this gave her.

Clare was happy for Diana when she married the Irish policeman. She had a son now, and he would be the same age as Owen. She had known her as a poor struggling actress, but the ordeal she had suffered and the way she had carried on with her life, and made something of herself, had been inspirational to many women. Of course, the sad part of it all was that Ella had never been found, and nobody truly knew whether she was alive or dead.

203

She interrupted her thoughts to glance at Esme, fifteen years old and excited to be visiting Britain, and she tried to put herself in Diana's place. She knew she would not have been so brave if she had lost her daughter. It might be fifteen years now, but she would not be able to visit Diana, because it would simply bring up bad memories and mess up the new life Clare had now.

Not having had a proper family life, and being left to fend for herself, had made Clare rather desperate to be a mother herself to fill that void. Meeting Max, getting married and having her own family now, had made her fulfilled and happy. She had given them all her unconditional love and, because she was a mother, she could feel even more for Diana having her baby taken so soon after birth, and then having to live for the past fifteen years never knowing where she was. So she was sad she could not go and see her, but still the curse of being in the Spencer family would continue.

Anna Price looked contentedly around her magnificent home, which nestled deep into the Yorkshire Dales. The only downside of being married to a politician was the fact that Alan was at Westminster during the week, and only able to get home at the weekend. But as an artist, it meant she could paint to her heart's content, lost in the beauty of the area, totally immersed in her own world.

Alan had his own flat in London where he spent the week, and then he was home for the weekends. It might not have suited some couples but it worked for them. Anna had sold quite a few of her paintings for a good price; not that she needed the money, but it was heartening to know that her talent was appreciated.

Alan was ten years older than her, divorced with two children of his own when they met, and he was not concerned about having any more, which was just as well, because Anna did not want to go through another ectopic pregnancy. Her stepson and daughter were initially frosty towards her, but in time they grew to like her, and she found it was nice to have them to stay, but equally nice to get her own time back to do as she wanted when they returned to their mother.

Living in the farmhouse suited her very well. She had become a loner because she had to after that day which had changed her life forever. Looking back now, after fifteen years, she realised that her infatuation for Neil had very nearly landed her in prison. The only person she had told was Daddy, and he had got her out of that mess, firstly by getting Neil out of the studio flat at Bodmin, and then by giving her a safe haven in Yorkshire. If she had not come to Yorkshire, she would not have met Alan. He had a great interest in art, and when he saw her painting a cornfield with the rolling hills in the distance, he had bought the picture, and they clicked straight away. She didn't know he was an MP, he didn't go around announcing it, in fact he was a quiet thoughtful man, so different to Neil. They had now been married for fourteen years, and with each year that passed she had tried to block out that day when she had gone to the hospital to abduct baby Ella.

She had never told Alan much about her former life, but maybe she should. However, as an MP, he could not afford to have any sort of scandal touching him. The press would have a field day, they loved to knock people down if they could. So she had kept quiet, even when she heard about Neil Morris hanging himself. Having read the newspapers, she knew he had done many bad things, and he had talked her into doing something bad too. What a fool she had been, young and impressionable, and totally infatuated with that man.

But something she could never rid herself of was her conscience; that day would always haunt her. Being a fan of Diana Wilcox, she had seen her in many plays and films, as well as on TV, and she had always marvelled at how she had managed to carry on after her baby was taken. She had a successful career, and now at the age of thirty-eight, it was still flourishing. She was so glad that she had found love with Jake Maloney; he was a policeman who shunned the limelight, but she had seen a photograph of him. Thank goodness Diana had her own son now, but of course no child could ever replace Ella. She followed her on Twitter and Facebook just to keep up with everything that was going on in Diana's life.

Anna had assumed as each year passed, that she was safe, certainly Daddy would never say anything, but that day was to come back and haunt her. One Wednesday morning, just as she was getting ready to go out to do some painting, there was an announcement on the radio. Apparently Rachel Wilcox was in custody for abducting Ella, but they were now asking the woman who had handed the baby to her in the car park to come forward. Her crime had caught up with her.

Chapter Twenty-nine

Emma Williams had spent all of her fifteen years living in a remote Scottish village, and her accent was quite strong. Her red gold hair was not unusual, as many Scottish girls had that sort of colouring, and she wore it long and loose with a full fringe. Her mother's accent was less strong, and still carried a hint of South London, she didn't speak as fast as the local women, but her hair was the same colour as her daughter's.

Emma didn't remember ever having a father, and her mother had never spoken about him except to say he had died. Up until a year ago, Emma and her mother had been very close. She had always loved to be the centre of attention, her nature was a little outrageous, but also charismatic, and she was popular at school.

She was not particularly academic, but she did love drama; she also had a good singing voice, and her mother had paid for Emma to have piano and guitar lessons. She had a natural ability for music, and coupled with her strawberry blonde hair, and haunting green eyes, she made quite an impact. At school she was encouraged to develop these talents, and her desire at fourteen was to be a pop star and become famous. She knew she had a similarity to the actress Diana Wilcox, with her hair colouring and green eyes, and she followed Diana on Facebook and Twitter, and she wanted to be just like her when she was older; she wanted to be a star.

But when she told her mother about her dream, she had told her not to be stupid, there were so many talented girls out there who wanted the same thing and so few of them would achieve it.

Mother was firm, she needed to stay on until sixth form, work hard, and then do her best to get to university. There were so many more careers out there for her, and more suitable than show business, but she had to make the effort and work hard at school.

To Emma, this was like a slap in the face. After encouraging her musical talent, her mother now wanted her to do something else. She so loved to sing, she had been in so many concerts and choirs, and now her mother did not approve. It was that attitude that changed her overnight into a rebellious teenager, because nothing she ever did seemed to be right. Then she decided she would please herself, and as soon as she was old enough, she would leave her mother and lead her own life. Singing was going to be her life.

Rachel Wilcox had changed her name to Ava Williams fifteen years ago, and for very good reason. It may have been a long time ago, but it was imprinted on her heart; she would never forget that day, nor would her conscience ever give her peace.

When she looked back now she realised that, at that time, she had not been in her right mind. Having miscarried her own baby, to then find out that her sister was pregnant by Rachel's own husband had affected her deeply. The pain was so intense and nobody could possibly know how intense; she had been hoodwinked by a man she believed to be the love of her life.

She, Rachel, had been the clever sister, the stable and sensible one, or so she had thought, but it had turned out not to be true. She knew deep down that Diana had not encouraged Neil, and she believed he had raped her, but by accepting that, she was admitting her own weakness, her inability to see through him. So she had put the armour around herself, shut her beloved twin out of her life, and suffered ever since.

Curiosity to see Ella had taken her to the hospital that day. To her, being the daughter of her twin, made Ella almost seem like her own child. She had convinced herself that Diana would make a bad mother, because she had to try and ease her own conscience. But when she arrived at the hospital without any clear plan in her mind, someone was already holding Emma. Standing just outside the door of the ward she saw it all; Diana in her bed, the staff nurse holding Ella, then the buzzer going off, and finally the grey-haired nurse taking over.

208

Intrigued, she had followed the nurse towards the nursery, but she had not gone that way, she had gone out of a side entrance to where a car was waiting. When she called to her, by the car, and the woman turned, it was obvious to see she had mistaken her for Diana. She must have wondered how Diana had managed to get out of bed and dress so quickly, and then follow her. There was panic all over her face, and in her haste to hand Ella back to her, she knocked the grey wig sideways, and Rachel had a quick glimpse of a young woman with straight blonde hair. She wondered who the hell she was and why she wanted Ella?

She knew what she had to do; return Ella to her mother. But in that moment of madness, when she held her tiny niece in her arms, Rachel felt such an overwhelming love for her. All her life she had done the right thing, usually for her sister's sake when she felt Diana needed support, and often, when they were children, to cover up things that would have got Diana into trouble. But this time she did what she wanted, and took Ella.

She had taken the baby and the wig, whilst the woman was blubbering how sorry she was, and then got in the taxi waiting by the gate. But her mind was all over the place. It had been a spot decision and she had no clear plan.

So she had arrived at Heathrow and sat in the lounge wearing the grey wig, but then realised she would not get away with leaving the country with Ella. So she had abandoned the wig, and fled to the most remote part of Scotland that she could find. Before leaving she had thrown her handbag into the River Thames, and become Ava Williams.

The first night had been spent in a draughty B and B run by an elderly Scottish widow with such a broad accent it had been difficult to understand her. It was so remote, it was almost like being somewhere away from the world. There was no TV, and this particular village was quite behind the times. This is just how Rachel liked it, and she had soon found herself a cottage to rent, and was later able to buy it. She did rue the day she had left twenty thousand pounds in her account, but she had taken a job at the local hospital, trained to be a nurse, and after qualifying, had become a respected member of the local community. She couldn't continue to be a scientist, as it would be too obvious.

Whilst she was studying to be a mental health nurse, she realised that she, herself, had mental issues. She had behaved in

k

uncharacteristic fashion by taking Ella. But it was too late, she was now a criminal and had to live with what she had done.

She had changed the baby's name to Emma, and registered her birth in that name. She had not wanted to change her name, as she knew the baby had been named after their mother, but there was no other choice.

Rachel had taken her duty as a mother very seriously, and done her utmost to bring Emma up in a way that Diana would have wanted. Emma looked just like both the twins, with the same red gold hair and huge expressive green eyes. Her character was absolutely Diana; vivacious, dramatic, good at the arts, and also very loving. But there wasn't a day that went by when Rachel didn't regret what she had done and wish that she had the courage to put the situation right.

She had followed Diana's career with great pride, and admired her bravery after losing Ella. She knew what a wicked thing she had done to her, but Emma had become her whole life, and she could not bear to even think about losing her. Rachel was so happy when Diana married Jake, and thought it ironical that she, Rachel, had tried to protect her from him, and yet made such a bad choice of her own with Neil. Thank goodness Diana had become a mum and she had her son Andrew, even though she had lost Ella.

When Emma went to secondary school, her talent at entertaining became even more obvious. She had such an ear for music and her voice was captivating. Rachel encouraged her to learn the piano and guitar, but then became alarmed when she announced at the age of fourteen that she wanted to go on Britain's Got Talent. There was no way she could do that, or even pursue any sort of career on the stage. Emma looked so like her real mother, with the same talents, that the last thing Rachel wanted was for her to be in the limelight and be noticed, because then her deception would be revealed.

She knew she had not handled it very well. She had put Emma's back up, which was never a good idea with a teenager, and from that time on she had lost that close bond they had shared for so long. Even Jim Stewart, her music teacher, and also boyfriend of Rachel, had thought she should encourage Emma more.

Rachel and Jim had been an item for a year now. He had made

her very happy, and she had finally let her guard down and allowed her heart to love again at the age of thirty-eight. But then something had gone wrong with her health. She wasn't sure whether she was having an early menopause, as her periods stopped, and then she felt sick and ill and her stomach started to swell.

The local hospital was not that modern and up-to-date, but in the past that had never worried her as her health had been fine. But now it was different, because Rachel was convinced that she had stomach cancer. She had the symptoms, and that meant she would not have long left. So with a heavy heart, she knew she had to confess. Emma had the right to be with her real mother, and then she could go back to being Ella again.

That night she told Jim she could never see him again, and the look of pain on his face nearly broke her heart. She didn't want to say she had cancer, and then have him stay with her out of pity, so it was better for him to think she had stopped caring.

She cried herself to sleep that night, but by the morning she had composed herself; it was Emma's turn. So she told her how, soon after she was born, an unknown woman had taken her from the hospital dressed up as a nurse, and that she, in turn, had then taken her from that woman, and they had come to Scotland to lead a new life. Then she told her that Diana Wilcox was her mother, and also her twin, her real name being Rachel.

It took a few minutes for the shock of this very hasty confession to sink in with Emma; but when it did, a lot of things made sense. Rachel had always been a rather possessive mother, never letting her go far. She had thought it was because her dad was dead. Although she looked like Rachel, her nature was completely different; outgoing and vivacious. Then the enormity of her mother's crime hit her. The famous Diana Wilcox was her real mother, and because of Rachel's selfishness, Emma had been deprived of living with her true mother for all this time. She felt disgust for what her so-called mother had done and, at that moment, Emma found it impossible to love her.

Emma ran upstairs to her bedroom; her mind was in turmoil. Rachel sat at the kitchen table, her head in her hands. It had all come out so quickly. She had needed to shed this enormous secret, but in so doing she had lost Emma's love and respect.

Emma didn't go to school that day, and Rachel didn't press it.

211

After a shock like that, she could hardly concentrate on work. Rachel went up to Emma's room and tapped on the door. There was no reply, so she pushed it gently open to find Emma sprawled on her bed with her earphones in, listening to music. Her face showed her anger and pain towards the person she had always believed to be her mother.

"Emma, I can't live with this secret, you need to go and find your mother."

"Don't worry, I will, and you will end up in prison!"

Rachel flinched, but she no longer cared about herself as she was sure she didn't have long now. She couldn't blame Emma for wanting to hurt her; she had just ruined her young life. At least if she could make contact with her mother, when Rachel was gone, Emma would not be on her own. As she was only fifteen, Rachel could not bear the thought that when she was gone, Emma might end up in care; it must not happen.

Emma was finding it impossible to understand why Rachel had done such a thing to her own twin sister. It was hard to get her head round the fact that her mother was actually her aunt. She had offered no sort of explanation for her behaviour, so it looked like the truth lay with her real mother.

Because she was a well known figure, Diana had several homes, both in England, America and the South of France, and all with maximum security. Emma would never be able to get anywhere near to her, and she firmly refused any help from Rachel, who had told her she would give herself up to the police.

She guessed that somebody else took care of Diana's Facebook page, so she sent a personal message which she was sure would be passed on, it read:

> Dear Miss Wilcox,
>   I have been a fan of yours for many years, and I believe I may be related to you. Please can I have an address so I may write to you.
>   Yours sincerely,
>   Emma Williams.

*   *   *   *

When Diana's PA forwarded the message to her, she felt her mouth go dry. Could this be the contact she had been waiting for, fifteen years later. Jake was more cautious; they had been given false hope before, and he didn't want her to be let down again. However, they both decided that the fan club address could be given out, and then Emma's letter would be forwarded onto their private address.

When it arrived, complete with a photograph of Emma, they both knew without a shadow of doubt, this was her daughter Ella. Her likeness to Diana was so obvious, and there was also a photograph of Rachel, who, even after all these years apart, still looked so like Diana.

Diana should have felt hatred towards Rachel for depriving her of her daughter for all these years, but she could not. Her joy at finally meeting Ella soon, was tempered with the knowledge that Jake had reminded her that Rachel would be arrested, because she had committed a very serious crime.

It was arranged that Emma would be brought to their Chelsea home by private car, and Diana had requested that her twin Rachel should come too. She had made Jake promise that he would let them have some time together before reporting it to his office. He didn't want to break Diana's heart by arresting her sister, but somebody would have to.

But Emma had no desire to have Rachel with her; she was still very angry with her, and she arrived alone in the car. As the driver opened the car for her to step out, she looked around her with awe. It was hard to believe that her birth mother lived in this beautiful house, and she was just about to meet her. Was she dreaming?

The door opened, and the woman who resembled her mother so much stood there. She looked so familiar, it was as if she had known her all her life. She held her arms out to her, and Emma ran into them, feeling the warmth and security of her embrace. She was overwhelmed to think that the woman she had always worshipped as a star was her mother.

When Diana stood at the door, all the memories she had of the tiny baby that had nuzzled at her breast were gone. She had grown into a beautiful young girl, the sort that any mother would be proud of. She had missed all her baby years, she knew, but maybe she could play a small part in helping her through her teenage years. Remembering back to her own, Diana had been glad she had Rachel to help her. It seemed the most natural thing in the world to fold her young body into her arms, to hold her close and make her feel safe. She had never stopped loving her little baby, and now she had blossomed into this fine young woman.

When she finally released her, Diana could feel tears rolling down her cheeks, but they were tears of joy; all the pain and heartbreak of the last fifteen years had rolled away. Emma, as she now knew her, was sobbing too. For both of them, it was probably the most emotional moment of their lives.

Later, as they sat drinking coffee, Diana expressed her disappointment that Rachel had not come. Ella, as she now wished to be called, remarked:

"How can you bear to see her after what she did?"

"It's not as simple as you think," sighed Diana, wondering how she could explain without upsetting Ella, who was at a very impressionable age. "Your aunt Rachel suffered her own miscarriage, then her husband left her, and she was not in a normal state of mind."

"I see." Now Ella could feel a little bit more compassionate towards Rachel, and try as she might to ignore it, she felt like she was still her mother. She had two mothers with different personalities. It was really all a bit confusing. Then she asked the one question that Diana had been dreading.

"Who is my father, and is it true that he is dead?"

Diana swallowed, it felt like she had a huge lump in her throat. There had been so many lies and deceptions in the past, she had no choice but to speak the truth.

"Your father was Rachel's husband, so we thought, although it turned out later he had committed bigamy. He died some time ago. Unfortunately he went around deceiving women and stealing their money from them. He forced himself upon me. . ." her voice trailed off, as Ella looked at her in horror.

"He raped you. Why didn't you abort me?"

"My friend Clare wanted to adopt you. She had also lost a baby, but when you were born. . ." her eyes filled with tears as she remembered, ". . .the bond was there right away, I loved you, and I wanted to bring you up. I can assure you there is nothing of your father in you. You are good and kind, you take after myself and

214

Rachel. You must never judge Rachel, she was the best sister I could have had, always looking out for me; but your father was a sick man who came from a dysfunctional family, he was not right in the head, so we have to forgive him too. Life is too short to do otherwise. I have lived by that belief, and my prayer has been answered because I have finally got to meet you."

Ella felt quite moved by these words. What a story it was, and although she was only fifteen, it was apparent that not everything in life was black and white. Her Aunt Rachel had suffered by being led on by a man that she thought she could trust; even going through a marriage ceremony, no wonder she had flipped, and then she had to deal with a miscarriage. Diana had been raped by her sister's husband; how traumatic that must have been, and how degrading for Rachel. It sounded like that man had been the cause of all the trouble. She, Ella, had been the result of that rape, but it had not stopped Diana from loving her; what greater love could a mother have for her child than that? This knowledge made her feel very proud. Her sick father had not been able to spoil that. But there was just one more question she needed to ask: "Who was the woman that stole me, and why did she?"

Chapter Thirty

Rachel looked at her swollen stomach in the mirror; it felt very tender when she touched it. Up until now she had resisted going to a more up-to-date hospital for a scan. Being a nurse and knowing about symptoms was scary; she was convinced she had cancer. As she turned, she felt a huge flush come over her. Damn the menopause, but this flush seemed to be never ending, and she felt the sweat pouring off her. Then a pain ripped through her body, so intense she was doubled up in pain. As she attempted to sit down on the bed to try and bear it, she slipped, sliding onto the floor and hitting her head on the leg of the bed, dazing herself.

Jim had been wondering what was wrong with her. He had been planning to ask her to marry him, and then she had gone cold on him. He couldn't believe they were over, just like that. She was a beautiful intelligent lady, and she could have had any man, but he had always sensed a sadness inside her, and he had spent the last year gaining her trust. He was so in love, and all he wanted to do was take care of her and Emma, her feisty talented daughter.

When he knocked on the door, he noticed her car was in the drive, so she was in. But there was no reply, so he pushed gently and it opened. In this village, people rarely locked their doors during the day. He called as he went in, as he still didn't like invading her privacy. Sometimes she could be a very private person.

Was that a muffled cry from upstairs? Jim's long legs took the stairs two at a time, and when he arrived in the upstairs hall; he could hear her more clearly, calling for help. When he entered the bedroom, he saw her on the floor, dressed only in her dressing gown, holding her stomach and clearly in pain.

He ignored all her protestations that she was all right, and took out his mobile to ring for an ambulance. It wouldn't be very quick, nothing was around here, but he didn't dare move her, so he covered her with a quilt to stop her getting cold, put a pillow under her head, and sat down on the floor beside her.

"Where is Emma?" he enquired, thinking she would have to know about her mother's predicament, and she would probably want to come home.

"She has left me!" she said dramatically. "And when I tell you why, you will too, you won't want to know me!"

Jim squatted next to her, brushing her hair with his fingers and stroking her brow.

"Nothing you have done would make me stop loving you. I know you are a good woman and a great mother. And when we get you sorted, then I want to marry you."

His words meant so much to Rachel, but he didn't realise he had no future with her. She told him about the cancer and he didn't even flinch, he was going to stand by her no matter what. Then she poured out everything about her life, and why Emma had gone because she wanted to find her real mother. But he still looked her steadfastly in the face and promised he would be there for ever to take care of her. If ever there was a test of love, that must be it, and by the time the ambulance arrived, Jim knew everything he needed to know about her, and he wasn't going anywhere.

Jake liked Ella very much; she was as talented and feisty as Diana, and even Andrew seemed impressed by his new sister. At thirteen he didn't much like girls, but having a new sister felt cool, and he couldn't wait to share the fact with his friends.

It was heartening to finally see Diana with her daughter. They were so comfortable with each other that it was like they had never been apart. But this reunion was not going to be entirely happy because Rachel had committed a very serious crime. Diana had said she would not press charges, as there was no one better to raise her daughter than her sister, but he didn't think a judge would see it that way. When Ella asked who the stranger was who took her, he wondered too. Rachel had taken her from the stranger, but her crime had been not to return Ella to her rightful mother.

He had no choice but to return to the case again and appeal for that woman to give herself up, whoever she was, and to explain why she did it. Maybe it had been Clare, he just didn't know, but he wanted to solve this case once and forever.

Ella's mobile rang whilst they were talking, and she excused herself and turned to answer it. Maybe it was Rachel. Then he saw her face go pale whilst she was talking; whatever it was, he could see it was serious. She turned towards them, and her face had tears rolling down. It had been such an emotional day, and now the person she had believed to be her mother needed her. She could not just turn her back on her.

"I have to go home. That was my mother's boyfriend." Oh hell, she had said it again, it was her aunt!

"She collapsed on the floor this morning and is now in hospital. They have done tests on her; she has a growth in her stomach, but they did say it's not malignant, and also she's twenty-five weeks pregnant!"

They all stood there digesting the news, and then Diana spoke first.

"You must go, she needs you, and I am coming with you."

"You have a job tomorrow," reminded Jake, although he knew Diana and expected nothing less of her.

"Oh, just cancel it. There are plenty more jobs, but only one sister!" said Diana with feeling. Their roles were reversed now, and it was her turn to help her sister. "I am going to get packed."

Jake had so much admiration for her. She didn't waste her life with bitterness about what might have been; Diana was truly a remarkable woman. He felt he owed it to his wife and her sister to try and find this other woman, and wrap the case up. Maybe with a good solicitor, and a plea of diminished responsibility, Rachel might get a light sentence. He did hope so.

Diana took time out from work and stayed to be near to Rachel whilst she was in hospital. Their reunion had been so emotional for both of them. Rachel's guilt was obvious, but Diana shrugged it off, saying they must make up for lost time, they both only had one life. Rachel's shock when she was told she was pregnant turned to joy. They were going to remove her lump and they felt they could operate without harming her baby, so now, more than anything, she wanted to live.

Ella still loved the woman she had believed to be her mother, and there was such a strong bond between the twins anyway, she felt like she belonged to both of them. Now that everything was out in the open, with the blessing of both Rachel and Diana, she was going to enrol at a school for performing arts, and when she was sixteen she was going to try and audition for Britain's Got Talent. If she succeeded, she could stay with them in Chelsea whilst she was competing on the show.

Jim had promised to wait for however long it took, to marry Rachel and take care of her and their baby. In the meantime, Anna had come forward to explain her part in the abduction, because she couldn't live with herself if Rachel took all the blame. Her husband took all the flack from the press, but he was well used to it since his marriage broke up, and he hired a very competent barrister who he felt would be able to minimise the punishment Anna would get.

When Anna gave her statement to Jake, it all made sense. Neil Morris had ruined the lives of all these women in one way or another. This court case was going to be the sensation of the year, but as a family they would cope, like they always had done.

Jake and Diana both liked Jim. He was a typical Scot, he had red hair, and his brogue was strong so they didn't get everything he said, but he adored Rachel and would be her rock forever. He was also in favour of nurturing Ella's musical talent, as he had spotted it when she was eleven.

Rachel's baby son arrived six weeks early, only weighing five and a half pounds, but young Angus was a fighter, and he had the familiar red hair and strong nature of the rest of his family. It was a poignant moment for Rachel when she left hospital to go into custody. She didn't want to leave him behind, and the pain she felt was a reminder of just how Diana must have felt fifteen years earlier.

Diana had been stalwart throughout. Initially she stayed on in the cottage to care for Angus. He was thriving now and putting on weight, and Jim was so grateful for her help, as new babies were quite a mystery to him.

Jake and Andrew understood it was something she had to do, although they missed her; then after six weeks, she returned home and went back to the job she loved so much.

Soon Rachel's court case was coming up, but because the sisters were so united now, Jake didn't believe she would have such a long sentence, especially as she had a new baby.

Ella was working hard at her performing arts school in London, and during holiday periods she spent time with her new baby cousin. Helping to care for him cemented the bond between them. She was excited to learn that Jim had been offered a post at a London School, and as there was no need to hide away any more, they were going to move down to London, and get their new home ready for when Rachel was free.

Diana was delighted that her sister was going to be living close to them again. Jake was pleased for her, and found it amazing that through everything that had happened, it had not broken the bond between the twins. It was obviously Diana who was the caring one, because Rachel had been the one to cut herself off. Curiosity made him ask:

"Diana my love, tell me, having missed out on so much with Ella; her first steps, her first words, and when she started school, but to name a few landmarks, how were you able to forgive Rachel?"

Diana smiled, and put her arms around him, kissing his perplexed face.

"I have often asked myself that question, and I think it stems back to losing our parents. I was so frightened; no one could replace them, and the one thing that remained constant and got me through was Rachel. My sister was my rock, and until Neil Morris came along, she never changed. That man ruined so many lives, I was determined when we were reunited, that he wasn't going to do it again. I have always loved Rachel; it's part of being a twin, the bond that can never be broken."

"So you must be so pleased they are moving to London then."

"Yes, I am pleased, we are going to be like an extended family."

"I am hopeful that with her psychiatrist and barrister working in her favour, Rachel won't have to serve time for long."

At this reminder, Diana looked sad.

"Yes, Rachel has been punished for the last fifteen years, and now she's missing out on the early part of Angus's life too."

Jake didn't like to see her sad. Diana meant the world to him, even if he didn't say it that much. Her next words moved him a great deal.

"Jake, I would not have got through losing Ella and Rachel, if it had not been for the fact you came along just when I needed you that was my strength."

"Nonsense, enough of this serious talk. You are a strong feisty lady, as is your daughter, and I won't have another word said about it!"

Diana's face broke into a smile; she had some news that would make him very happy.

"I know at thirteen Andrew might not be thrilled at my news, and he now has his sister Ella, but I think you will be. In six months time we are having another baby. I won't miss out on anything with this one, and Angus will have a new cousin to grow up with."

Jake couldn't believe his ears. The baby they had tried so hard for, after eleven years, was now a reality. And it was true, this baby would be less than a year younger than Angus, so they could grow up together.

"You clever girl," he murmured. "It must be all in the genes."